CRUEL PRINCE

AN ACCIDENTAL PREGNANCY ROMANCE

LILIAN MONROE

PREVIOUSLY TITLED KNOCKED UP BY PRINCE GALLANT

*If you'd like access to the Lilian Monroe Freebie Central, which includes bonus
chapters from all my books (including this one), just follow the link below:*

http://www.lilianmonroe.com/subscribe

Lilian
xox

WANT THREE BOOKS DELIVERED STRAIGHT TO YOUR INBOX?
HOW ABOUT THREE ROCK STAR ROMANCES THAT WERE *WAY* TOO
HOT TO SELL?

GET THE COMPLETE *ROCK HARD* SERIES:
WWW.LILIANMONROE.COM/ROCKHARD

1

JO

THE DOOR SLAMS, and my boyfriend of two years becomes my ex-boyfriend, as of right now.

I stand in the middle of my studio apartment, staring after Ryan. He's gone. I'm not even sure how I feel about it. Offended? Relieved? Indifferent?

Glancing over at my laptop screen, I flinch. A grimace lingers on my lips as I read the form letter for the fourth time. It's yet another rejection email from a publisher, and it stings. I'm more hurt about their rejection than Ryan's—and that's probably exactly why he left. Apparently, I care too much about my flagging writing career and not enough about his ego.

Should I care that he's gone? Does the fact that I don't make me a bad person?

I'm not heartless, I swear. Ryan was nice, I guess.

But he kept talking about marriage, babies, and me being a stay-at-home mom. Never once did he ask me if I really wanted that.

I stare at the door again, and then back at the email. I

scan my body, and decide that I do, indeed, care more about the publisher's rejection than I do about my ex.

My shoulders slump, and I sink down onto my desk chair.

Ryan's and my relationship was probably over a long time ago, but I'd hung on in the vain hope that something would change. Our relationship was just like every other relationship that I've ever had—and like my short stint in college, or my current writing career: Another failure.

Just like this email. Rejection never gets easier—even if it's the thirtieth refusal letter I've received this month.

Reading the email over and over again, my heart sinks. Every publisher's snub is the same. It's professional, yet it cuts deep into the fabric of my once unshakeable confidence.

My manuscript didn't grip the editors, it says. The beginning wasn't compelling enough.

How much of my book did they read before rejecting it, I wonder?

I rub my hands over my face, sighing. That was the last publisher on my list. My book is dead. I'm single, broke, and apparently a big, old failure.

Look away while I wallow for a while, will you?

I push myself off my chair and stare around my apartment. My shifts at the restaurant aren't covering all my expenses. My freelance work has dried up, and I'm not sure how I'll make rent next month.

I came to New York City six years ago with big dreams and bigger expectations, and they haven't quite come to fruition. By 'haven't quite' I mean I should probably tattoo FLOP in big letters across my forehead. I've ended up with a big pile of rejection letters and a very small bank account.

Ryan was offering to help me out with my expenses until I got a book deal—but that's obviously not going to happen, now.

"That's fine," I say under my breath. "I didn't want your money anyway." I talk to the closed door, as if my ex-boyfriend can hear me.

Ryan used his money as a chain around my neck, always making me feel guilty for not having enough of my own. He'd make a big show of paying for things whenever I couldn't—which was often. I hated it.

But not anymore. I won't use him as a crutch. I'll figure this out on my own. I press my lips together and widen my stance. Pushing up my sleeves, I swing my eyes from one end of the room to the other.

Is my sofa worth anything? I don't even sit on it that much. Maybe I could get a hundred bucks for it. The TV can't be worth much—it's an old-style thing with knobs on the front and no remote—but maybe a hipster will want it in an ironic kind of way. My dining room table has three mismatched chairs and a lot of rings from coffee mugs on it. I doubt I'd be able to even give it away for free.

My eyes flick around the tiny studio apartment, cataloguing all my belongings. Only my two most precious possessions aren't for sale. My laptop and the little leather-bound notebook where I stuff all my ideas. Those two items will stay with me until I croak.

When my eyes land on my dresser, I pause. Maybe I could sell my dirty panties on the Internet, or something. Don't people pay a lot for those?

Shaking my head, I try to build myself back up again.

I'm not a screw-up. It's not failing until you stop picking yourself back up. Isn't that on a motivational poster somewhere?

Things will work out—they always do. I'll pick up a couple of extra shifts at the restaurant. I'll put my groceries on my credit card. I'll hustle harder for some freelance writing work. I'll sell my panties, if needs be.

I'll make it work. I can do it.

I stretch my neck from side to side and try to build myself back up. Maybe if I rewrite the book—revise it for the millionth time and make the beginning more gripping—maybe then a publisher will pick it up. I'll get a nice advance cheque, and my problems will be solved.

It'll happen. I have faith.

Confidence starts to creep into my heart. A sense of calm washes over me, and a smile drifts over my lips.

I haven't been rejected by my ex-boyfriend—I've been *freed*. I can do anything. I can *be* anything! I'm not Jolie, failed writer and tired waitress. Not anymore. No, I'm Jolie, the independent and successful boss-lady! Watch me blossom!

My smile grows wider as my belief in myself grows. I slam my laptop screen down with a thud as a giggle bubbles up inside me.

Laughter tastes sweet, even if I'm alone in my apartment. I throw my head back and let out a big belly laugh, leaning into the feeling.

Freedom.

It feels good. Great, even! I build myself higher, and higher, and higher...

...and then reality brings me crashing all the way back down when the lights in my apartment flicker off.

I hear the refrigerator shut down, too, as the power to my entire apartment is cut.

"Shit, shit, shit." I rush to the switch on the wall. I flick the lights on and off, but nothing happens. Using the flashlight on my phone, I find the electrical panel and turn the breakers on and off again, but nothing works. I try it again, and again, and again...

...nothing.

Groaning, I sink down to the floor. I drop my head in my hands and I admit to myself what I've known since the lights went off:

It's not the breaker. It's the bill.

To be precise, it's the red-marked bill currently sitting on my kitchen table, unopened and unpaid.

Tears sting my eyes as an overwhelming sense of failure creeps into my heart. How did I think I could do this? When I moved away from Farcliff, I truly believed I could make it in the world. I had eight hundred dollars, half of an English Lit college degree, and an ego the size of Farcliff Kingdom. I was invincible.

I got myself a work visa to the United States and I moved to New York, full of hope and dreams and naivety.

Bright-eyed, I fell in love with the lights and noise of the city.

Now, the lights are off and it's deathly quiet.

I've failed. Professionally, personally, and philosophically flopped.

My lower lip trembles as I squeeze my hands into fists. I dig my fingernails into my palms to try and get a grip on myself. I'm working the closing shift at the restaurant tonight, and the last thing I need to do is show up with puffy, blood-shot eyes and a red nose from crying.

I shut my eyes and try to pull myself together.

It feels like I'm teetering on the brink of a breakdown. A strong gust of wind would knock me into meltdown mode. I keep swinging between highs and lows every few minutes, and it's making my head spin. So, I just stay huddled on the floor, with my hands balled into fists and my eyes squeezed shut.

I count to a hundred. The lights still haven't miraculously come back on, and I'm still single and broke—but at least I don't feel like I'm going to break down and cry anymore.

Picking myself up off the floor, I stand up and find my work uniform. I'll work my shift tonight and scrape together enough money for the bill. The power will be back on in no time.

I repeat the words to myself over and over until I almost believe them. I take extra time to do my makeup and hair like I'm putting on war paint. I stare at myself in the mirror, fake-smiling at my reflection. I wonder if I look as miserable as I feel.

My phone rings, interrupting my pity-party. It's my mother.

"Hey, Mom."

"Jolie, don't panic."

You know when people say, 'don't panic' and you immediately start panicking? And then instead of explaining themselves, they pause, as if the silence hanging between you will do anything to calm your racing mind?

My mother is an expert at that. She wrote the book on dramatic pauses—which, coincidentally, is more than I can say about my own book-writing career.

"*Whatsgoingon?*" I breathe the words out as one.

"It's your father." My mother sighs.

My heart takes off at breakneck speed, trying its best to make me faint. "What happened?"

Is this the gust of wind that will knock me over the edge into a full-on breakdown?

"The cancer's back," she says quietly.

"No. No, no, no. How, Mom? How?"

"The oncologist said it's treatable, and we caught it very early this time. We're going to have to move back to Farcliff

City. We have to be near the hospital now. There aren't enough medical facilities out here in Westhill."

My parents have been living at the Westhill Palace, in the heart of the forests on the western edge of the Kingdom. My father has been in charge of the Westhill Royal Rose Gardens for about five years. The two of them moved to Westhill after I left for the United States. Being appointed to the Westhill Rose Garden was the greatest honor that has ever been bestowed upon my family.

For my parents to be moving away from the Westhill, it means my father's illness is getting very, very serious.

"What about the garden?" My voice squeaks, and I clear my tightening throat.

My mother sighs. "We're going to have to leave it behind. Harry Brooks will be in charge of it."

"Harry Brooks? Last time you left him in charge of the roses, you practically had to start over. He killed nearly all of them—you were complaining about it for months."

"Jolie..."

"Mom... How bad is it?"

Leaving Westhill on such short notice, *and* leaving the incompetent Brooks in charge of the Royal Rose Gardens means something is seriously wrong. My heart is racing and I'm finding it hard to see straight.

My mother sighs. "We just need to be closer to the hospital, that's all. He needs to start another course of chemotherapy, so we'll be in and out of the hospital every week. We can't travel two hours each way from Westhill to Farcliff. It's just not feasible."

"Every week?"

Mental breakdown, here I come.

"The doctors had to up the frequency of his treatment this time."

7

"I'm coming home."

"Jo, stop. You don't have to. Your father didn't even want me to tell you that we were moving, but I wanted you to know. Everything will be fine. He'll recover—we just need a bit more care for him this time. It's precautionary."

"Chemo isn't precautionary, Mom. *Aggressive* chemo isn't a precaution."

My mind is reeling. I can't stay here. I can't be in a foreign country, struggling to keep my lights on, when my father is in and out of the hospital.

"I'm coming home," I repeat.

"No, Jolie. You can't put your life on hold for us. You're doing so well in New York! It keeps your father and I going to know that you've been so successful."

I almost start laughing.

Successful? Me?

I'm the very definition of failure. I'm so far from success that I might as well not even know the meaning of the word. I've never told them how much I'm struggling, of course. What would that accomplish?

But the truth is, I wouldn't be giving anything up by coming home. I need to be close to my family. There's nothing left for me here.

Taking a deep breath, I try to think of an angle that my parents will agree to. "Well, what if I tended the rose gardens?" The words slip out of my mouth before I even know what I'm saying.

My mother pauses, and the words hang between us. "What do you mean?"

"I mean, I'm better at gardening that Harry fucking Brooks—"

"*Language*, Jolie."

"Sorry. All I'm saying is, I'll be closer to you. At least I'll be

8

in the Kingdom. That way, Dad won't have to worry about the gardens going to shit—sorry, I mean he'll know the gardens are being taken care of. I can write from there, too. A bit of solitude in the country will do me good. I've been wanting to get away from the city, anyway."

I can hear my mother breathing on the other side of the line. She's thinking about it.

"Darling, the Prince..."

"I can handle the Prince."

"He's not well. Ever since he had his daughter..."

"Who cares? I probably won't even see him. You've lived in the Westhill for years, and you've only seen him a handful of times."

"Jo..."

"Mom, I want to be closer. If you won't let me stay with you in Farcliff, at least let me help out with the gardens. Dad will want to show some flowers at the Annual Rose Festival, no? How would he feel if he wasn't able to show any flowers at all?"

Mom sighs, and I can hear her starting to give in. "I'll talk to your father."

The tightness in my chest eases, and I nod. "Okay. I'll start packing."

I've always been decisive, but this is quick—even for me. The power isn't coming on in my apartment, though, and the refrigerator isn't going to magically fill itself with food. I can't be struggling here when I should be closer to my family in Farcliff.

Taking my father's place at Westhill is my only choice—even if I won't admit that to my parents.

2

GABRIEL

I HOLD my brother's letter in my hand, staring off into nothing. The garden is mostly quiet, with only the calls of a songbird disturbing the silence. The roses are still only green, prickly bushes, but I can already see tiny buds starting to form on them. It'll be at least a month before they bloom, before the garden is bursting with color and scent. It'll be the most beautiful place in the Kingdom, and the one place that makes me calm.

Today, though, not so much. Nothing would make me calm after reading the King's letter.

It's the ten-year anniversary of the King's crowning, and I'm invited to attend the celebrations at Farcliff Castle. 'Invited' might be the wrong word. 'Compelled to attend' is more accurate. My brother has left no room for negotiation.

I know I should be there. To see my brother celebrate his first decade as King of Farcliff would be a great moment for the family, especially after everything that happened when he ascended to the throne.

That's not what worries me.

His letter also mentions someone else. Someone who

hasn't seen Farcliff Castle since she was an infant. I took my daughter away from Farcliff nearly six years ago, and I hoped I'd never return.

Charlie's letter is very clear about it, though. My presence is required—as is Flora's.

As if my daughter can sense my turbulent thoughts, I hear her voice coming nearer.

"Daddy!"

Flora comes into view at full-speed. She's sprinting through the rose bushes, barreling toward me as she grins from ear to ear. I stand up to catch her, bracing myself for impact.

Another child might slow down, or even come to a stop. Not Flora. She accelerates toward me, leaping into my arms at top speed. As I spin her around in the air, she giggles so hard spittle goes flying from her mouth.

I set her down and a smile cracks on my lips.

"What are you so happy about? You shouldn't be running, Flora. You know what the doctor said."

"Look!" Flora ignores my worries. She reaches into the pocket of her dress. Flora insists that all dresses should have pockets and refuses to wear ones that don't—probably because of situations exactly like this one. Her pockets routinely hold all types of treasures that a six-year-old finds.

Flora pulls something out, cupping it gently in her hand. I sit down on the bench and lean toward my daughter as she takes a step toward me.

"I found it in the forest," she says, still hiding the object in her palm.

It could be anything. A beetle, or even a frog. It could be a little stick that she liked the shape of. It could be a foil-wrapped chocolate, flattened and melted from the heat of her body. It could be squirrel poop, or a funny-shaped leaf. When I say it could be anything, I mean *anything.*

And my daughter, ever the actor, loves to heighten the drama. Her lips tug into a mischievous grin.

"Ready?"

"Show me."

She uncurls her fingers to reveal...

...a rock.

"Wow," I say, unconvinced.

"Wait." Flora licks her finger and rubs it over the rock. Once wet, I can see all the sparkles and parallel lines of shimmering blue that striate its surface. She tilts it in the sun and more dazzling colors appear. Smiling, she glances at me. "Isn't it beautiful?"

Flora brings the rock up within an inch of my face. Her eyes are wide, a hopeful smile hanging on her lips.

In that moment—in every moment with Flora—I forget about Charlie's letter. I forget about Farcliff Castle, and all the bad memories that go with it.

I just take the rock between my fingers, and I look at it.

Copying my daughter, I lick my fingers and wet the surface of the rock, which has already started to dry. The brilliant blues and teals that line the rock reappear, and I angle them in the sunlight.

"It's beautiful, Flora." I smile, handing the treasure back to her. Flora is the only person in my life with the ability to make me see the beauty in the small things. To her, everything is magical—even a simple rock. Her cheeks are rosy today, and she almost looks like a normal, healthy child. On days like today, I forget about the pain and suffering that her illness has caused us.

"I got it for you," Flora says, tucking it into my front pocket and patting my chest. "It's good luck."

"Is it?"

"Uh huh." She hops up onto the bench beside me and points to the letter that lays forgotten. "What's that?"

Leaning back on the bench, I stare up at the bright blue sky. Westhill Castle has been my oasis. It's been my refuge from the controversy and evil that lurks in the streets of Farcliff.

But it's also been my prison—and Flora's

Now, it might be time to walk out of my prison and back to my home.

Taking a deep breath, I take the letter between my fingers and stare at it. "It's a letter from your Uncle Charlie. He wants us to come visit."

"Visit Farcliff?" Flora's eyes widen.

I nod. "Yes. Would you be willing to come with me?"

Flora stares at me for a moment, and then startles me when she springs off the bench and onto her feet. She yelps and jumps, doing a little dance. There's no weakness in her— no paleness, or coughing, or pain in her eyes. Today, she's a normal kid, excited to be going on a trip.

"Farcliff Castle! I'm going to Farcliff!" She sings and jumps around me, laying a big kiss on my forehead. "When do we go?"

"Next week."

"Woohoo!" Flora wiggles her body in front of me, laughing so much I can't help but laugh along with her. The tension in my chest eases, and I start to wonder if this trip to Farcliff might actually be a good idea. It's time for Flora to see the capital. She's a princess, after all, and she should know her Kingdom. Even though I want to keep my daughter safe in Westhill, it's time for me to show her where I came from— where *she* came from—even though the few months she spent there as a baby were chaotic.

Mrs. Grey, the head of staff at Westhill Castle—and Flora's closest approximation to a mother figure—appears at the end of the pathway and tuts at my daughter, who's still dancing and jumping.

"Your Highness, that is *not* appropriate behavior for a Princess of Farcliff. It's time for your physiotherapy."

"Yes, Mrs. Grey," Flora says, snapping her spine straight. She glances at me, winking, and I wonder what I've done to deserve such a daughter. She's brave, and happy, and loving —all the things that I don't see in myself at all.

Mrs. Grey curtsies, and I nod my head. The older woman produces a bottle of water and three pills, which Flora takes without complaint. My daughter's illness is inherited, and a small part of me has always blamed myself. Both her mother and I carried the gene that caused her cystic fibrosis. I've watched Flora go through chest infections, difficulty breathing, and countless other difficulties—enduring it all with a smile on her face.

She's six years old, and she's the bravest person I've ever met. These days, her illness is manageable with the help of our in-house medical team, about sixty pills a day, and Flora's unrelenting positivity.

Flora slips her hand in Mrs. Grey's, and the two of them disappear down the pathway. I hear the Rose Garden gate open and close, and once again, I'm alone with my thoughts.

I pat my breast pocket with my hand, feeling the small lump where Flora's pebble lies against my heart. If she's right —and this rock brings me luck—then going to Farcliff for the ten year anniversary of my brother's coronation will be a good thing. Bringing Flora into society will be a positive experience for both of us.

If she's wrong, though...

Rustling at the far end of the rose garden pulls me from

my thoughts. Marcel, my rose gardener, comes into view. He's leaning heavily on his wife, Violet. Marcel brings a handkerchief up to his mouth and coughs into it, stopping in his tracks and bending over double. Violet holds his arm as he coughs, and then pats his back as he rights himself.

The gardener's eyes drift up the path and land on me. His eyes widen, and his mouth moves up and down without uttering a word.

"Your Highness..."

"Marcel. Violet."

Violet curtsies awkwardly while Marcel struggles to bow.

I frown. "Are you all right?"

They exchange a glance. Violet steps forward. "Your Highness, my husband isn't well. We thought Bertrand would have told you..."

"Bert hasn't told me shit."

Marcel motions for his wife to back up. He steps in front of her, wringing his handkerchief in his fists. "Your Highness, I'm going back to Farcliff for treatment. I'll be gone at least three months. But don't worry, the Royal Rose Garden will be in good hands."

I stare at the two of them for a moment. I can sense the fear coming off them in waves. Is it me they're afraid of? Or just my reputation?

I nod. "Good. You've done a fine job with the garden this year, Marcel. If last year's garden is anything to go off, we'll have a good showing at the Annual Rose Festival."

A faint blush appears on Marcel's cheeks. He nods. "Thank you, Your Highness."

For a moment, there's a silence—and then I say something I hadn't planned.

"I'm told you knew my mother."

I tilt my head, staring at the couple. Marcel and Violet

have been at the Westhill Castle about five years and worked on other royal estates before that. Marcel has been one of the best rose gardeners in Farcliff for as long as I can remember.

And yet... I know nothing about him. I hadn't even realized he was sick.

"Her Majesty was a treasure," Marcel replies, his eyes shining. "She understood the care and effort that goes into tending roses."

I nod, making a soft noise in agreement. My mother loved this place. She was killed when I was a toddler, and I have only a handful of memories of her.

Everyone that I talk to gets that soft look in their eyes whenever they talk about her. It's simultaneously touching and infuriating that she had such an impact on the people around her, yet I never got to experience it for myself. I was robbed of those memories before I even had a chance to form them.

One of the only memories I have of my mother is right here, in this garden. I was a toddler, and my mother was healthy. I remember her throwing me up in the air and catching me. We had laughed, and laughed, and laughed. My cheeks ached and my stomach hurt from giggling so much, and I was completely, utterly happy. The memory sticks in my mind like a bright light—a flagpole for a feeling that I haven't experienced since that moment.

Well, except with Flora. My daughter shatters through the darkness in my heart and brings light into my life. I pat the pebble in my pocket, staring at Marcel and Violet.

Maybe that's why I came to live in Westhill after all the shit that went down in Farcliff—Westhill is the last place I was happy.

Marcel clears his throat, and I'm dragged from the past back to the present. I motion to dismiss him, and then pause.

"Who is replacing you?"

"Well, we've trained Harry Brooks to upkeep the garden," Violet starts, glancing at Marcel. I can see an unspoken conversation between them.

"Brooks?" I snort. "Are you sure there will be a garden to come back to?"

Marcel clears his throat, glancing at Violet. It's almost as if he doesn't want to say what he's about to say. He drags his eyes back up to mine and nods once. "Our daughter will be coming back as well. She has the touch. She grew up with roses."

I nod, frowning.

A daughter? I don't remember them having a daughter.

I dismiss Marcel and Violet and watch them walk away. I still don't know what his illness is, or anything about his daughter.

I know most of the staff's names, bar a few new faces. I keep a close eye on what happens at Westhill. Typically, I vet all the new arrivals. I have to keep a close eye on the people in the castle—otherwise I'd be putting Flora at risk.

But I didn't approve Marcel's daughter, and right now, I don't have time to do anything about it. I have my own daughter to worry about. King Charlie is commanding me to come back to Farcliff for his anniversary.

I'll have to expose her to that city and all its evils. Its history. *My* history. My pulse quickens, and I clench my jaw. My hand drifts to the scar that cuts a jagged line across my face.

My scar is a reminder of everything that happened in Farcliff, everything that happened when Flora was born, and everything that made me leave.

Now, I have to take her back there.

I turn around and walk back toward the palace. My boots

crunch on the gravel, and I focus on the breath that passes in and out of my nostrils.

This garden is where I feel most peaceful. When the roses bloom, the beast inside me quiets down and I can find stillness. I can hear my own thoughts without feeling like I'm drowning in them. I can see a future for myself and for my daughter. I can push away the memories of the past that do nothing but hurt and betray me

Here, I can be at peace with myself.

But when the flowers start to wilt, and their petals flutter to the ground, I know that the darkness in my heart won't be too far behind.

3

JO

THE JOURNEY from New York City to Farcliff takes five hours by bus, plus about an hour to go through customs at the border. As soon as I cross into Farcliff, my heart beats easier and my shoulders relax. I lean my head on the headrest and close my eyes. With a deep sigh, I let a smile drift over my lips.

I'm home.

I never thought it would feel this good to be back here.

This time, I'm not here for just a short visit. I'm not coming home to see my parents for two weeks. This time, it feels like I'm coming home forever—and to my surprise, I *like* the feeling.

I thought I wanted to be Miss Independent, living in the Big City. I thought I wanted to make my own way as a writer. I left Farcliff with stars in my eyes, not remotely prepared for the struggle and the grime that would paint the next six years of my life.

Coming home is like being thrown a lifeline. There's nothing for me in New York anymore. All I've left behind are failed relationships and unpaid bills. Over the past few days,

I've sold off what furniture I could, and given away the rest. It took me less than a week to get all my affairs organized, scrape together enough money for the bus ticket, and lock my apartment door for the last time.

My landlord didn't even blink when I said I wasn't coming back.

When the bus crosses into my home country, I feel more at ease than I've felt in the past six years. I grip my backpack to my chest and watch the countryside turn to a cityscape. My heart thumps, and I feel like I'm starting a new chapter.

Coming home isn't moving backward—it can be a fresh start, right? Maybe in Westhill, surrounded by the gardens and solitude, I'll be able to find my voice. I'll rewrite my book and I'll finally be able to convince a publisher to pick it up. Maybe I'll write a new book. My father will get the treatment he needs, and my family will find a bit of stability.

As we drive into the city, I feel more at ease than I've felt in a long, long time.

Farcliff Castle juts out into the sky up ahead, and the tree-lined streets of Farcliff City greet me. My heart sings. I never thought I'd be so happy to see this place, but I can't wipe the smile off my face.

At Farcliff Central Bus Station, my mother stands waiting for me. She wraps her arms around me with tears in her eyes. When my mother pulls away, she keeps her hands on my arms and draws her eyebrows together in concern.

"Jolie, you're so thin! Have you been eating? You look tired. Look at the bags under your eyes! You're working too much, aren't you? And your hair! It's brittle!"

I snort, pinching my lips together. "Nice to see you too, Mom."

My mother fusses over me and leads me to the car. I drag

my suitcase behind me and sling my backpack over my shoulder. These two bags contain all I own in the world.

The past couple of years have been a struggle to make ends meet, and I think I kept going out of sheer stubbornness. The only thing holding me in New York was a shitty relationship with Ryan and my own damned ego. Leaving that dingy, old apartment behind is like being unchained. It makes me feel like I can take on the world.

My mother wraps me in another tight hug before getting behind the driver's seat. I load my bags into the car and slip into the passenger's seat, glancing at the city as excitement blooms in my heart.

Hanging on every lamppost are pendants celebrating the King's ten year anniversary—both of his coronation and his marriage. The city is exploding with color. There are flowers planted into every available space and fluttering banners flying high. There's an energy in Farcliff that I haven't felt in a long time.

I grin, forgetting for a moment that I'm flat broke, homeless, and that my father is seriously ill.

"So, I was thinking I'd head over to Westhill the day after tomorrow." I glance over at my mom.

"So soon?" Her eyebrows draw together. "There's the ceremony in three days! You could stay in Farcliff until then, at least. Your father and I would love to spend some time with you."

"I think Dad would agree that we shouldn't leave Harry Brooks in charge of the roses for too long."

My mother lets out a dry laugh and nods her head. "That's probably true."

She tells me a thousand and one things about the garden, the Prince, his daughter, and everything that has happened since we last spoke on the phone. We head towards their new home and I settle into my seat, only half listening to my mother's rambling voice. I watch the trees and buildings zip by us, and I inhale the fresh air in the Kingdom.

I'm home.

My parents are staying in a small rental apartment near the hospital, and have a blow-up mattress set up for me on the living room floor. I look at the makeshift sleeping arrangements, and decide that I definitely won't be staying longer than two nights.

"Jolie?" My father limps out of the bedroom, wearing a big smile. He looks weak, but happy. "Thank you for coming back, kiddo." He wraps his arms around me in a big bear hug. "I appreciate it."

"I'll make sure the rose garden is in good shape for when you come back."

My father gives me a tight smile that doesn't quite reach his eyes, and I wonder if he thinks he'll be coming back to Westhill Palace at all. My chest tightens, and I try to ignore the feeling of dread that crawls into my heart.

My father could be dying.

That weighs on my mind as I spend the rest of the evening with my parents. My father struggles to move around, and he's lost the bounce in his step that he once had. He coughs into a handkerchief often, and goes to bed early.

I watch him, biting my lip. My leg bounces up and down whenever I sit down, and I find it hard to eat anything. Every time I look at my father, knots form in my stomach.

THE NEXT DAY, my father pats a chair beside him. I sit down and his face grows serious.

"Now, remember, Jolie," Dad says before pausing for a coughing fit. "You have to water the roses twice a week—but don't soak them. I've made sure the soil is draining well, but you'll still have to keep an eye on it. You might need to add some mulch. Keep an eye on the leaves, some of the other gardeners in the area have said there are some beetles—" My father coughs again, and my chest tightens.

"I know, Dad. Don't worry."

He dabs his mouth with his handkerchief.

"They should start to bud soon. I planted some repeat bloomers on the southern side of the garden. They looked like they were in good shape when we left, so they should produce flushes of flowers every month or so."

"Okay, Dad." I squeeze his arm. "Don't worry. Everything will be fine. If you're still concerned, I can video call you every day from the garden." I grin, winking at him.

"You don't have to do that." A smile quirks his lip. "Every second day will do."

I laugh, kissing my father's cheek. He pats my hand and lets out a sigh. I can tell it's killing him to leave the garden behind, and I do my best to sound confident. The most gardening I've done in the past six years has been killing a few house plants. An award-winning Royal Rose Garden should be a breeze, right?

My father nods and kisses the side of my head. "I know you'll do great, honey," he says. "You have a better touch with the roses than I do."

"I don't know about that, but I'll do my best."

"The Prince..." My father's face pinches.

"What about him?"

"He's... *troubled.*" Dad glances at me. "I think it would be best if you kept your distance."

"Troubled?"

My father nods and takes a deep breath. "I know you can

handle yourself, Jo. I'll stop fussing. I'm a bit tired. I might go lie down for an hour before dinner."

As I watch him shuffle toward his bedroom, my heart breaks all over again. I know that the only thing I can do for my parents is make sure the rose garden is well taken care of. I can't heal my father or make him feel better, but I can provide that peace of mind.

WHEN IT'S time for me to leave in the morning, I pack up my things and give my parents another big hug. My mother drops me off at the bus station and asks me if I have enough money. I just smile and nod.

"I'm fine, Mom. Things are going well," I lie.

"I'm proud of you." Her eyes shine, and she holds my cheeks in her hands. She kisses my forehead, patting my cheek. "Thank you for coming back. Your father was relieved when I told him you'd take care of his flowers. The doctor said he had to relax as much as possible, so who knows? You might be helping him heal, too."

"I hope so."

After one last hug, I get on the bus for Westhill and settle into my seat. As the bus pulls out of the station, a warm buzz courses through my body. My chest feels light, and a smile starts to stretch across my lips.

I pull out my notebook and start jotting ideas down. I love this little book. It holds bits of scenes, turns of phrase that pop into my head, fragments of story ideas, and anything else that sticks in my brain. Interspersed between the pages are messy to-do lists and scratchy doodles.

As I write down my rush of ideas, they become too much to record in my humble notebook. Instead, I pull my laptop out of my backpack and open it up. I click to create a blank document, staring at it for a few thrilling moments.

Is there anything more beautiful than a blank page, ready to be filled with magical, inspiring words?

My lips curl into a grin. I don't want to re-hash the book I've already written. Maybe the rejection letters were right. I tried to write a fast-paced thriller, but maybe my first attempt just wasn't gripping?

For the first time in months, I want to write something *new*. Something fresh. I stare at the blank page in front of me, and my heart starts to thump. I glance out of the bus window at the passing landscape, and the words start to flow.

I didn't even know the words existed inside me, but they come out like an avalanche. I can hardly type fast enough to keep up with my own mind. The two-hour bus journey goes by in a flash, and I look up from my screen, exhausted.

I've written three chapters of a new story—another thriller —and the spark of inspiration coursing like a wildfire inside me. I close my laptop and stuff it back into my bag, slinging it over my shoulder as I step off the bus. My smile is wide, and I have a bounce in my step. The bus driver helps me haul my suitcase out of the bus's cargo compartment, and I glance around me.

Only two other people have gotten off in Westhill, and I immediately understand why. Westhill is a small village at the foot of the Westhill Palace. There's not much here except a decrepit-looking community garden, a library, a shop, and a school. The houses look well-kept, though, and the air here is sweet and fresh. Intersecting the only road through Westhill is a street called 'Palace Lane'.

Seems like an obvious place to start looking for the palace.

I drag my suitcase down the road, already knowing I

made the right decision to come here. If the first few chapters of my new book are anything to go by, Westhill could be the birthplace of some of my best work.

At the end of the long road, there's a tall, ornate, cast-iron fence. By the time I get to the gates, I'm sweaty and my arm is sore from dragging my suitcase. My heart speeds up as I get closer.

The gates are elaborate, with designs of roses and snarling beasts intertwined in them. The Palace estates are vast and sprawling, enclosed by the intricate fencing as far as I can see. In the distance, at the end of an even longer drive than the one from the town to the gate, Westhill Palace sits. It rests among well-manicured lawns and topiary, with beautifully flowering beds lining the entire drive.

My mouth goes dry, and I gulp.

The Farcliff crest is engraved on both pillars that stand either side of the gates. I take a deep breath, and then start walking toward the intercom on one of the pillars. I press the button and wait for a response.

"Yes?"

"Jolie Beaumont," I say into the speaker. My voice trembles slightly, and I take a breath to steady myself. "I'm Marcel and Violet's daughter. I'm here to tend the rose garden."

The intercom clicks, and for a moment nothing happens. I frown, glancing around me. My parents warned the staff that I'd be here, right?

The early May sun is warming my back, and a bead of sweat trickles down the side of my face. After an interminable moment, the gates swing inward without a sound.

I take a deep breath, chewing my lip, and then I step through. My pulse hammers, and I can hardly believe I'm here.

Maybe I'm not a failure, after all. Maybe I just needed to

find some time and space for myself—and maybe Westhill is exactly that.

I've only taken half a dozen steps when a car appears at the far end of the long driveway. Even from a distance, I can tell it's a royal vehicle. I drag my suitcase off the road, and stand to the side, waiting for the car to pass. I take care not to step in the flowerbeds. There's nowhere else for me to stand unless I want to crush all these flowers with my suitcase.

The car is travelling at high speed, zooming down the narrow drive faster than I would find comfortable if I were driving. I glance at the flowerbeds again, wondering if I can jump over them to get out of the way. They're too wide, though, and I know I'd end up crushing the plants.

My throat turns dry, and I grip the handle of my suitcase as hard as I can.

The vehicle slows down only the tiniest bit as it approaches me. The windows are tinted, so I can't see anyone in the car—but I already know who's inside.

I can feel Prince Gabriel's eyes on me like hot coals burning into my skin. I can sense his presence, and for the briefest moment as the car passes, I think I actually enjoy it.

The car zips through the front gates and I let out a sigh, staring after it. Then, I turn back toward the royal grounds and continue my long walk toward the palace.

4

GABRIEL

GLANCING IN THE REAR-VIEW MIRROR, I catch a glimpse of the young woman walking towards the castle. She drags her suitcase behind her with her head held high.

I come to a stop outside the gate and glance in the mirror again, watching her ass sway from side to side as she walks down the drive. Is she Marcel's daughter? She has to be—I haven't heard of anyone else arriving this week.

I wouldn't expect the short, portly man with the frizzy white hair to have a willowy daughter like her. Her long, chocolate brown hair is gathered up in a high ponytail, cascading down to between her shoulder blades.

As if she senses my stare, the girl pauses and turns to look over her shoulder. I know she can't see me, but it feels like she's staring straight into my eyes. For just a moment, I forget about the celebration in Farcliff, about my brothers, about the past and all the memories that await me in the city.

I just stare at the girl, and she stares at me.

We stay like that for a few moments, until Flora clears her throat from the back seat of the car.

"Who's that?"

Turning back to the road in front of me, I let out a sigh. "No one."

"Why is she at the castle?" Flora asks, twisting in her seat.

"She's taking care of the rose garden."

Turning out of the gates, I step on the accelerator and drive toward the city. Flora starts asking me a thousand and one questions about Farcliff, and I answer them as patiently as I can. It's a two hour drive, but I can probably do it in an hour forty.

So, why am I slowing down?

I find myself driving slower than the speed limit, flexing and unflexing my hands as I make my way toward the capital at a snail's pace. Even my daughter notices.

"Are you okay?" Flora asks from the back seat.

I glance at her in the rear-view mirror and try to force a smile. "I'm fine, Flora. You want to watch a movie?"

"No," she answers simply, turning to stare out the window.

My hand drifts to my jaw, where that six-inch long scar mars my face. I rub it, remembering what happened the last time I was in Farcliff.

I remember the pain of the knife as it slashed my face. I remember the blood. I remember the shame.

Most of all, I remember the ice-cold fear that spiked through me when I thought I'd lost Flora.

Going back there is a terrible idea. She doesn't even know what happened, and I'm bringing her back to the beginning of it all.

That stupid book started the chaos. If I'd have known that my ex would write some trash about our relationship, I never would have gotten involved with her. I knew she was just interested in fame, but I didn't listen to my instinct—or maybe, I just didn't care.

32

Until she got pregnant, and I became a father.

Then, I started to care. It wasn't about me and my demons anymore, it was about Flora. My daughter. My savior. My life.

I ended up disgraced, scarred, and too afraid to set foot in my own home city—not that I've wanted to.

My heart beats a little bit faster as I slow the car down even more. A rickety old camper van passes me on the freeway, and the driver gives me a slight courtesy wave. I wave back, knowing the windows are too tinted for the driver to see me.

When we cross into the Farcliff city limits, sweat is gathering under my arms and I feel like I can't breathe right. I snake through the streets, thankful for the darkened windows of my car.

People stare at the car—they know it's a royal vehicle—but no one knows it's me and Flora inside. That anonymity is a blessing.

I make it to the Farcliff Castle gates, which open without even questioning who I am.

They're expecting us.

Flora lets out an excited squeal and asks me another slew of questions about the castle itself. Up the driveway I go, sucking in a breath as memories flood my mind. I do my best to answer my daughter's questions, but I'm not sure I'm making any sense.

The castle looks just the same as I remember. It hasn't changed a bit. I park the car near the wide front steps and exit the vehicle. A valet appears beside me, and I drop my keys in his hand with a nod. I open Flora's door just as she unbuckles her seatbelt. She slips her hand into mine and gives me an encouraging smile.

"Did you bring the good luck rock?"

"Got it right here," I say, patting my pocket.

33

"Good," she nods. She squeezes my hand and we turn toward the castle. The heavy double doors at the top of the steps swing open, and my brother's butler appears with a bow.

I take a deep breath.

Charlie, my eldest brother and the King of Farcliff, fills the doorway. For a moment, my nerves are almost too much to bear. Being in Farcliff is surreal.

But Charlie's face splits into a smile and he starts bounding down the steps toward us. His kids beat him to it, though, dodging around his legs and flying in to hug me. I catch all three of them, laughing and ruffling their hair.

"Uncle Gabriel, you came!" Prince Charlie, the King's eldest, smiles at me.

"Of course I came." I cluck his cheek with my finger.

Their only daughter, Thea, slips her hand into mine. "Come inside. We made cookies for you." She smiles at Flora. "Hi." They've met at Westhill, but they haven't seen each other for almost a year—an eternity in a six-year-old's life.

My heart squeezes when I see Flora next to her cousin. Both girls are about the same age, but Flora is a lot smaller. It's her illness. *Failure to thrive*, one doctor explained to me with a nonchalant glance. I fired him shortly thereafter.

The two girls study each other for a moment, and then Flora reaches over to give her cousin a hug. The top of her head just about reaches Princess Thea's shoulder, and the two of them smile at each other.

Charlie winks at me and extends his hand for me to shake it. "Good to see you, Gabe. I wasn't sure you'd make it."

"Wouldn't miss it for anything," I lie. He practically had to drag me out of Westhill by force, and I'm only here for two nights. As soon as these celebrations are over, I'll be heading back to Westhill with my daughter.

Back to safety and isolation.

I let the kids lead me inside to one of the smaller living rooms, and I accept a burnt cookie from Thea. It looks more like a hockey puck than edible food. I bite into it—or at least, I try to—as Thea watches me with a hopeful smile.

"You like it?"

"Delicious," I nod with a grimace as crumbs fall off my lips. I crunch through the cookie, slightly worried I've chipped a tooth. Thea grins, twirling in a circle.

Flora looks at her cookie suspiciously. "It looks burnt."

Thea's face falls, and Flora glances at me. I give her a loaded look, and she nibbles at the cookie before making an exaggerated noise and rubbing her belly. "Deeeee-licious," she says.

Thea's face brightens, and the two girls run off to play. My nerves crank up a notch as Flora disappears out of my sight, but I force myself to calm down with a deep breath. She's in Farcliff Castle—arguably the safest place for her, besides Westhill.

Charlie nods to the garbage can. "Quick, while Thea's not looking."

I grin, tossing the calcinated cookie away. "She's not quite a star baker."

"Not quite, no," Charlie laughs.

My brother hands me a beer and takes a seat next to me. Neither of us say anything for a while, until Charlie finally breaks the silence.

"Thanks for coming." He glances at me, his eyes piercing into me.

My heart squeezes. How could I have considered avoiding this event? It would have killed him. I may be a recluse and a bit of an asshole, but Charlie has done everything for me and our brother Damon. He investigated our own father, and discovered that the former King had murdered our mother. After that bombshell, Charlie ascended to the throne even though he didn't want to.

When things went to shit for me, he gave me Westhill Palace as my own.

My brother is a good man, and the least I can do is be here to celebrate his ten year anniversary with him.

Charlie clears his throat. "How does it feel to be back in Farcliff Castle?"

"Weird."

The King grunts.

"Last time I was here, my face was sliced open and my picture was plastered over every newspaper."

"I remember it well." He glances at me and then takes a sip of beer. "You ever talk to her again?"

"Who? Paulette? Fuck no. If I never saw her face again, it would be too soon. I don't exactly want to get my cheek slashed again, and I can't put Flora in danger by being around her."

Charlie makes a soft noise in agreement as the side door opens. Our middle brother, Damon, pokes his head through. His face splits into a smile when he spots me. He strides over to me, wrapping me in a hug. He's gained a bit of weight over the years, but the gaunt lines in his face have disappeared. He looks happy.

Surprisingly, I start to feel happy, too.

While I catch up with my brothers in the castle where I grew up, I feel almost comfortable. The fears that gripped my heart on the way here start to ease, and I even smile.

"So, the ceremony tomorrow will be televised." Charlie eventually turns the talk to business. "We'll start at the castle and then have a procession through the town."

I sip my beer and nod. "Okay. What do you need me to do?"

"Just sit beside me and look pretty."

"Easy," I grin. "Even with a six-inch scar, I'm still better looking than the two of you."

My first evening in Farcliff lulls me into a false sense of security. Coming back here is strange, but I feel almost comfortable. That night, I sleep in my old bedroom, and wake up with my nephews and nieces jumping on my bed. I eat breakfast with my family like a normal human being.

I keep Flora's good luck rock in my pocket, and I touch it whenever unease creeps into my heart.

Flora seems happy here. She's always gotten along with her cousins, but she seems extra excited to be in Farcliff. Her energy levels are high, and she has color to her cheeks. She looks healthy. For the first time since I received Charlie's invitation, I start to think that coming back to Farcliff might have been a good idea.

But when the ceremony starts, I realize how wrong I am.

We begin in the Great Hall, and I see a face in the crowd that I hoped I'd never see again.

Paulette.

It's just a split second, and then she disappears.

I blink, wondering if I imagined it. It must be my brain playing tricks on me. All those memories I've been pushing away are coming to the surface.

Paulette would never have been admitted to the castle. Of course it wasn't her. It's impossible. I'm seeing things.

Shaking my head, I turn back to my brother.

King Charlie makes a speech and spreads his arms wide to the crowd in the room. Applause erupts. I clap my hands and try to smile. My gaze drifts over to the spot where I saw my ex's face.

I put a protective arm over Flora's shoulders.

I was imagining it. I had to be.

I follow Charlie, Damon, and their wives, Elle and Dahlia, out through the main double doors. We enter the royal cars, convertibles, so that we can wave to the crowds that line the streets to see us.

Perfect for the weather and the occasion.

Very much imperfect for me.

It's too open. Too public. Too exposed.

Flora slips her hand into mine and gives me an encouraging squeeze. Shouldn't it be *me*, comforting *her*? I'm her father. I'm the adult. She's just a six-year-old girl.

As usual, she surprises me. She lifts me up and helps me when I need it, giving me more strength than a child should.

It feels difficult to take a full breath. When the cars pull out of the castle gates and I see the crowds for the first time, I feel like I'm going to pass out.

As we drive down the streets, Flora waves to the crowds and flashes them her most dazzling smile. People point and take pictures, and I hear the swell of excitement at the sight of my daughter.

The whole city is jubilant. There's a frantic sort of energy in the air that leaves an electric taste on my tongue. My heart beats erratically, and my mouth is a little too dry to be comfortable.

I'm exposed, naked, on display.

Flora is, too. I can see the people pointing at her—at the mysterious princess who's been kept out of the public eye. At the young girl whose birth was surrounded by so much controversy. At the one person in the world who means anything to me.

Damon leans into me. "You okay?"

I gulp. "I'm fine. I just don't like crowds."

"You've been too isolated out in Westhill."

"Maybe."

The people lining the streets meld into one mass of humanity. I can't pick out individual faces. All I hear are screams getting louder and louder and louder. Arms wave, mouths stretch open to shout at us, and eyes pierce through me.

In an instant, I'm carried back to six years ago.

Those same faces, those same voices, but not quite the same screams. Today, they're jubilant. Back then, they were menacing.

My hand flies to my face and my scar feels hot to the touch. It burns my face, slicing it open all over again as the images of that day fill my mind.

Damon puts his hand on my arm, squeezing it gently. I swallow a breath, staring at the back of our driver's head as I try to regain control over myself. Flora waves to the crowds on the other side of me, and it takes all my self-control not to tell her to stop.

I'm on the edge. I know this feeling—I've been here before. The beast inside me is trying to break loose. I'm shaking—trembling in my seat, trying to maintain control over my own body.

Damon's hand feels heavy on my forearm. My heart beats wildly, and my breath comes in short, staggered gasps. I can't get enough air. I can't fill my lungs. There's a weight pressing on my chest, and a giant hand squeezing my head.

Then, I do the one thing I shouldn't do. I look up at the crowd...

...and I see her.

Paulette.

Looking as attractive and venomous as she did six years ago. Dressed in a skin-tight dress, showing off her perfect, intoxicating body. Her pink lips curl into a cruel smile and her eyes drill into mine.

The moment our eyes meet, the barricade holding the crowds back breaks. They rush at our car. At me. At Flora.

People scream and jump forward, running toward our vehicle as panic mounts inside me...

...and I lose the battle with the beast.

My scar throbs, my heart races.

And I roar.

Jumping over Flora, I rip the car door open. I lunge toward the crowd. Cheers turn to shouts as people shrink away from me. I fly toward them, roaring and swinging my arms wildly from side to side. My fist clips someone's jaw, and I roar once more. I shrink further and further inside myself, letting the wildness take over. I taste blood in my mouth, feeding off the adrenaline that courses through my veins.

Screams buoy me further as I rush the crowd. My vision is fuzzy. People rush away from me, back behind the barricade as photos flash in my eyes.

I feel like a caged animal. My family screams behind me, and the crowd shrieks in front of me. Reaching the edge of the crowd, I lean over an untoppled section of the barricade and climb up on top of it, searching the crowd for the woman who ruined my life.

I'll rip the head from her shoulders. I'll slash her face, just as she slashed mine. I'll do anything to make sure she doesn't hurt my daughter. I'll *kill, kill, kill.*

But she's gone.

Maybe she was never there to begin with.

My chest heaves as I grip the barricade, hundreds of terrified eyes staring up at me as cameras continue to flash.

Smartphones stay pointed at me as I stare into them, seeing nothing.

An arm pulls me off the barricade. I'm dragged back to a different car, thrashing and screaming until the door slams and I'm driven away.

5

JO

MY NOSE IS inches from the television screen. My breath catches as I watch Prince Gabriel leaping toward the crowd. He looks feral. Even on the television screen, I can see the whites of his eyes. Sweat is beading on his temple, and his cheeks are bright red.

His daughter cries in the car behind him and my own lip trembles. My heart breaks for her as the news cycle shreds Prince Gabriel to pieces. His outburst overshadows the entire ceremony, and Flora's crying face stays frozen on the screen as reporters dissect every moment of the Prince's breakdown.

Is this what my parents meant when they said he was troubled?

I put my hand to my chest as my eyebrows draw together. Tears sting my eyes as I watch Prince Gabriel's reaction to the crowd get replayed on an endless loop.

The network plays it from a multitude of different angles, in slow motion, at regular speed, over and over and over again. Grainy, shaky smartphone footage in interspersed with official television recordings. He's dragged back to a car, kicking and screaming, and the entire ceremony descends into frantic damage control.

They interview the man Prince Gabriel punched, who calls the Prince an animal. A tear rolls down my cheek. His outburst was unprovoked, but the way he's being treated in the media is downright savage.

Leaning back in my seat, I let out a deep breath and wipe my tear away. As reporters replay the Prince's attack yet again, disgust wells up inside me and I flick the television off. I toss the remote away and sigh, rubbing my palms over my eyes.

"They're animals, aren't they?" A voice says behind me.

I turn to find Mrs. Grey's head poking through the door. I'm in the Gardener's Cottage, my new home. It's at the back of the Westhill Palace grounds, tucked away in a copse of trees.

Mrs. Grey, the no-nonsense woman who runs the castle, steps through the door. She shakes her head. Her salt-and-pepper hair is tied back in a low bun, and she wipes her hands on her apron. "The press, I mean. Jumping on poor Prince Gabriel like that when they should be focusing on the King. And poor Miss Flora! This has ruined her first public appearance."

"What happened? It looked like he just snapped."

Mrs. Grey tuts. She pulls a rag out of her pocket and starts dusting some shelves. My parents left most of their belongings here, which is a good sign that they think they'll be coming back. My father is an avid reader, like me, and he has shelves and shelves of books in the cottage. He still has all my books from when I was a kid, too.

Mrs. Grey dusts the books without looking at me. "Prince Gabriel is a complicated man," she says, not really answering my question. She puts her hands on her hips and turns toward me. "Anyway. I came here to make sure you had everything you needed."

I nod. "I'm all set."

"The rest of the staff and I prepared a bit of a welcome lunch for you today. We figured you'd be tired yesterday, but we'd like to officially welcome you to the castle."

"Really?" My eyebrows jump up. "Wow, I... Thank you."

Mrs. Grey smiles at me, and my heart swells. Since my arrival yesterday, I've met half a dozen people who've made me feel more welcome than I've ever felt before. Maybe it's because I've been living in New York City for so long, and I'm used to strangers being rude to me. Maybe I'm just happy to be back in Farcliff.

Whatever it is, there's a sense of community in Westhill that warms my heart. It makes me feel like coming here was the right decision—for myself as well as my parents.

Mrs. Grey motions to the door, and I follow her back to the main castle. She points out the various areas of the grounds to me as we make the ten-minute walk back.

"This is the servant's entrance," she says. "So you'll be coming in and out of here every day. We serve lunch from noon until one. If your shoes are dirty, clean them here. I don't want you tracking dirt all over the kitchens. Your father was a nightmare for that."

I grin, imagining my father going toe-to-toe with Mrs. Grey. I think he'd rather face the cancer than get on the wrong side of her.

The hallways in the servants' quarters of the castle are a bit too narrow for the two of us to walk side-by-side, so I fall in behind her. She points out a couple of bathrooms, a linen closet, and finally the kitchens. I can hear the sounds of pots and pans clanging, intermingling voices, and lots of laughter.

We turn the corner and the smell of something delicious fills my nostrils. I inhale the scent and sigh in contentment.

"Is that a roast?"

"With all the trimmings," Mrs. Grey smiles. "George is a fabulous cook—fit for a king." She winks.

George bows to me. He's wearing a white chef's jacket and a matching cap. "At your service, Madame."

His hair is jet black, poking out under his cap in thick curls. He has a slight French accent.

"You already know Harry," Mrs. Grey continues. I nod to the young man. Harry Brooks is broad and strong, with sun-kissed skin bronzed from hours working in the gardens with my father. I met him yesterday, when I first checked out the rose garden. He winks at me, and I blush.

"This is Samantha," Mrs. Grey continues. "The head of housekeeping."

"Sam," the young woman corrects. She has curly red hair and ruddy cheeks, and I like her instantly. "You're Jolie?"

"Jo," I say, and we both smile at each other.

I'm introduced to a dozen more staff, including Bertrand, Prince Gabriel's personal butler. He's tall and bald, with a hooked nose. He doesn't say anything to me, but gives me a low bow and studies me with his sharp, dark eyes.

I take a seat next to Sam and accept a plate from George.

"Welcome to Westhill," he says in a deep, friendly voice. "We loved your parents. They always spoke highly of you."

It only takes a few moments for me to feel at home here. I've lived alone for so many years, struggling to make ends meet—this is almost too much for me to take in.

The staff laugh and joke with each other throughout the meal. Most of them have worked and lived in this castle their entire lives. It feels like a big family. By the end of the meal, both my heart and my stomach are full. My cheeks hurt from laughing, and I have no doubt that I've made the right decision in coming here.

Harry takes my empty plate and nods to the door. "I can show you around the grounds, if you like. You can let me know if you need any help with anything in the rose garden."

Something in the way Harry's eyes sparkle makes me uncomfortable, but I just smile in response and agree. When we walk toward the door, his hand drifts to my lower back, and I pull away, clearing my throat.

His touch feels too insistent, and I don't like it.

Still, I've just been welcomed into this tight-knit group with open arms, and Harry is one of them. He has jet-black hair and objectively, he's very handsome. I don't want to be rude on my second day here. It's just that every time Harry smiles at me, an uncomfortable feeling crawls up my spine.

Harry leads me outside and to a golf cart. We take off. I grab on to the handle above me as Harry points out various areas.

"We'll go to the creek first. It's the wildest area of the castle grounds. It's actually a protected wildlife reserve, so we don't do much work there. The Rangers monitor it." He nods to a little brick building on the edge of the reserve. We drive along the perimeter of the forested area, and Harry glances at me.

"You're pretty," he says. "Better than I expected you to be."

"Um, thanks?" I frown. Was that supposed to be a compliment?

"Yeah, although if you keep eating as much as you did today, you'll probably put on a few pounds" He glances at me, dragging his eyes up and down my body. I shift in my seat uncomfortably, not answering. How long is this tour going to last? Not long, I hope.

Harry drives over to the hedge maze at the western end of the grounds. "You want to go inside?"

I glance at the tall hedges and clear my throat. The last place I want to be is stuck in a maze with Harry's wandering eyes—or any other parts of his that may be prone to wandering.

I shake my head. "Maybe some other time. I was hoping to get some work done in the rose garden today."

"Straight to work, hey?"

"That's why I'm here," I smile awkwardly, and Harry turns the golf cart back toward the castle.

"You know, Prince Gabriel really loves the rose garden. I hope you'll be able to keep it up to his standards." Harry glances at me, giving me what I'm guessing is his best roguish smile.

I nod. "Thanks for the vote of confidence."

"You're a bit uptight, aren't you?"

When I don't answer, Harry continues: "Yeah, the Prince was pretty tough on your father. You think you can handle it?"

"What do you mean? Tough on my father how?"

Does this have anything to do with Prince Gabriel's outburst at the parade? What kind of person is Prince Gabriel, really?

"Oh, you know, His Highness is just very particular about how the roses should be kept."

"Well, I learned from the best, so I'm sure I'll be able to handle it. Thanks for the tour." I jump out of the golf cart before it even comes to a full stop. Harry reaches his hand toward me, and then reconsiders. He grins at me, and with a wink, he drives away.

I watch him leave, trying to ignore the prickly feeling at the back of my neck. Yesterday, Harry Brooks told me he's the youngest head gardener ever to be in charge of Westhill. I think he resents that my father was in charge of the rose garden.

Whether or not he's a threat to me, though—I'm not sure.

I'm inclined to think he's mostly harmless, and maybe just used to having girls crawl all over him. Harry is muscular, and quite handsome—but I just broke up with another up-himself, arrogant prick. I have no intention of falling into bed with another one.

The last thing I want to do is have *any* kind of romantic relationship that would jeopardize my position at Westhill.

I shake my head and turn back to the Westhill Rose Garden.

It's enclosed in a low, wrought iron fence, similar to the one that encloses the palace grounds. I push the gate open. It's a miniature version of the front gates I walked through yesterday.

The roses are just beginning to bud, and I take my time walking among them. I grew up surrounded by these flowers, since my father has always been a rose gardener. When he got the position at Westhill Palace, he looked happier than I've ever seen him—and now, it's my turn to make him proud.

I run my fingers over one of the tiny rose buds, letting my heart settle after a hectic few days. I spin around in a slow circle, taking stock of the small patch of land that will become my own little kingdom over the next few months.

Inhaling the fresh air, my mind starts sparking with ideas. I take out my precious leather-bound notebook to make notes of all the things that need to be done for the roses before slipping it back into my pocket.

My mind flits back to the story I started writing on the bus. Walking to the shed, I can't stop smiling. I grab a bag of mulch and start spreading it out wherever it's needed, all the while thinking of my story.

Surrounded by my parents' hard work—and wanting to make them proud—I feel more inspired than I have in years. Finally, I have a stable base from which to live my life. I have a house, and food, and a garden to tend.

Most importantly, I have ideas.

In this rose garden, I think I've found my muse. If I can keep my distance from the Prince, I might just be able to make a home here.

6

GABRIEL

I DRIVE BACK to Westhill in the dead of night. Flora sleeps in the back seat, and I check on her in the mirror often. I don't want to see anyone or talk to anyone. I know I lost control. I know I ruined the ceremony. I know that Charlie isn't happy with me.

But how could I help it?

Paulette was *there*. I saw her. She probably orchestrated the whole thing—the barricade falling over and the crowd surging forward.

I saw the way she looked at Flora, like a lion salivating at the sight of an antelope. That woman is evil, and I don't want her anywhere near my daughter.

Of course I snapped. Of course the beast took over. How could it not?

I'd kill for Flora.

I drive into the Westhill Palace gates and park the car in the garages. Bertrand greets me with a bow. He takes the car keys from me without a word as I gather Flora in my arms.

She makes a soft grumble, but doesn't wake up. Her breaths are shallow, and I worry that the trip to Farcliff will cause her to get another infection. I carry her down the quiet hallways toward the East Wing.

Westhill Castle is smaller than the one in Farcliff City, but no less ornate. As soon as I make it to our wing of the castle, my shoulders relax. I lay Flora in her bed and tuck her in. I make sure she's comfortable before flicking the lights off. Then, I head next-door to our live-in nurse. She nods to me, and then slips into Flora's room to check on her.

I sigh, finally at ease. Flora is safe. I'm safe. We're home.

Going to my own chambers, I kick off my shoes and let my toes sink into the plush carpet. In the silence of my own home, reality starts to set in.

I fucked up. I know I did.

Flopping down onto the bed, I rub my hands over my face and groan. Charlie hardly said a word to me after the ceremony, and I left before I could really talk to him. Now that I'm here, in the silence and isolation of Westhill, I feel like an idiot.

Why did I have to rush the crowd? I *punched* someone. I punched one of my own subjects! I'm a prince, for Farcliff's sake! What was I thinking? I can only imagine what the media are saying about me. They're probably dredging up old footage of my face getting knifed, and grainy videos of me lunging toward Paulette.

Maybe they're talking about Flora. That thought makes my gut churn. The last thing I want for Flora is for her to be dragged into a messy fight with the media.

Paulette probably loves this, though. Her book sales will go through the roof. Even though her book was banned in Farcliff years ago, I know it still gets smuggled into the country and sold in the back of dingy bookshops. That drivel she wrote about me made her a millionaire—and it turned me into a recluse. She's still making money off her lies, and she's probably loving all of this.

I rub my hand over my jaw and push myself off the bed. Heading to the window, I gaze down at the Royal Rose Garden below. The rose bushes are still here, silently working to create the explosion of scent and color that will soon happen.

Movement catches my eye. It's the girl from the driveway. She's walking through the bushes, inspecting the tiny buds. I crack the window open, and I can hear the sound of her voice. I frown.

She's *singing* to them.

I lean against the window frame, hidden in the shadows. What did Marcel say his daughter's name was? Did he even tell me her name? I frown, watching her. The sounds of her melody float up toward me, and the tension behind my eyes begins to ease. The pounding headache that's plagued me ever since I left Farcliff starts to fade.

The girl pauses under my window, glancing up toward the castle. I shrink away from the glass, and I'm not quite sure why. I don't care if she sees me—it's my castle.

Still, I don't want to ruin this moment for her—because that's what I do. I ruin things.

I ruined my own life. I ruined Flora's health by giving her this disease. I ruined Charlie's ceremony.

Everything I touch turns to ash.

My new gardener's eyes drift past my window, and I watch her take a deep breath. Her voice grows more and more faint, and she makes her way out of the rose garden and towards the Gardener's Cottage. I watch her until she slips out of view.

What kind of young woman would accept a position here? What kind of person would take her father's place in an isolated palace at the edge of the Kingdom? The only people who come to Westhill are ones that grew up here, or they're running away from something.

I know which I am. I've been running away from myself since I was a toddler.

What is she running from, I wonder?

I already know I won't sleep tonight. Truthfully, I don't sleep most nights. Insomnia is like a devil sitting on my shoulder, poking me every time my eyelids start to droop. Some nights, when the demon cackles in my ear, my eyelids don't droop at all. When that happens, I'll wander the castle and the gardens, or I'll stare at the ceiling. If all else fails, I'll go to my studio and I draw feverishly through the night.

Tonight, I decide to head down to the garden. The evening still has a bit of a chill to it, but it zips through me in a pleasant kind of way. I wander through the roses and glance up at the window where I'd been standing.

Usually, being in the rose garden makes me calmer. The flowers creep around me and push the beast inside me down. Tonight, though, I'm restless. I wander up and down the rows of rose bushes, not daring to touch the flowers. I know that their thorns will prick me if I get too close.

The roses have a mind of their own. When they bloom, I can hear them singing all day and all night. When they die, their petals flutter to the ground like hundreds of falling tears. Their songs fade as quickly as their colors, and the magic in the garden dies.

Tonight, as the flowers bud, the garden feels like it's full of energy buzzing right below the surface. Energy like this is dangerous. I know it, because it's the same energy that flows constantly just beneath my skin.

I take a deep breath and walk along the waist-high fence. At the gate, my eye catches a small, brown leather notebook.

Leaning over to pick it up, I turn it around and flip through its pages.

Tight, scrawly handwriting stares back at me. I read notes about people and places, quotes, half-formed ideas, and to-do lists that look like they've been jotted down in a hurry. It looks like a writer's notebook.

I lick my finger and turn the pages over, sinking deeper and deeper into the mind of whoever wrote these words. It's bursting with ideas.

Interestingly, the people described in the book are dark and the places are seedy. The bits of dialogue are biting and sharp. I don't know how long I stand there, reading words that will never make sense to me. It feels like I've opened a notebook into the depths of its owner's mind, flipping through the pages of their innermost thoughts.

Dark thoughts. Fragmented thoughts.

Then, I turn another page and I see one last to-do list.

Mulch roses, ask George about food scraps for compost, buy more fertilizer.

A smile tugs at my lips. The mind that I've just split open, whose most innermost thoughts and images I just read?

It's my new rose gardener's mind.

I lift my eyes towards the Gardener's Cottage at the far end of the grounds. Before I can stop myself, my feet are carrying me towards it.

Maybe I'll just slip the notebook in the mailbox or leave it at the doorstep—but the lights in the cottage are still on, and I know I won't be able to resist knocking on the door.

As I get closer, my heart starts to beat harder. The dangerous energy zipping beneath my skin grows more frantic, and I can feel every hair on my skin standing on end.

The grass is dewy, and by the time I make it to the cottage, my pants are damp up to my mid-calf. I wipe my feet on the welcome mat outside the front door, and I glance around the front of the building.

I can't tell if there are any changes since Marcel and Violet left—I haven't been out to the cottage in months.

As I stand there, a curious noise comes to my attention. It's the tapping of fingers on a keyboard, as if my new rose gardener is typing at light speed. I lean toward the door, listening for anything else. A chair creaks, and footsteps sound as she starts pacing up and down the room.

She's talking, and I frown. Is someone else in there with her? Who would be with her at this hour? A lover?

Why does that thought bother me?

Dirty, green jealousy flares inside me, and I don't even understand why. I don't even know this woman's name, and I've never seen her up close.

No one responds. The pacing stops, the typing resumes, and the voice falls quiet. She was talking to herself.

I turn the notebook over in my hands, and then raise my fist to knock on her door.

The typing continues, and I drop my hand again. I stare at the notebook, and I wonder what her words look like when they've moved from her notebook to her computer screen.

Sighing, I shake my head.

Another damn writer—it's always a writer.

At least this one is honest in her writing—or at least her notebook seems that way. I place the little leather-bound book on the welcome mat, then turn around and walk back to the palace.

7

JO

"Thanks for bringing my notebook back." I smile at Mrs. Grey across the breakfast table. "That thing keeps me sane. My whole life is in that notebook! Everything I've ever done, am doing, or will do in the future is written down in it." I laugh, shaking my head. "Losing it would be a disaster."

Mrs. Grey frowns. "Your notebook?"

"Yeah. It was on my doorstep this morning. I hadn't even realized I'd lost it."

"I didn't bring anything back, Jo," Mrs. Grey says, shrugging. "Must have been someone else."

I glance at Sam, who shrugs as well. "Wasn't me. Harry, maybe?"

I grimace at the thought of Harry Brooks showing up at my place unannounced. The look on my face makes Sam laugh.

"Didn't enjoy the tour Harry gave you, I take it?" She asks.

"No, I did." I insist. "It's just..." I look around the room, not wanting to gossip on my third day at the castle.

Sam grins. "Don't worry. I get it."

Harry walks in with his chest puffed out. He flicks the back of one of the young gardener's heads, who yelps in pain.

Sam rolls her eyes, and I stifle a giggle.

I touch my pocket, where my precious notebook lives. The thought of Harry showing up at my door doesn't exactly make me feel comfortable. At least he didn't want to come inside.

Sam nudges me with her shoulder. "How about a tour of the *inside* of the castle today? I can show you around after breakfast."

"Really?"

"As long as you're not too busy in the garden."

"Well, there's always something to do, but I wouldn't mind seeing some of this place. It's so huge!"

Sam smiles, spooning another dollop of porridge into her mouth. I turn to my eggs. When I take a bite, I moan in pleasure. "Mrs. Grey, you weren't joking. George is a master. I never knew scrambled eggs could be this good."

"Wait until you try his cream puffs."

"*Choux a la crème,*" George corrects with a shake of the head. "I refuse to call them *crème* puffs." He tuts, slinging a tea towel over his shoulder. With a judgmental glances at us, George turns his nose up. "Heathens—all of you."

Ever since I've arrived here, I haven't stopped smiling. I feel like I've found a new family. No wonder my parents never wanted to leave. The only person that I'm not sure about is Harry—but truthfully, he's fine. Just a little awkward, I think. Hopefully, he'll move past his lame attempts at flirting with me, and then things will be more comfortable.

Sam pushes her chair back and clears her plate. "Let's go," she says, nodding to the door. "Before Mrs. Grey finds something better for us to do."

We put our dishes away and slip out of the kitchen door.

Sam leads me down a narrow hallway that opens onto a much larger one. My feet sink into the plush, intricately designed carpet. The ceiling is lined with crown molding, and chandeliers dripping with crystals give the whole place a soft glow. Ceiling roses weave above the chandeliers, and I crane my neck to look at them.

We walk for a minute, until we reach a small alcove in the hallway. A shiny, silver suit of armor stares back at me.

I laugh, reaching out to touch it. "What is this thing?"

"Apparently it's like, six hundred years old or something." Sam pulls out a polishing rag and wipes away the smudge my finger left. "They're all over the castle."

We keep walking, and Sam glances at me. "So, are you excited for the fair?"

"The what?"

She stops dead in her tracks, staring. "Excuse me?"

I frown.

"Did you just say that you didn't know what the fair is? The Westhill Town Fair?"

I shrug. "Is it famous, or something?"

"Jo! It's only the biggest event in Westhill!"

"Okay, well, yeah, I guess I'm excited then."

Sam huffs, shaking her head. "I can't believe this. You mean to tell me that you came to Westhill and you haven't even heard of the Fair?"

"What is it?"

"It's the one time a year that the entire staff gets the night off—except for the medical staff, obviously. They stay with the Princess. The whole town of Westhill transforms! Last year, your parents had a booth selling roses. They raised, like, three thousand dollars for charity."

"Did they? They never told me that."

Sam nods. "They were great. I'm sad they're going to miss

59

it. This year, apparently the Mayor of Westhill hired some professional acrobats. It's a huge event! People come from Canada and the States, too. It's all for charity." She stares at me, smiling. When I don't respond, Sam shakes her head. "You'll see. When we go to the Fair, you'll understand why it's such a big deal." She nods down the hallway. "Come on, I want to show you the library."

The hallway stretches on forever, opening onto a multitude of formal living rooms and dining rooms. All the while, Sam tells me in great detail about the Westhill Town Fair. I nod and pretend to be excited—but how good can a regional town fair be, really?

Finally, we get to a set of tall, arched, double doors. The Farcliff crest is carved into the wood.

Sam smiles at me. "The library. Ready?"

"As ready as I'll ever be."

She throws the doors open. I wasn't ready.

When I was a child, I'd dreamed of having a private library. I'd close my eyes and imagine rows and rows of books, stacked high up to the ceiling. I wanted one of those sliding ladders all around the room, and big, comfy chairs.

I never thought I'd see it in real life—but it's here, and it's glorious. The library of my dreams stares back at me. It's intimidatingly grand and comfortably snuggly at the same time. The roof is domed, with an intricate scene painted on it from wall to wall. At the far end of the room, massive windows dominate the wall, staring out onto the vista of the castle grounds.

We enter, and I run my fingers along the spines of the books, unable to wipe the smile from my face. I make my way to the windows and let out a soft breath as I stare out.

Then, I sit down in one of the plush sofas near the window. I sigh, staring up at the painted ceiling. There are thousands of tiny roses painted above me. A smile drifts over my lips as I lose myself in the details of the painting. It's just like the front gate, and the fence around the rose garden, and the carving on the library door. Everything is so detailed and so beautiful here. It takes my breath away.

My heart sings. To think that in only a few days, I've gone from a tiny, rat-infested apartment in New York City—where my doormen were junkies and drug dealers—to *here*. To the lap of luxury.

I'm living next door to the Prince of Farcliff, and his daughter, the Princess.

Of course, this luxury isn't mine. I'm only the rose gardener, and the Prince is notorious for his short fuse and legendary temper.

Not exactly the perfect neighbor.

Sam and I aren't even supposed to be here, but I can still enjoy it for a few moments...

...until the library door opens, and Prince Gabriel steps through the doorway.

Sam yelps, clapping her hand over her mouth. I jump up from the sofa as if it's burned me, smoothing my hair down and stammering as I half-bow, half-curtsy at the Prince of Farcliff.

He takes another step closer, and my breath catches.

The Prince is taller than I expected—and wider. He's wearing slim-fitting pants and a t-shirt under a tailored sport coat. It hugs him in all the right places and makes him look like he belongs in a place like this.

Of course he belongs here. He's the Prince of Farcliff, for crying out loud.

Me, on the other hand? Wearing dirty jeans and a ripped tank top I use to garden in?

I'm not exactly Farcliff nobility.

The Prince's sharp blue eyes drill into mine. His dirty blonde hair is swept back from his face, but a stray strand falls across his forehead. Every step he takes toward me fills me with fear and a deep, pulsing excitement. His eyes make me feel like I'm on fire. His lips part, and for the briefest of moments, I wonder what they'd taste like to kiss.

I shoo the thought away. Why would I think that?

"What are you doing here?" The Prince's voice is low and commanding. My stomach clenches as delicious heat curls around it.

"We were just leaving." Sam shifts her weight from foot to foot, darting toward the door.

Prince Gabriel swings his eyes from mine to hers and holds up his hand to stop her. "That doesn't answer my question."

When he looks at me again, I notice the faded white scar that passes from his chin, over his jaw, and up across his cheek.

I remember watching the reports on television when he got the scar, and hearing all the rumors that surrounded his relationship at the time. I remember him lashing out—just like he did at the ceremony this week.

I gulp.

Didn't my father tell me to stay away from him?

"You're my new rose gardener."

"Yes," I answer, even though it wasn't a question.

"What's your name?"

"Jo."

"Jo," he repeats, tasting my name on his tongue.

"Short for Jolie."

Not that you asked. Stop talking, Jo.

His eyes slide over my body, and I've never felt so alive. The Prince takes another step toward me, and I feel like he sucks all the air out of my lungs. His presence fills this massive room, and I can't look anywhere except into his deep, blue eyes.

"Did you get your notebook?" He tilts his head, and his gaze darkens. Something flits across his face. Contempt, maybe? Interest?

My lips part in shock, and the Prince's eyes follow the movement. His own tongue slides out to lick his lips, and heat roars in the pit of my stomach.

The Prince of Farcliff brought my notebook back to the cottage for me?

My cheeks burn and I try to respond, but all I can do is stammer. Finally, I manage to thank him and do another awkward bow-curtsy. The Prince waves a dismissive hand and checks his nails.

He leans against a bookshelf, dragging his eyes back up to mine.

Yep, definitely contempt.

"You shouldn't leave your things lying around."

Anger flashes through me. "Well, it was hardly lying around intentionally. I dropped it," I snap.

His eyebrow arches. I clamp my mouth shut.

"Is that any way to speak to your Prince?" He takes a step closer to me, and fear grips my chest. "Your father was a lot more docile. Shame you had to take his place."

I frown. "Excuse me?"

"Judging by your presence in my private library, you're not as adept as he was at following *rules*." Prince Gabriel emphasizes the last word, and my jaw tightens. "Maybe you should take some time to figure out how things work around here."

I desperately want to talk back. I want to tell him to stop talking to me like I'm worth less than the dirt under his shoe.

I want to tell him that he's lucky I'm here, because otherwise he'd be left without a rose garden.

But he's the Prince of Farcliff, and I'm just Jo.

The Prince nods, taking a step to the side to signal that we can leave. I hate that I waited for his permission. My jaw ticks, and I start walking to the exit.

In order to get out, though, I need to pass right in front of the Prince. My heart hammers and my mouth turns dry as I get closer to him. Every step makes my pulse quicken, as heat curls in my stomach. It's a mix of anger and desire, and I struggle to walk normally as the heat teases between my thighs.

I hate that I'm attracted to him. He's your typical arrogant, self-serving jerk. The Prince hasn't lifted a finger in his life, but because his title is 'Prince', he thinks he's better than me.

I want to keep my eyes on the door. I want to hurry past him—but I can't help myself. I'm not the type of person who keeps my head down. My chin lifts and my gaze meets the Prince's as I walk past him.

He catches my hand in his.

My heart jumps to my throat and rage flares through my chest.

How dare he grab me? *Touch* me? *Hold me back*?

My pulse thunders through my veins. I'm so close to him that I can smell his fresh, manly scent. My hand burns where he touches it.

The Prince turns my palm over, and runs his fingers over it more gently than I expect.

"Your hands feel too soft to be a gardener's." His eyes drag up to mine, and my whole body burns.

"I wear gloves," I snap, "and I haven't had a garden in a while."

"Well, don't fuck it up."

Rage.

The Prince stares at me blankly, and I desperately want to gouge his pretty, blue eyes out.

Still holding my hand, the Prince nods at me. My eyes drop to his lips, and once again my thoughts are treasonous. Is he a good kisser? That brutishness, beastly side of him—does it come out in other ways?

In *good* ways?

Shut up, brain!

Finally, the Prince drops my hand, and the moment is over. I stumble out of the library and close the door behind me, leaning against it as I try to catch my breath.

Sam waits there for me, biting her lip.

"Oops," she whispers. "Sorry."

"It's fine." I shake my head and try to smile, even though my head is spinning and I'm trying my best not to pass out. "I had to meet him sometime. Bit of an asshole, hey?"

Sam's eyes widen, and her freckled cheeks turn an unnatural shade of red. She glances behind me.

I hope he heard me. It's the truth. He's a complete and total ass.

We head back the way we came.

"What's that way?" I ask, pointing down the hallway.

"That's the East Wing," Sam says in a hushed whisper. "It's forbidden. That's where the Prince's chambers are. His and his daughter's. Only them and the medical staff are allowed over there.

I stare down the hallway, and then back at the library door. My heart is still hammering, and I can't make sense of what just happened. I let Sam drag me back to the servants' quarters. I'm still in a daze when I stumble out into the rose garden to get back to work.

8

GABRIEL

I WATCH my new rose gardener leave the library, and a low growl rumbles through my chest. She shouldn't have been in here. Anyone else, I would have fired on the spot.

But not Jo.

I stare after her, and my whole body pulses. I want her.

I want her in a way that I haven't wanted anyone in a long time.

I want to consume her body, her mind, her soul. I want to tear her apart and watch the ecstasy pour out of her. I want to hear her scream, and moan, and laugh. I want to taste her, devour her, destroy her.

Fire roars through my body. I haven't felt this way since the early days with Paulette. It scares me, this feeling. I know that I'm not far away from tumbling into mania, from losing control of myself again.

I'm not chaste—I've been with women in the past six years. Lots of them. But that was more like scratching an itch than really fulfilling a need. I know I could call Bertrand and ask him to bring me a willing woman, or two, or three—but I don't want a willing woman without a name.

I want Jo.

Short for Jolie.

My blood pumps hot through my veins and I breathe in through my nose, slowly and deeply. I stare up at the ceiling, and I already know I've lost the battle against her.

I already know I'm going to pursue my rose gardener. I know I'll claim her, I'll ruin her, and I know it'll tear me apart.

The wildness inside me is waiting to be unleashed. Ever since the ceremony in Farcliff, I've been holding myself back —white-knuckling through my urge to destroy myself and everything around me.

All it takes is one doe-eyed girl to send me over the edge.

Another fucking writer, to be exact—because that went so well for me the first time.

But still, I do love to ruin things. Why not ruin myself?

Stalking out of the library, I head over to the East Wing. I need some time away from people so that I can think. Before I get there, though, I pass by large picture windows at the front of the castle. Three cars coming up the drive.

Frowning, I wait for them to get closer. My shoulders drop.

It's my brother, the King, and I know why he's here. It's not to congratulate me on my decorum and poise at the coronation ceremony.

I trudge down to the front doors to meet him. The motorcade of cars pulls up outside the steps, and Charlie steps out of the middle vehicle. His face is dark.

I glance behind him, but no one else comes out. He didn't bring his family. He's not here on a social visit.

"I need to talk to you," he says as he walks up the steps.

I nod, motioning to the door. Charlie brushes past me

without a word. I follow him straight through the castle, all the way back to a small study overlooking the rose garden.

"Close the door," Charlie orders without looking at me. He stands near the window, staring out with his hands clasped behind his back.

I close the door, anger flaring in my chest. It teases the inside of my ribcage, singing my bones as I fight to regain control over myself. I'm not used to being spoken to like this —even if Charlie is the King. This is *my* castle. *My* domain.

Standing by the door, I watch him for a moment.

Finally, my brother sighs and turns to look at me. "What the fuck, Gabe?"

"What?"

"*What?* You're seriously going to stand there like you've done nothing wrong? I told you to come back to Farcliff for two days for the ceremony. You couldn't handle yourself for *two fucking days!*" He shakes his head. "And then, you left without a word, and you stand there asking 'what'."

"What was I supposed to say? I know what I did."

"Oh, I don't know, maybe 'sorry', to start?"

I scoff, shaking my head. "What would that achieve?"

Charlie glares at me. He turns back to the window and lets out a heavy sigh. "It was my ten-year wedding anniversary, Gabe. Ten years since I was crowned King, ten years since I had my son. Then, you just show up like a fucking hurricane and destroy it all."

"What did I destroy? All I did was leave the parade early."

"Those videos of you lunging at the crowd have gone viral, Gabe. That ceremony started with as much chaos as my reign did. And what about your daughter?"

"What *about* my daughter?" My voice has a dangerous edge to it.

Charlie holds my gaze. "What about the introduction you've given her into Farcliff society? Huh? What about that?"

"Fuck Farcliff society. We don't belong there."

"Don't you think you should let Flora decide that?"

"Flora is six fucking years old—so, no. I don't think she should decide anything, except maybe the color of her socks in the morning. I'm her father, and I decide that she's better off here, in the care of her medical team and away from the cesspit of Farcliff City."

Charlie sinks down into a chair and sighs. He leans back, staring at me. In the past ten years, Charlie has lost his rebel edge and grown into a true King. He's reasonable, and kind—but doesn't tolerate any shit.

Including mine.

"This has got to change, Gabe," he starts. "You're going to stop hiding away in Westhill, and you're going to resume your duties as Prince of Farcliff."

"My duties?"

"Charitable work, to start."

"I already do charitable work."

Charlie arches an eyebrow. "Like what?"

"I employ all the people at this castle, don't I? Keep the village running? Keep the castle in good shape?"

"You call that charity? Living in the lap of luxury?"

I bristle, even though I know Charlie's right. I know I've been shirking my duties, and that I've been isolating myself out here. He's given me an easy ride—probably because of Flora. I've had time and space and resources to deal with my shit.

Instead of dealing with anything, I've just grown more isolated, and now it's hurting the people I love... including my daughter.

I hate that Charlie's right. I walk over to the window and

lean against the frame, gazing out without really seeing anything.

"So?" Charlie asks.

"So, what?" I sound like a child, but I hate being told what to do.

"Don't start, Gabe."

I don't answer.

Charlie sighs. "Well, since you claim to be so good for the town of Westhill, you can start there. When I was driving in, I stopped in to see the Mayor. They're preparing for the Westhill Town Fair—there's lots of work to do this week. I also noticed a pretty decrepit community garden. The library needs a new roof. Should I keep going?"

"You want me to plant fucking tomatoes and help people sell corn dogs?"

"And smile while you do it. In fact, the Mayor was ecstatic to hear that you'll be participating in the dunk tank."

"Dunk tank?"

"The wonderful residents of Westhill will be able to pay to have you dropped into a bucket of ice-cold water."

I stare at my brother, unmoving

His eyes flash. "What? Not happy about that?"

"Are you being fucking serious right now?"

"As fucking serious as can be, little brother. Maybe a little bit of public humiliation will shock you out of all this wallowing you've been doing for the past six years."

"I'm not wallowing. I just don't like people."

"Well, you're a Prince of Farcliff, so you need to learn to like people."

"No."

Charlie shakes his head. "You don't get a say in this, Gabe. If you don't do this, you're on your own. I mean *on your own*. You and Flora won't have this castle at your disposal, or the resources of the Crown to leech off. No more teams of doctors at your disposals, and pretty, young gardeners to take care of your roses." Charlie nods toward the window. "When did you hire her, anyway?"

My eyes flash.

Charlie arches an eyebrow, shrugging. "From now on, everything you do will be in service to the Kingdom."

I turn back to the window, trying to contain my frustration. What will it help to have me at some stupid dunk tank? How the fuck is that in service to the Kingdom?

Movement catches my eye outside, and I see Jo wheeling a wheelbarrow over to the garden. She pauses to wipe the sweat off her brow, and then continues over toward the roses.

"Charlie..." I start, sighing.

"No," my brother cuts me off. "You don't get a choice anymore. You've had time to work on yourself, and you've done nothing. You came back to Farcliff and embarrassed the whole family, not to mention leaving a black stain on my ten-year wedding anniversary. If you're going to continue living on the Kingdom's resources, you're going to contribute."

"How is an idiotic dunk tank *contributing*?"

Charlie's lips curl into a grin. "Call it your punishment for making an ass out of me this week. After that, I promise I'll never bring it up again." He pushes himself up out of the chair and stares at me. "It's either this, or you give up your position and join the real world. I don't know what marketable skills you've developed while skulking around in this castle, but you'd better make use of them now. Either that —or plant some fucking tomatoes and sell some fucking corn dogs."

He strides out of the room, leaving me at the window.

I watch the rose gardener shoveling mulch around the base of a few plants. She touches the leaves and inspects the buds. Every movement is delicate and precise. She moves purposefully, as if there's nothing more important than tending to her father's roses.

Jo has a purpose—even if it's a modest one.

And what do I have?

Sighing, I turn away from the window and stalk back to my rooms in the East Wing.

9

JO

I'M STILL SEETHING when I make it back to the rose garden. How dare the Prince talk to me like that? How dare he mention my father? Doesn't he realize my father is sick?

I shake my head and work the afternoon away. Deciding not to have dinner in the castle kitchens, I make my way to the Gardener's Cottage. I saw a can of soup in the cupboards —that'll do for dinner tonight.

My muscles ache and my mind is exhausted. It's been an eventful first week at Westhill. I'm looking forward to having a bit of food and collapsing into bed. Maybe I'll put a movie on and zone out.

I don't get to do that, though, because when I walk into the cottage, I spot a little blonde head poking up over the back of the couch.

"Um, hello?" I say.

A young girl turns around and smiles. She gets up off the couch and dips down in a graceful curtsy—much more delicately than I ever could.

"You must be Mr. Marcel and Mrs. Violet's daughter. They told me you were coming."

I close the door, nodding. "I am—and you are...?"

"Flora." She walks toward me with her hand extended, and I see a book tucked under her arm. Noticing my gaze, the little girl takes the book out. "Mr. Marcel used to let me come and read here some evenings. It's quieter than the castle."

I stare at her face. She looks familiar, but I can't quite place her. I've seen her somewhere before... but when? I rack my brain, but the information is just on the fringes of my memory.

I nod to the couch. "You mind if I join you?"

Flora breaks into a wide smile. "Not at all. Your dad said I'd like you."

I chuckle. "I'm glad."

We sit down next to each other, and Flora returns to her book. I notice it's a novel, and I stare at the girl. She's so tiny. How could she possibly be reading a book?

"How old are you?"

"Six and three quarters," she answers without looking up from the page.

Then, it hits me.

Flora.

As in, *Princess Flora*, the daughter of Prince Gabriel.

"Are you...? Is...?" I stammer, clearing my throat. I stare at her, wide-eyed.

"Am I the Princess?" Flora asks. "Yes. But Mr. Marcel said you wouldn't mind." She finally looks up from her book, smiling at me.

"Of course I don't mind." I answer. I glance at the book again. It's a Nancy Drew mystery—the exact copy that I used to read when I was younger. "You can read that, and you're not even seven years old?"

"My tutors tell me I read at a fifth-grade level," Flora says with a big, toothy grin. "I read a lot. Sometimes I have to be in

76

bed for a long time when I'm sick, so I have more time to read than normal kids."

"I used to read a lot, too."

The Princess nods, and turns back to her book. Not knowing what to say, I decide to grab my laptop and do a bit of writing. As surreal as it is, I sit beside the Princess in comfortable silence and type.

After a time, she closes the book and stands up.

"See you around!" Without waiting for an answer, Flora leaves the cottage.

I stare after her, speechless. How could such a smart, polite, gracious little girl come from that brute of a father? How could *he* create *her*?

FROM THEN ON, Flora shows up at the cottage almost every day. She asks me about my writing, and I give her book recommendations. The girl is a borderline genius. She tears through books faster than I do, even offering some critiques of the plots when she's done.

I'm not surprised my parents loved her and let her have free rein in the Gardener's Cottage. My father probably kept my old books specifically for her.

In a way, the times that I spend with Flora—reading and writing quietly beside each other—are some of the most pleasant moments of my first couple of weeks at Westhill.

I catch a glimpse of Prince Gabriel once in a window, and then I don't see him for two weeks. I don't mind though, the kind of energy he instilled in me in the library was almost too much to bear.

I remind myself that I'm here to take care of the roses, so my father will have something to come back to. Beyond that, I need to finish my new book. I'm not here for any other reason. Not for the Prince, and definitely not to act on any rogue desires.

I speak to my parents almost every day, and make sure to send my father lots of pictures of the roses. Settling into life in Westhill is easy. For the first time in a long time, I don't feel like I'm on the brink of failure. I actually feel like I'm doing well.

As the days fly by, I hear more and more about the upcoming Westhill Town Fair. Sam's cheeks turn bright red whenever she tells me about it, and her fiery orange curls bounce with excitement. It's contagious. By the end of my first few weeks at Westhill, my body is tired from the manual labor in the garden, but my mind is buzzing with thoughts of the Prince, my new book, and my father.

Three weeks after I arrive at the castle, the Westhill Town Fair officially opens.

It's the event of the year, according to Sam. I'm as excited as the rest of the staff to get off the grounds and relax a bit. We'll have funnel cakes, caramel popcorn, corn dogs—the works. Not to mention riding the Ferris wheel and playing carnival games.

Apparently, people from all around come into Westhill for the Fair. I'm not quite sure what to expect. After living in New York City, I can't really bring myself to believe it'll be all that exciting, but I'm glad to have a night away from the castle.

"Be ready at seven," Sam says to me on the night of the Fair's opening. Her blue eyes are shining. She brushes some dirt off her maid's uniform and glances at me. "You want me to pick you up at the cottage?"

"I'll come to the kitchens and we can leave from here." I

don't know if Flora is allowed at the cottage officially, and I don't want to get her in trouble. I feel oddly protective over the little girl, even though I've only known her a couple of weeks.

"Perfect," Sam smiles. "You're going to love the Fair."

Most of the staff at the castle is abuzz with excitement. Even Bertrand, Prince Gabriel's stone-faced butler, has cracked a couple of smiles today.

I have a few things to finish up in the garden, and then I head to my cottage to get freshened up. By the time I make it to the kitchens again, the sun is starting to set.

"Excited?" Sam asks, hooking her arm into mine.

"Definitely." I try to match her enthusiasm, but I just can't see how a country fair will be anything to write home about. I've just moved from New York City, where everything is hustle and bustle all the time, and I can get any kind of cuisine I want. I can't help but wonder if the excitement in the castle is just a result of their being cooped up in here too long.

A horn honks, and I see Harry Brooks in the driver's seat of a beat-up car.

"Come on," Sam smiles.

Even Mrs. Grey is coming out tonight, wearing her best dress. We all pile into Harry's car, and another carload of staff follows behind. We call ourselves the Westhill Castle Contingent. Harry glances at me in the rear-view mirror, and I ignore the slimy feeling his gaze sends down my spine.

I'm still skeptical—right up until we arrive at the Westhill Town Fair. Then, I finally understand the excitement.

The entrance is a huge garland of vines and flowers, towering overhead. We walk through to see thousands of twinkling lights strung up over the fair ground, and dozens of tents set up on a big field. There are booths offering food and games all around us, and a Ferris wheel at the far end of the grounds.

Sam jumps up and down in excitement. "I *love* funnel cakes. I look forward to this all year!"

"I've never actually had a funnel cake," I say, allowing her to drag me further into the fairground.

"Excuse me? Did you live on the moon?"

I laugh at the outrage painted on her face, and follow her to the nearest funnel cake stand. A band is playing on a small stage nearby, and acrobats are walking through the crowd. I don't know where all these people have come from, but the fairground is packed with smiling faces.

"The profits from the Fair are split between Westhill and the neighboring towns," Sam explains. "So you can spend as much as you want without feeling bad—it's for charity!"

I laugh, glancing at the carnival games. "I'm sure they're experts at taking our money."

"Come on," she says. Harry stands on the other side of me, and our little group walks through the fair ground.

I'll hand it to Sam—funnel cakes *are* delicious. Harry wins a teddy bear at a shooting game and presents it to me with a solemn face. I eat my way through all the food stalls.

After the stress of moving countries, all the work I've put into the garden during the day, and my writing at night, it feels good to have a night out. The Westhill Castle Contingent are good company, and pretty soon my cheeks are sore from laughing, and I'm so full of food I feel like I'm going to pop.

I can see how this would generate quite a bit of money for charity—I've already spent half a weeks' wages, and all I've done is eat.

I'm not ashamed to say I was wrong. The Westhill Town Fair *is* the event of the year.

An announcement booms over the loudspeaker, and all the heads in the fairground turn up to listen.

"Ladies and gentlemen," the voice proclaims. "Now, for the main event!"

Spotlights swirl in the sky and then land on the main stage. A curtain drops, and a large tank of water is revealed. Sam jumps up and down, squealing.

"*Dunk tank!*"

"What?"

"The dunk tank! They haven't had it in years. I wonder who they'll have up there." She grabs my hand and starts dragging me toward the stage.

"What is it?"

Harry, Sam, and even Mrs. Grey turn to stare at me, wide-eyed.

"Are you serious?" Harry says with a mocking grin on his face. "You don't know what a dunk tank is?"

"Someone sits on that platform," Sam explains, "and then another person throws a ball at that target." She grins, glancing back at me. "If you hit the target... *sploosh!*"

I laugh, and we all move closer to the stage. The first person who appears on stage is a clown in full makeup. He bounces around the stage to laughter and cheers from the audience, and then props himself up on the dunk tank.

I've never seen so many people excited to throw a ball. The gatekeeper at the bottom of the stage has a hard time managing all the people who line up to compete. Harry pushes himself forward and manages to buy a ticket for himself.

I'm not a huge fan of Harry's, but I have to hand it to him —he's a good showman. He winds his arm back as far as it will go, and pretends to throw the ball. The clown in the dunk tank yelps, and the crowd eats it up. Everyone laughs and cheers, and pretty soon, Harry is the hero of the show. The two of them play off each other until all of us watching are in stitches.

"He's good," I say to Sam.

She laughs. "See? I told you it would be fun."

Harry finally throws the ball for real, and the clown drops into the water. The crowd cheers, and Harry raises his arms in triumph. I can't stop laughing. It's so silly, but the atmosphere in here is contagious. Three more people step up to throw, and another one of them manages to hit the target.

By now, the clown on the platform is drenched, his makeup running off his face as he clambers down from the dunk tank. With a deep bow, he exits the stage to clamorous applause.

Sam leans her head against my shoulder, sighing happily. Surrounded by all the staff from the castle, watching something as ridiculous as the dunk tank, I feel like I belong. I haven't felt this good in a long time.

Even if the Prince is intimidating, I've only seen him once in person in the three weeks I've been at the castle. If I can stay out of his way, I could see myself staying at Westhill for a long time. It already feels like home. The staff is like an extended family, and Flora brings a smile to my face whenever she comes over to read with me.

It's nice here. Maybe next year, I'll be as excited as the rest of them for the Fair.

Harry comes back down from the stage to rejoin our group, and George, the chef, gives him a big pat on the back. Even Mrs. Grey shakes Harry's hand, and another gardener claps him on the shoulder. Harry's eyes flick to mine, and a blush creeps over my cheeks.

I'm not interested in him—and plus, it's too soon after my breakup—but in this kind of carnival atmosphere, it's nice to be surrounded by fun and happiness, and maybe even a bit of male attention.

The master of ceremonies on stage raises his hands, and a hush falls over all of us. I'm giddy, and I can't stop giggling. I never expected to have this much fun.

"Tonight," the emcee booms, "we have a special guest."

I throw a questioning glance at Sam, who shrugs.

"Put your hands together for our next *dunkee*. The wild and untamable, mysterious and brooding, the one and only, Prince Gabriel of Farcliff!"

Total silence is probably not what the emcee wanted or expected, but that's what he receives. A second ago, the crowd was buzzing. Now, the fairground might as well be empty. Even the music stops.

The Prince steps onstage, in all his brooding glory, and my panties turn as wet as the Prince is about to be.

He's wearing jeans and a white t-shirt, and his hair is falling across his forehead. He searches the crowd for a moment, and then heads to the dunk tank. He doesn't smile, or nod, or do anything to indicate that he's happy about this situation.

He hates this, and everyone can tell.

I gulp.

With the clown, there was a rush of people trying to get up onstage to try to dunk him. There was an excited energy.

Now, though?

Total silence. Dread. Fear.

Not a single person steps up to the stage. The Prince takes his spot on the platform, his legs swinging gently off the edge. He turns to look at the crowd, scanning all the faces in the audience as we all stand there, unmoving.

When his eyes fall on me, fire ignites in my veins.

Prince Gabriel stares at me just as he did in the library,

and I feel naked, and hot, and alive. It feels like there's only him and me, and the entire fairground drops away.

I wait another few moments, and then I know what I need to do. Maybe a small part of me *wants* to do it, if only to get back at him for being so arrogant in the library. My feet carry me toward the stage without me really realizing what I'm about to do. Sam tries to call after me in a hushed whisper, but it's too late.

The crowd parts in front of me, and I walk in a straight line toward the stage. I pull out a couple of crumpled bills to pay for a ticket, and then I step up to the platform.

Whispers pass through the crowd, and I accept the ball from the emcee with a trembling hand. His eyebrows are drawn together, and he holds the microphone away from his mouth.

"Are you sure about this?"

"Well, it's too late now." I force a smile, and the man frowns.

The ball is heavier than I expected. I feel the weight of it in my hand, and then take my spot on the small 'x' taped on the stage.

Then, finally, with a few hundred sets of eyes on me, I lift my gaze to meet the Prince's.

10

GABRIEL

JOLIE LOOKS TERRIFIED. Her big, brown eyes are wider than I've ever seen them. She moves the ball from one hand to the other.

A grin tugs at my lips. Maybe my brother was right—maybe charitable work *is* fun.

No one else in this crowd was brave enough to do this. But here Jo is, looking like she's about to jump off a tall building with no parachute.

None of the men in the crowd stepped forward. None of the people that know me—the ones that have worked at Westhill castle for years.

No, the person that volunteered to stand there is the one woman that I've been trying to avoid.

The writer. The rose gardener.

Jolie.

She takes a deep breath, and I watch the way her chest rises and falls. She has a short, sunflower-yellow summer dress on, and her long legs are tantalizingly bare. My mouth waters as I watch her dry her palm on her dress.

I'd love to slip the shoulder strap off and run my fingers

over her skin. I'd love to taste her lips, and hear her whisper dirty words into my ear.

Jo glances at me once more, and then sets her shoulders. My eyebrows arch, and my grin widens.

She's actually going to do it. She's going to throw that ball and send me falling into this vat of ice-cold water. Even when I saw her accept the ball, I wasn't sure that she'd throw it—but now, I know. A slight breeze picks up, and Jolie shivers. She closes her eyes for a moment, and then opens them to look at the target.

When she pulls her arm back, a collective gasp escapes the audience. They can't believe she's doing this either—but I love it. I love the cheek of it. The attitude. The little rebel rule-breaker inside her.

Everyone has seen the news reports about me. They've probably read the drivel that Paulette wrote. They think I'm a monster. They think Jo's making a mistake, and that I'll punish her for doing this.

And who knows? I might.

But her jaw clenches, and she does it anyway. Jolie launches the ball across the air, slicing toward me faster than I'd expected. The crowd gasps again, and someone cries out.

The ball hits the dunk tank with a dull thud, and I squeeze my eyes shut, bracing for impact...

...and nothing happens.

She missed.

I open my eyes to see Jo's chest heaving and her cheeks bright pink. She glances at me and lets out a sigh.

"Try again," I hear myself say.

Jo's eyes widen. "What?"

"I said, try again."

"I only bought one ticket."

"You're not getting out of this so easily. How do I know you didn't miss on purpose? Throw the ball again."

The man with the microphone picks the ball up and hands it back to Jo. I think I see him mouth 'I'm sorry', and it makes me grin.

I'm loving this. I love how much they don't want Jo to do it. I love seeing the whole crowd squirm uncomfortably as I sit on this perch, waiting to be soaked. My favorite part is the innocent, hesitant look in Jo's eye, and the way she bites her lip as she stares me down from across the stage.

"Don't miss this time," I grin.

Something shifts in my rose gardener's face. Her mouth sets in a pinched line, and she arches an eyebrow. "As you wish, Your Highness." She gives me a tiny little curtsy and straightens up to aim.

The fucking attitude on this girl, I swear.

Desire roars through me. If we weren't on a stage with a few hundred people watching, I'd tear her clothes off right now. I'd devour her, claim her as my own, fuck that sass out of her until the only thing she wanted to do was scream my name.

The scar on my face pulses as I think of driving my cock inside her. Even when she reaches back to throw the ball, I'm thinking about how she would look if I came on her tongue. As the projectile flies through the air, and her mouth drops open, I'm imagining what those pink lips would look like wrapped around my cock.

Even when the ball hits the target, and I hear the mechanism thunk, I'm thinking about fucking her to oblivion.

It's not until I hit the water that I'm jarred back to my senses. I sink down, deeper than I'd expected, and then push off the bottom with my feet to stand.

The water is chest-high, and I inhale sharply. It's fucking freezing.

I'm greeted with complete silence. Jo is standing on the other end of the stage, looking like she just killed someone. Every face in the crowd is painted with shock and horror.

Then, I do something I haven't done in a long, long time —I laugh.

I laugh at something other than my daughter's antics. It bursts out of me, surprising even myself. As ice-cold water runs down my face and I brush my soaking-wet hair off my forehead, I laugh harder.

Maybe Charlie was right—maybe this is exactly what I need.

Who knew charity was this much fun?

As I laugh, I feel the tension in the air start to dissolve. The first cheer comes from the back of the crowd, and pretty soon the entire fairground is alive with whoops and hollers.

I climb out of the dunk tank and stand on stage in an ever-growing puddle. I raise my arm toward them.

Toward the subjects of Farcliff.

Toward my people.

They cheer for me, and for the first time in my life, I feel like I belong up here. I feel like their cheers are lifting me up, and not drowning me out. My smile splits my face open, and I laugh some more.

Turning to look at Jolie, I see her smile shyly at me. She nods her head slightly, and then exists the stage via the stairs she'd climbed to get here.

The crowd parts again for her, and she rejoins the castle staff. One of the gardeners—Harry—puts his arm around her, and a flash of jealousy makes my lips turn downward. I drop my arm, staring at them. I can feel the anger welling up inside me.

Jo looks over her shoulder at me, and gives me the tiniest of smiles.

It's enough to snap me out of my anger, and I turn around before it grips me again. I walk backstage and away from the hundreds of prying eyes. I brought a change of clothes, and once I'm in them, I head out to the waiting car behind the fairground fence. Before I get in the vehicle, I look to the crowd once more.

The other gardener doesn't have his arm around Jolie anymore. She's laughing with one of the maids—a redhead. Again, she feels my gaze and glances toward me. It's as if she can sense me, just as I can sense her. Her chin dips down and her lips tug into a smile. Then, I get in the car and drive away.

"That was wonderful, Sir," the driver says as he takes me back to the castle. "You were great."

"All I did was sit there."

"You did a lot more than that."

I nod, staring out the window as we drive back. Once home, I go to my chambers, but I already know I won't sleep. Instead, I walk the hallways of the East Wing, and then make my way down to the rose garden. The buds are growing, and they'll be blooming within weeks, if not days. Soon, the scent in the rose garden will be just as I remembered it as a child. I'll be happy and calm for the few weeks that the garden blooms.

I take a seat on my favorite bench, and then sink down to lie across it. I stare at the sky, sighing. Jolie's face appears in my mind's eye, at the exact moment when she realized she'd hit the target. I can picture it perfectly—the mix of shock, horror, and maybe a little bit of pride.

Alone in the rose garden, lying on the bench, I laugh some more, and I feel better than I've felt in years.

11

JO

ONCE THE ADRENALINE of the dunk tank wears off, tiredness sets in. The rest of the group is enjoying themselves, so I tell Sam that I'm going home. After listening to a string of protests, I finally split off from the group. I start walking out of the fairground, a tired smile painted on my face.

There's something I love about walking at night. The sounds of the Westhill Town Fair fade behind me, and soon, all I can hear are my own footsteps, the occasional car, and the hoot of an owl.

Night air is fresh and crisp, and it tastes better than the air in the daytime. I walk quickly to ward off the chill—I didn't bring a jacket, and my thin summer dress isn't providing much warmth. Rubbing my hands over my arms, I speed up.

The air is sweeter in the country, and my freedom tastes sweeter still. My father is responding well to treatment, and my book is coming along nicely. Some evenings, I even work on a brand-new book. It's completely different from my usual thrillers—it's actually a middle grade children's book. The protagonist reminds me of Flora. Bright, happy, and ultra-intelligent.

Maybe, one day, she'll read it and see herself in it.

I smile to myself, no longer feeling cold as I make my way back to the castle. Back to my *home*. Despite the fact that I just dunked the Prince into a vat of water, I have to say that things are going well for me. Besides, even if he does hate me forever, the look on his face when he fell in made it all worthwhile.

Serves him right for being an ass in the library.

When I make it to the castle gates, I buzz the intercom and walk through when they opened, just as I did the first day I arrived. Unlike the first day, though, now I actually feel comfortable. I thought I'd be isolated out here on my own, but I'm not. I feel more comfortable in this castle at the far reaches of the Kingdom, than I did in my own place in the city. There's a bounce in my step, and I walk around the castle toward the Gardener's Cottage.

Glancing down at the rose garden, I change my trajectory. My father always said that roses can feel the presence of those who take care of them, and they need to be fed with love as well as water and fertilizer.

Tonight, I have a lot of love to give them.

The energy bubbling inside me is too much for the little cottage, and I feel like I need to visit my flowers. And yes, even within a couple of weeks, they already feel like *my* flowers. It's a good feeling—like I belong here. Like I've been accepted.

I push the gate open and step into the garden.

"Hello, Miss Rose," I say to the first plant. "How was your evening?" I brush my fingers over the budding flower, laying a soft kiss on its emerging petals. Then, I start walking along the garden's pathways.

This was always when my father was most excited about the garden—right before the flowers bloom, when the plants are working their hardest. He used to tell me that he could feel the pulse of the roses. I pull out my phone from my purse and snap a couple of pictures to send to him.

"Do you always talk to your plants?"

The Prince appears from behind a bush with an irresistible smirk on his face. I make a strangled sort of yelping sound, and he laughs. His hair is still wet, but his clothes are dry. He must have changed.

Why does he have to be so goddamn handsome, and so goddamn arrogant? He walks toward me, his eyes darkening. Every step has a swagger, and I wish I wasn't this attracted to him. My body almost leans toward him, as if he has a magnetic pull that reaches deep into my gut and drags me in his direction.

"Not always," I answer. "Just when I feel like they need it."

"And they need it tonight?"

"Maybe I'm the one who needs it tonight," I grin. "I've had a very stressful evening."

"You didn't look too stressed. You looked like you enjoyed yourself."

"Which part? The part where you looked so smug up on that platform, or the part where you fell in?"

The Prince's eyebrow quirks as if he can't believe I'm talking to him like this. To be honest, *I* can't believe I'm talking to him like this.

I shrug, continuing. "There's something about sending a member of the royal family falling into a big barrel of cold water that cranks up the cortisol in a person's body."

"I wouldn't know," he says, taking another step toward me.

My breath catches. He's so... *big*. In the library, I got a sense of how strong and tall Prince Gabriel is, but standing beside him here, shivering in my sun dress, he towers over me.

The Prince shrugs off his jacket and drapes it over my shoulders. His fingers brush the skin of my collarbones, and a wave of goosebumps follow. My breath catches. His touch feels good—too good.

"I didn't realize you knew how to be a gentleman," I quip.

"I think the words you're looking for are 'thank you'."

The timbre of his voice sends shivers through my stomach, and I fight back a smile.

"Thanks," I say. I stare at a rose bud, touching it gently.

"You know, you're pretty arrogant for a rose gardener."

"*I'm* arrogant?" I spin toward him. "Take a look in the mirror, buddy."

"Buddy?"

"Your Royal Buddy Highness." I clamp my mouth shut to stop the word vomit from continuing. What is wrong with me? This is the *Prince* I'm talking to. Literal *royalty*.

Royalty that happens to have a legendary temper. I'm prodding the bear, and I can't stop myself.

But instead of snapping at me—instead of losing that notorious temper of his—Prince Gabriel just chuckles. I drag my gaze up to his. For the first time, I notice that he has little flecks of brown in his eyes. From a distance, they look completely blue. He stands close to me, his hands moving up to hold the edge of his jacket. His thumbs brush the skin below my clavicle again, and heat blooms under his touch.

"Took a lot of guts to come up on stage," the Prince says, tilting his head to the side. "Although, judging by how comfortable you made yourself in the library, I have a feeling that you're not the type of person to play by the rules."

"You've got me all wrong, Your Highness. I'm a rule

follower." I laugh, shaking my head. "I'm so far from a rebel, it's not even funny."

"And yet, every time I see you, you're doing something you're not supposed to."

"What about now? I'm not supposed to be in my own rose garden?"

"*My* rose garden," he growls, sending thrills straight through my stomach. "The Royal Rose Garden."

I clench my thighs together, biting my lip.

"Maybe you make me want to break the rules," I say in a hoarse whisper.

My heart thumps. Did I just say that? I gulp, standing still as a statue before him. The Prince's hands fall away, but he doesn't step back. I'm rooted to the ground, intoxicated by his presence. I can smell his cologne—faint and fresh as it envelops me.

My tongue slides out to lick my lips. My head is spinning. I can't string a sentence together or make sense of my swirling thoughts. All I know is I need to get away from the Prince. He's what's making me feel off-kilter. He's the one my parents warned me against. He's the one I just sent tumbling into a vat of ice-cold water while hundreds of people watched.

I shrug the Prince's jacket off my shoulders and hand it to him. "Thank you for that," I nod. "I should get to bed."

"Keep it on," he says. "It's cold out. I'll walk you home."

Not wanting to refuse royalty—and maybe, wanting to remain in his presence—I nod in response. I turn toward the gate, and the Prince's hand floats to my lower back.

Unlike Harry's touch, the Prince's hand on my back fills me with a delicious tingling sensation. Whether it's his touch, or the cold, I'm not sure, but my nipples pucker beneath my dress and goosebumps erupt all over my skin. We walk in silence for a while, until the Prince clears his throat.

"You have a pretty good arm, you know."

"I played softball when I was a kid," I say. "I guess I've still got it." I glance up at him, grinning.

"You certainly do."

We're halfway across the lawn on our way to the Gardener's Cottage. My heart is in my throat, and my stomach is clenching nervously.

A couple of weeks ago, I was living in a shitty apartment in New York City. Now, I'm walking across the palace grounds with the Prince of Farcliff by my side.

I want to ask him about the ceremony in Farcliff, and about his daughter, and about the rumors that surrounded her birth. I want to find out who he is—under the brooding layers and aura of mystery—but the words stick in my throat, and I can't get them out.

It's not my place to ask them, anyway.

We make it to the cottage, and stand on the front step. I shrug the Prince's jacket off and hand it back to him. He nods in thanks, slinging it over his arm.

I play with the keys in my hand, not wanting him to leave, but not knowing what to say to make him stay. Lifting my gaze up to his face, a thrill passes down my spine when he stares into my eyes.

The Prince lifts his hand up and brushes his fingers over my cheek. I close my eyes and lean into his touch, relishing the sparks that fly across my skin. My heart hammers as my breath catches in my throat.

When I open my eyes again to look at him, the Prince's gaze is still on my face. He drops his eyes to my lips, and desire teases my thighs. His hand drifts over my jaw and across my chin. I lean into his touch, not daring to move, or breathe, or speak.

I want to kiss him. The urge is overwhelming. I want his lips crushed against mine, his arms pulling me into him. I want him to take me and claim me and never let me go.

But the Prince drops his hand and takes a step back. "Goodnight, Jolie," he says softly.

Without another word, he turns around and walks away.

12

<hr>

GABRIEL

My steps are unsteady as I walk back across the grounds toward the castle. My hair is wet and cold against my head, but the rest of my body is burning up.

I want her. I can't deny it.

Another fucking writer.

I shake my head and take hurried steps back toward the castle. Reaching up to rub the back of my neck, I try to ignore the pulsing blood between my legs, or how much I wanted to tear Jo's clothes off, slam her against the wall, and make her mine.

I replay the evening over and over in my mind, from the moment Jo stepped up on stage, to the moment I said goodnight.

The devil on my shoulder giggles in my ear, whispering that I should have entered the cottage with her. She wanted it —I could tell by the way she leaned into my touch. Her thin summer dress left little to the imagination, and it took all my self-control to walk away.

But why?

Why walk away when I could have had her? What would

it change? What would it hurt? I'm the Prince of Farcliff, I'm single, and we're both willing.

The devil whispers to me, urging me to turn back and knock on her door. Go back to her and claim her. Bring her to ecstasy and enjoy every moment of it.

The animal inside me rages, and I clench my fists to hold it back. Desire and anger are my two worst triggers—and these past couple of weeks, I've had a healthy dose of both.

As soon as I'm inside the castle, I lean against a wall and let out a breath. I think of Flora, my beautiful daughter, and what I owe to her. I touch my pocket, where I still carry the rock she gave me. Who knew it would give me so much strength? A simple rock, given to me by a child, is providing me with more strength than I've been able to muster on my own.

Feeding the beast will only bring Flora pain. Jo may seem harmless, but so did Paulette. I gave in to my desires with Flora's mother, and I ended up with the scar on my face to show for it.

I have to think of my daughter. The last thing I need to do is bring more trouble into her life. Charlie's right—it's time for me to move beyond my past and introduce Flora to the Kingdom. It's time for me to forget about Paulette and re-enter the royal world.

And Jo? She's too much like the past. A writer—a beautiful one—who stokes the flames of my desire like few other people ever have. I need to look to the future—to Flora's future as well as my own.

I can't get involved with Jolie. Every time I see her, I feel like I'm on the edge of losing control. And when I lose control, disaster always follows.

Padding through the castle hallways, I head toward the East Wing. The energy inside me is still sparking, and the devil on my shoulder still speaks in my ear. It's a dangerous feeling, knowing that I could lose control again.

I snapped at the ceremony. I snapped when Paulette released her book. I snapped once, when Flora was little—when the doctors told me there was nothing they could do for her.

I can't let it happen again.

Making my way to Flora's room, I poke my head inside and find her sleeping in her big four-poster bed. I tiptoe my way to the side of her bed and stroke her hair as she sleeps.

My angel, my savior, my sweet, little daughter. She's the one who calms me down, who teaches me what's most important.

Jo isn't important. Catering to my carnal needs isn't important.

Only Flora matters, and she's the one I have to put first. My daughter sleeps softly, and watching her brings me the peace I'm looking for. I creep softly out of her room and let out a sigh.

I won't sleep tonight, so I go to my study and get to work. Charlie left me with lots of affairs to sort out with regard to the work to do in Westhill, and I sit at my desk to settle in for a long night.

I don't need coffee to stay awake—my mind is more than capable of doing that on its own. When the sun comes up, I lean back in my chair and stretch my neck from side to side. Charlie's done his research—there are detailed proposals for the community garden in Westhill, and improvements to the library and the school.

I'll be involved with them all.

I let out a heavy sigh. My eyes feel tired, but my mind is still awake. Noise at the window draws my attention, and I turn to see Flora running toward the rose garden. Mrs. Grey hurries to catch up, calling out after her. I grin, watching my daughter.

She has wildness inside her, too—except hers is good, whereas mine is all rotten. Flora pushes the gate open just as Jolie comes into view with a wheelbarrow. Jolie pauses, inclining her head at Flora. I'm too far away to hear what they're saying, but Flora's face breaks into a smile.

I watch Jo point to the rose bushes, taking a stem in her hand to show Flora something. I lean forward, as if it'll help me hear what they're saying.

Usually, I'd be mad. Mrs. Grey has strict instructions to keep Flora away from everyone except people that I've approved—and I certainly haven't approved Jolie. Any stray pathogen could trigger a life-threatening lung infection. Her body is too weak to sustain any harm.

But as I watch the two of them, my heart warms. A smile drifts over my lips as Flora laughs, and I can tell she's comfortable around my rose gardener.

Mrs. Grey appears, and I can almost hear her chastising my daughter. The old woman's cheeks are bright red and she's puffed from chasing after Flora. Flora drags her feet, and then reaches into her dress's pocket. She pulls something out and presents it to Jo.

My forehead touches the window as I try to see what my daughter gave her. Jolie just smiles and inclines her head, and then tucks the item into her own pocket.

Flora skips away with Mrs. Grey, and I move away from the window.

I should be mad. I should discipline Mrs. Grey, or tell Jolie to stay away from my daughter. Surprisingly, though, I'm not. Watching the two of them together felt natural. Flora looked so happy.

Frowning, I head to the East Wing. Bertrand has brought

my breakfast up to my chambers, but I don't have the appetite to eat. Tiredness comes over me like a wave, and I fall into bed without another thought.

I'M awoken by the sound of voices down the hall. I frown. There shouldn't be any voices down here. The only people allowed here are me, Flora, Bertrand, and Mrs. Grey. The medical staff doesn't even come this far—they stay at the other end of the corridor. I rub my eyes to clear the drowsiness from them, surprised at how deeply I slept.

Stretching as I stand up, I make my way to the door. I crack it open and peer out, but the voices are too far away.

"Mr. Marcel told me that roses can hear what we say to them, is that true?" My daughter asks.

"My father certainly thinks it is," a voice responds. I know that voice—I've thought of it every day since I first heard it singing in the rose garden.

I frown. It couldn't be—Jolie must know she's not allowed in this end of the castle. But she comes into view, holding my daughter's hand. Flora is smiling up at her, and the two of them turn toward Flora's chambers. My daughter opens the door.

"This is where I keep my books. See?"

"I would have loved to have this when I was your age," Jolie says. I can hear the smile in her voice. I poke my head out of my own door and crane my neck to hear what they say. Panic worms its way into my heart. Jolie shouldn't be up here. No one should be up here! She could be tracking any kind of bacteria into Flora's room. She could be putting my daughter's life in danger!

"Look, this is my favorite book," Flora says excitedly. "I can't wait to read the one you gave me."

"*Charlie and the Chocolate Factory* was my all-time favorite book when I was younger. I was a bit older than you, but you're a better reader than I was," Jolie laughs.

"I'll read it tonight and bring it right back to you."

"Don't worry about it, Flora. Take your time."

Flora? *Flora?* Did my fucking rose gardener just address a royal princess by her first fucking name? Who the hell is this woman, and why is she so comfortable being insolent?

"I really should get back to the garden."

"When I finish it, can I swap it for another?"

"Of course," Jo replies. She says goodbye to my daughter as I seethe behind my own door.

This has gone beyond breaking the rules. It's gone beyond trespassing. Jolie has crossed a line, and I intend to let her know just how unacceptable her behavior has become. There is no fucking way I'm putting my daughter's life in danger just so she can start a fucking book club with a six-year-old.

The rage inside me mounts, and the demons on my shoulder start to laugh, and laugh, and laugh.

"YOU MET THE PRINCESS?" Sam asks in a hushed whisper. "She brought you up to her chambers?" Her freckled cheeks are bright red, and a stray tendril of curly red hair has escaped her bonnet.

I frown, glancing from my plate of food over to her. "Yeah. You haven't? She says she knew my father, I thought she was pretty close with the staff." I don't tell Sam about our little reading parties in the evenings.

"The closest I've come to her was seeing her get into a car from a distance. His Highness keeps her away from everyone except Bertrand and Mrs. Grey."

"That's a bit sad, don't you think? Poor kid. Doesn't she have any friends? She was so excited about getting a new book."

Sam chews her lip and shakes her head. "The Prince has always kept her away. She's sick, you know."

"Yeah, but that doesn't mean she isn't a bright, young kid. She still needs to socialize. What kind of parent isolates their daughter from everything? The kid is a genius. She should be making the most of it."

"Ever since Prince Gabriel brought Flora here when she was an infant, he's kept her away from everyone and everything. The incident in Farcliff changed him. I've worked here my entire life, and when he used to visit when he was younger, he was different. Less angry. Less alone." Sam shakes her head. "I'd stay away from the Princess if I were you, Jo."

"That incident was right around the time I left for New York," I say, chewing thoughtfully. "What happened, again? A fight with his ex?"

"More than that." Sam glances around the kitchen. We're alone at our end of the table, so she lowers her voice and continues. "His ex wrote this tell-all book that became a best-seller. It had *all kinds* of crazy details about him—even their sex life."

My eyes widen. "Really? I don't remember that."

"Uh huh. The King had the book banned, but it still sold like crazy. Prince Gabriel went nuts one day, when he was mobbed by the press about it."

"Is that when he was knifed?"

Sam nods gravely. "In the street. His ex was having a press conference, accusing him of stealing her baby. He was accusing her of neglecting the Princess and keeping his daughter away from him..." She shakes her head. "It was messy. I think there's still video of it on the Internet."

"This must not have made international news, because I don't remember any of this."

Sam shrugs. "It was a big deal in Farcliff."

"Maybe I was too focused on trying to pay my bills."

Sam leans in toward me. "Apparently, the ex left the baby at home unsupervised. A three-month old! Who does that? Prince Gabriel found out, took the Princess into his care, and confronted his ex about it."

"Holy shit."

Sam shakes her head. "He's crazy about that little girl. Like I said, Jo, I'd stay away from her if you value your job—and your life."

Bertrand appears in the doorway, and we both straighten up. I feel like a guilty child, caught doing something I shouldn't have done. My cheeks burn as the Prince's butler swings his eyes over to me.

"Miss Beaumont, the Prince would like to see you."

Silence falls over the kitchen as all eyes turn to me. Even the scraping of utensils over plates stop.

I swallow the last bite of food in my mouth. "Me?"

Bertrand nods, gesturing to the door. I wipe my mouth on my napkin and pick up my plate, but Sam stops me.

"I'll clear it," she whispers. "You should go."

"What's going on?"

My friend shrugs. "I don't know. This doesn't usually happen."

My heart thumps as I push my chair back. I jerk up to stand and bump the table, sending the water in Sam's glass sloshing over the edges.

"Sorry," I whisper.

"It's fine. Go."

I smooth my hands over my legs and take a quick breath. As I follow Bertrand down the hallway, I pick at the skin around my fingernails and try not to trip over my own feet. My limbs feel heavier than usual, making every movement clumsy.

Why would the Prince want to see me? Am I going to be fired? My father would be devastated. Is this because of the Princess? Does he know that she's been coming to the cottage since my father and mother were here?

I knew I should have refused to follow her to her chambers—Sam told me the East Wing was forbidden—but she was so insistent and so proud of her little library. How could I refuse? She's royalty, too.

I clear my throat and Bertrand glances at me. He says nothing to calm me down, and my mind spins out of control. My movements become even jerkier. I run my fingers through my hair and rub the back of my neck as sweat starts to gather under my arms and between my shoulder blades.

Bertrand comes to a stop outside a set of double doors. We're not far from Flora's room, just the other side of the hallway. The doors are less grand than the library, but the sight of them fills me with terror.

This is the end of me. I'm done. I'll be fired, disgraced, and I'll have to go back to Farcliff with my tail between my legs. I've only just started my new book—based on Flora— and I feel like I've found a new family and a new home.

I can't leave now. It would kill my father—literally. Every time I talk to him on the phone, all he wants to know about are the roses. If I ruined this for him...

The Prince's butler knocks on the door, and then pushes them open. He bows deeply, and my eyes flick to the end of the room, where the Prince sits at a small desk.

"Thanks Bertrand," the Prince says, putting a bundle of papers down and turning to face us. He waves a hand. "Leave us."

The butler arches an eyebrow, but says nothing. I stumble inside the doors, and they close behind me silently. Suddenly, the room is stifling. I can't breathe. I don't know where to look. The Prince's eyes are glued on me, and I just want to disappear.

I can't move. I can't even curtsy, or bow, or whatever the heck I'm supposed to do. I just stand there and sweat. The room is small, with a desk and a couch opposite each other.

Another set of double doors leads to a massive bedroom. I'm in the Prince's chambers.

"Miss Beaumont," the Prince starts. His voice reverberates through my body, and I gulp.

I don't feel sassy or confident right now. I feel completely, utterly terrified.

"Your Highness."

The Prince stands up from his chair and walks toward me. Every step he takes makes my nerves crank tighter. He keeps his hands folded behind his back. His brow is dark as he surveys me.

"The East Wing is forbidden," he growls.

This is it. I'm going to be fired, or arrested, or worse. My life is over. Done. Finished.

The Prince arches an eyebrow. "You told me you weren't a rule breaker."

"I... I'm not," I stammer. "The Princess asked me..."

"What my daughter says shouldn't supersede the rules of this castle. She's a *child*."

I say nothing, inhaling sharply as Prince Gabriel takes a step toward me. His eyes are dark and stormy, his face impassive. He's so broad—so strong.

Is it wrong that I'm still attracted to him? Even when I see the darkness inside him. Even when he's angry and imposing. Even when I know I can never have him.

I close my eyes. I can't look at him. Every time I stare into his face, a lump forms in my throat and he steals the words from my lips. The only way I'll be able to say anything is if I'm not looking at him.

"I'm sorry," I whisper.

"You should be," he growls.

With my eyes closed, I can sense every movement he makes. The Prince takes another step, and I can smell his cologne. I can feel the heat of his body just inches from mine.

I've ruined everything. I won't get to take care of the roses for my father, I won't get to finish my new book. I've failed again, just like I always do. At least I'm consistent, right? If I can count on anything, I can count on my ability to fuck something up.

"Look at me," the Prince commands.

I take a breath and force myself to open my eyes. Prince Gabriel is standing just inches away from me, in all his towering glory. I've never met a man like him before. The danger in his eyes is tantalizing, and he makes me melt. He makes me think about everything naughty, everything wrong, everything *right*.

"I should have you fired…"

"Your Highness…" My breath hitches.

"… but my daughter seems to like you." He tilts his head, his eyes flicking down to my lips.

Fire burns in my veins and I waver on my feet. I can't speak, or think, or move. I just soak up his presence and try to stop my head from spinning.

The Prince steps toward me, and I step back. His lips tug at the corners, and he takes another step. I move back.

It's not that I want to move away from him. Quite the opposite, actually. I want to throw my arms around him and kiss him like I've never kissed anyone before. I want to give myself to him—mind, body, and soul. I want to surrender to this feeling inside me and never look back.

But he's *royalty*.

And who am I? I'm just the gardener's daughter.

Once more, he steps toward me. This time, when I take a step backward, my back hits the door. The Prince grins, bringing his hands up to cage me in against it.

My pulse hammers. He leans in toward me, his breath tickling the base of my neck. The Prince's lips brush the skin just below my ear, and a growl rumbles in his chest.

My fingers act of their own will, curling themselves into his shirt and pulling him closer. Torturously slowly, the Prince moves his lips up my neck and over my jaw. Everywhere he touches sends sparks flying over my skin. His body cages me against the wall and I submit to the desire inside me.

I arch my back toward the Prince, pressing my chest against his. My fingers curl into the fabric of his shirt, pulling him close to me. His lips tease me, trailing over my jaw and across the corner of my lips.

When I roll my hips toward him, Prince Gabriel chuckles.

"Jolie," he chides. "You *are* a rule breaker."

"What rule am I breaking now?"

I lift my eyes to his, and the tension between us heightens. His lips part, but I don't wait for his response. I lean toward him and press my lips to his.

I don't know what's come over me. I'm not usually this forward. I didn't come here to kiss him.

It's just that his aura is engulfing me, and I can't resist any longer. I pull him closer to me, fusing my body against his. Swiping my tongue across his lower lip, I part my lips as I kiss the Prince of Farcliff.

For the briefest of moments, I can feel his hesitation. He pauses, feeling my lips against his as his body traps mine against the door.

It's only a moment, though, and then something inside him snaps. It's almost an audible shift in the energy between us, like thunder breaking overhead.

Sweet, irresistible thunder.

Prince Gabriel roars, slamming his body against mine as

he crushes my lips with his kiss. His hands move from the door to my hips, and then around to my ass. He pulls me closer, grinding his hips to mine as he deepens the kiss.

It's electric. It's animalistic. It's wild.

He claws at my body, lifting me up so I wrap my legs around his waist. I hook my arms around his neck, kissing him fiercely as I moan into his mouth.

His hands slip under my shirt. The feeling of his bare hand against my skin sends red-hot shivers coursing through my body.

I can feel the fire burning inside him. I can sense the wildness just beneath the surface, and it makes my heart hammer against my ribcage. My fingers curl into his blond locks and I swipe my tongue into his mouth.

Prince Gabriel tastes like danger. He smells so intoxicating it feels immoral to be this close to him. I moan again, and he kisses me harder. His hips roll toward me, and I feel his length. He's hard—for me. I moan into his mouth and he grinds himself against me again.

It's better than I'd imagined. Desire consumes me whole, and I give myself over to him.

I'm ready.

I want him.

I don't care about the consequences. I don't care about anything except what's happening right here, right now...

...but just as suddenly as it starts, it's over. The Prince pulls away, unwrapping my legs from his waist. I drop to my feet and he takes a step back.

"Go," he says, his eyes flashing.

"But, your Highne—"

"*Leave!*" He howls, and fear spikes through me.

I scramble for the door, my hands shaking as I tear it open. I don't even take the time to close the door again. I just run down the empty hallway, straightening my clothing as tears sting my eyes. My cheeks burn and shame coats the inside of my mouth.

I run all the way to the Gardener's Cottage, not speaking a word to anyone. I don't stop moving until I'm safely inside with the lock bolted.

Then, and only then, do I break down and cry.

14

GABRIEL

I SLAM the door shut and stand in the middle of my ante-room, panting. My blood pumps hot and fast through my veins. My chest heaves. My legs tremble.

Fuck.

I shouldn't have done that. I brought her here to fire her —and instead, I kiss her?

No, that was more than a kiss. I was seconds away from losing control. If she'd stayed a moment longer, I'd have torn her clothing to shreds and fucked her senseless. I'd have given in to the beast and lost control.

Slumping down onto my chair, I let out a sigh.

I shouldn't have screamed. I shouldn't have kicked her out. I saw the tears fill her eyes when I yelled, and the frantic edge to her movements. I heard her footsteps running away from me.

And she should run away from me, the demons whisper. *Everyone should.*

Charlie wants me to do charity? He wants me to re-enter the royal life? How could I possibly do that, when I can't even control my own urges?

My face feels hot, and there's a tickle in my throat. I crumple away from the door, slouching in my chair as I struggle to come to terms with my own behavior.

She's just like Paulette—or is she? The kindness in her eyes is genuine. Jolie is good. I know she is.

Would it be that bad to sleep with her, just once? To give in to these urges a single time?

I inhale sharply, rubbing my palms against my eyes. Something has shifted inside me, and I don't know how to fix it. Does it need to be fixed?

To want someone as badly as I want Jolie—is that a bad thing, or a good thing? What does *she* want? Why would she kiss me? Why would she break every rule in the castle, and then shatter my defenses with one bat of her eyelashes?

She's going to destroy me—but destruction feels too good to say no.

The echo of her footsteps in the hallway rattle in my mind, and I let out a sigh. I shouldn't have treated her that way. What did she do to deserve it, except show kindness to my daughter?

My mind pulls me in a thousand different directions, but in the end, my body wins. My feet carry me out of my chambers and down the hallways. My footsteps follow hers as I walk out of the castle and across the lush, green lawn toward the Gardener's Cottage.

There's a tingling in my fingertips and a hollowness in my chest and all I can see is the small building at the edge of the grounds. My steps are hurried as I make my way across, and all I can hear is the rushing of blood in my ears. My mouth tastes bitter and I inhale deeply as I step onto the flagstones that lead to the cottage's front door.

Twice, I've stood here before—and twice, I've hesitated.

Not today.

Without pausing, I bring my fist up and knock on the door.

"Jo!" I call out, leaning toward the door.

I can hear rustling on the other side of the door, but it doesn't open.

"Jolie," I call out again, a little more quietly. I knock once more, then pause.

Her footsteps come closer, and I think I hear her inhale. The lock scrapes open, and the door swings inward. Jolie stands in the opening, her eyes shining and her mouth set in a thin line.

"Your Highness?"

She's stunning. More than stunning. She's the embodiment of everything I want, from her thick, wavy hair, to her willowy body. Even the hostility in her face doesn't put me off.

I take a deep breath. "Can I come in?"

She doesn't react for a moment, watching me. Then, with a sigh, she opens the door wider. "I guess it's as much your cottage as it is mine."

When I'm inside, Jolie closes the door behind me and takes a step away from me. Her eyebrows arch in question.

I take a step toward her, but she holds up her hand.

"Not this again." She shakes her head, averting her gaze.

"Not what again?"

"You. Not *you*, your Highness." She raises her gaze up to mine, and the determination in her face nearly knocks me back. She continues: "You can't kiss me like that and then scream at me to leave. You can't treat me like a toy that you can pick up and put down again. If you want me to leave Westhill, I will—but I won't be treated like that."

Her shoulders tremble.

"I'm sorry." I say the words softly, and to my surprise, I

mean them. I don't remember the last time I apologized to someone and actually meant it.

She swallows thickly. "Thank you."

Neither of us moves, and I feel like I'm being torn apart. All I want to do is wrap my arms around her again. I want to feel her body pressed up against mine again, taste her lips, curl my fingers into her hair. I want to devour her, ravage her, and ruin her until she begs me for more.

But an invisible wall stands between us, and I know that I'm the one who put it there.

"I'm not used to this," I say.

"To what?"

"To wanting someone like I want you."

Her eyes widen ever so slightly, and I can see the pulse thumping in her neck.

"I'm just here to take care of the roses until my father is better," she responds quietly.

"What about the kiss?"

"What about it?"

"I know you want me, Jolie. No one kisses like that unless they want you."

"What does it matter if I want you?" She shakes her head, scoffing. "Of course I want you. How could I not? Look at you! But I don't want to be yelled at or treated like a cockroach whenever you feel like you've had enough of me."

My heart squeezes. I exhale slowly, raking my fingers through my hair. "I'm messed up in the head, Jolie," I say softly. "I have been ever since I was a kid. I don't know how to think straight sometimes."

"Oh, okay—that makes it all better. Let's have sex, then," she snaps.

I flick my eyes up to hers to see Jolie shaking her head.

Anger flares inside me, but a voice at the back of my head tells me she's right.

Jolie's deep, brown eyes are full of fire as she looks at me. "I may be nothing but a gardener and a struggling writer. I may be nothing to you—but saying that you're messed up isn't good enough. I've been with enough damaged men to know that I can't fix you, and I don't want to be anywhere near you when you implode."

I grind my teeth as a flush passes through my body. My ears feel like they're burning, and I ball my hands into fists to try and hold myself back.

"I'm your *Prince*," I say through gritted teeth.

"Congratu-fucking-lations." Jolie's eyes flash. "Are you going to command me to fuck you? Because the answer is still no."

I take a step toward her. "You have no right to speak to me that way."

"Neither do you."

"You should be on your knees in front of me." I take another stride.

"In. Your. *Dreams*," she spits.

The air between us crackles. The hair on my body is standing on end, and I can hardly contain the energy buzzing inside me. Jolie stands her ground, eyes blazing, arms hanging loosely at her sides.

When I take another step, my chest brushes against hers. She lifts her chin defiantly, holding my gaze. I bring my hand up to her jaw, and she smacks it away. Her jaw twitches.

And my cock throbs.

My breath is shallow. The two of us stand motionless before each other, the fury pulsing between us. I won't back down—I can't back down.

Every breath escalates the tension between us. Without a

movement, without a word, without a sound, Jolie makes the aching inside me more painful, until my whole body screams.

Still, neither of us moves...

...until Jo puts her hand on my chest, and I catch it in my own. The feeling of her skin against mine sends heat exploding through my body, and I can't resist it anymore.

I pull Jo's body into mine and crush my lips against hers. She melts into me without resistance, moaning gently as the wall between us crumbles, and desire wins over anger.

Our kiss is electric. Violent. Needy. Jolie sinks her fingernails into the nape of my neck and pulls me into her body. I claim her lips, relishing the taste of her mouth as she trembles against me.

Panting, I pull away. "You want this?"

Her nails dig into my neck. "Don't play the nice guy now, your Highness. Just shut up and kiss me."

15

JO

I HATE HIM. I want him. I need him. Anger fuels my desire as I wrap my arms around the Prince's neck, pulling him in for a deeper embrace.

The Prince grunts, sinking his fingers into my hips as he pulls me closer. His kiss is white-hot, and every touch singes my skin. As he grinds his hips against me, I moan.

The Gardener's Cottage is small. It's one large living and kitchen area, with a bedroom and a bathroom opening onto it. It almost feels like this space is too small to contain us both. There's too much heat in here to be held in by these four walls.

As the Prince walks me backwards, my thighs hit the back of the sofa. His broad, strong body presses into my own. Fire rips down my spine as desire comes over me in waves.

If I thought the kiss in his chambers was intense, I had no idea what was coming to me. This is more than intense. It's electric. It's angry. It's viciously needy.

Prince Gabriel drops his lips to my neck. He molds his body to mine as his lips trail down to my collarbone. With both hands, he lifts my shirt off over my head and growls as he sees my body. His hands slide up to my chest, ripping my bra down to my waist as his lips drop to my breasts.

I gasp when I feel his teeth graze my nipples, his hands holding me as if I belong to him.

Right now, I do. I hate it and I love it at the same time.

Running my fingers over his shoulders, I shiver at the feeling of his hard, warm muscles under my touch. His own hands drop to my ass, dragging me closer to him. The hardness of his cock through his pants makes the heat in my belly burn hotter. I gasp. The Prince lets out a low chuckle. His eyes are dangerous and flinty—anger and desire still war within him.

I scramble to unbutton his shirt. He watches me with hooded eyes, letting the garment drop behind him. My hands fly to his shoulders again, and he unclasps my bra, flinging it across the room.

Without warning, the Prince tangles his fingers into my hair and pulls my head back. He crushes his lips against mine, grunting as he grinds himself against me. My skin is on fire. Everywhere he touches sparks.

The press call Prince Gabriel an animal—and now, I see that it's true. With his hand still gripping my hair, he pulls my head back and watches me, panting.

"Do you still want me to leave?"

"I never wanted you to leave." My chest heaves and I force myself to hold his gaze. Everything inside me is screaming to submit. To comply. To give myself over to him completely.

His fist tightens in my hair, sending needles of pain and pleasure through my skull. The Prince's other hand drops to my breast and he brushes my nipple with his thumb. It's a gentle touch, but the look in his eye betrays something more.

My body screams for him.

As if he can hear it, the Prince drops his hand between my legs. A dark smile appears on his face when he feels the warmth and wetness between my legs, even through the fabric of my gardening pants. Without a word, Prince Gabriel unbuttons my pants and slips his hand down the front of them

Closing my eyes, I let out a long breath as his hand slides through my slit. My body arches toward him, and I know I've completely lost control over myself. I want him so badly I can't think straight.

"Open your eyes," he growls. "I want you to look at me while I make you come."

I do as he says. How could I not?

I love obeying his commands. I love the feeling of his fingers curled in my hair, while his other hand drags up and down my wetness. I love the darkness in his eyes as he watches the pleasure bloom across my face.

My heart hammers in my chest. The Prince licks his lips as he moves his hand toward my opening, and another wave of pleasure passes through me. I reach for his cock, wanting to feel its hardness in my hand, but he growls in warning.

"No."

"I want..."

"I don't care what you want." The Prince drives his fingers inside me, and my hands fall to the couch behind me. I grip the edge of it as he pleasures me. When I close my eyes, he commands me to open them again.

And I do. I'd do anything he tells me.

His fingers slide up to my bud and heat explodes across my thighs. My breath catches and a moan slips through my lips.

The Prince can sense the pleasure cresting. He tightens

the grip on my hair as I hold onto the couch. My legs buck, my back arches, and my body submits to him.

I come.

As Prince Gabriel brings me to orgasm, he kisses me hard. I moan into his mouth, unable to move, or think, or do anything except ride wave after wave of pleasure. Heat explodes through my veins. The Prince doesn't stop until I push him away, panting.

As soon as I push his hand away, I miss it. Shivers are still coursing through my body, but I already know I want more. With a quiet chuckle, he brings his fingers up to his mouth and tastes my wetness.

I watch him, struggling to catch my breath. As I lean against the back of the sofa, we stare at each other wordlessly. The Prince's gaze drops to my bare chest, to my unbuttoned pants, and back up to my flushed face.

"Did you enjoy that?" He grins, arching an eyebrow.

He's so fucking cocky. I gulp down another breath and shrug. "It was okay."

The Prince's eyes flash, and he's on me again. I yelp when he spins me around, pushing me down so I catch myself on the back of the sofa. He pushes my pants down to my knees as my heart skips a beat.

I glance over my shoulder just in time to see his palm come down across my ass. Yelping, I flinch as pain explodes into pleasure across my skin.

"Don't you dare move," the Prince growls. I hear his pants drop to the floor, and the next thing I feel are his hands on my waist.

Then, I feel his cock—thick, hot, and perfect. He slides it between my thighs and groans in pleasure. My pulse quickens and I grip the sofa even harder. I bite my lip, arching my back to feel him against me. He's not even inside me, and I'm already losing my mind.

The Prince slides himself against my slit, gripping my waist. One hand leaves my waist and comes down on my ass again with a loud crack. I inhale sharply, and then let out a laugh. My entire existence comes down to this moment. Nothing else matters except what the Prince does to my body. The pleasure he delivers to me is everything.

I push my ass back against him, and the Prince grunts. He pulls away, teasing me. I whimper.

"Do you want me?" He asks.

"Yes."

"All of me?"

"Yes," I pant.

The Prince slides his hand between my legs, groaning when he feels the wetness dripping down my thighs. I try to widen my stance, but the Prince stops me.

"I told you not to move." He smacks my ass again. "Stay right there."

His fingers slide inside me, but they're not enough. They'll never be enough. When he takes them away, I feel empty.

"Please," I whisper.

The Prince steps closer, pressing his cock against my ass as he leans over me. "What?"

"I want you," I whisper. "Please."

"You didn't want me earlier."

"I did—always."

Those words are enough to get me what I want—what I *need*. The Prince slides his cock inside me, inch by inch, until I'm completely filled. I squeeze my thighs together, arching my back as he moves even deeper.

It feels better than I expected. My fingers curl into the

couch and I grip it as tightly as I can. I know what's coming. I can feel the power coiled inside the Prince, and I know it'll be unleashed upon me.

I want it. I'm begging for it.

I push back into him and hear him exhale softly. His fingers sink into my waist and we stay there for just a second.

Then, the beast emerges. The Prince drags himself out of me and thrusts—*hard*. I gasp as pleasure explodes inside me, squeezing my eyes shut as a smile stretches over my lips. Then, he does it again, and again, and again.

The Prince's hands hold me in place while he drives his length inside me. I moan, gasping when he brings his hand down on my ass cheek.

He's rough, and I can't get enough of it. I brace myself against the sofa and slam my body back into his. Roaring in response, the Prince brings his hand down on my ass again. I scream, living somewhere between pleasure and pain.

Is it hatred between us? Or lust? Are we simply acting on a mutual desire, or am I giving him exactly what he wanted by submitting to him? Am I losing myself?

Do I care?

He drives his cock inside me again and I see stars. I scream once again, and the Prince runs his fingers over my ass. When he slides his thumb inside me, I make a noise I've never made before. He teases my most forbidden spot while his cock fucks me mercilessly, and I know I'm his.

I can't pretend anymore. I can't lie to myself and say that I don't love this. I'm a doll in his hands, and everything he does to me makes my body burn.

"Come for me," the Prince demands.

I obey.

My orgasm crashes into me without warning. My legs

quake as fire rips through my veins. It steals the scream from my lips as my whole body contracts.

The Prince grunts in response. Just as my orgasm begins to fade, and I start to go limp, I feel his body stiffen behind me. I gasp as he comes inside me, filling me with his seed as we both tremble against each other. It takes all my effort not to collapse until the Prince lets out one last growl. Then, I fall to my knees with a sigh.

16

GABRIEL

JOLIE IS BROKEN on the floor, and I'm struggling to stay standing. I suck in another breath and put my hand to my chest. My heart is racing so hard, I think I might faint.

With one more breath, I'm able to see straight. Jo is still panting on the floor with her pants around her knees. I lean over, pick her up, and carry her around to the front of the sofa. Flopping down on the couch, I cradle her in my arms. Her head lolls forward and rests on my chest, and we stay there for a while without speaking.

Jo's hand moves to my chest. "Your heart is beating like crazy," she says quietly.

"I thought I was going to pass out earlier."

"I think I did pass out." She laughs weakly, melting into my chest.

We doze off for a few minutes, or maybe longer. Finally, Jolie pushes herself off me. She tries to stand up, but her pants are still around her ankles. Stumbling, she lets out a cute little yelp and trips over herself. Catching herself on the edge of the couch, she manages to half-fall, half-lower herself down to the ground before dissolving into a fit of laughter.

"Was that graceful enough for His Highness, the Prince of Farcliff?" She grins, pulling her pants up and standing up.

"You should teach finishing classes."

Jo laughs and pours herself a glass of water. She takes a sip before offering it to me. I look at the glass, frowning.

Jo's eyebrows arch, and she laughs again. "Oh, I'm sorry Your Royal Highness, are you not used to drinking out of the same glass as us peasants? I don't have any crystal handy for you, and we did just fuck each other's brains out, so..."

I take the water with a wry grin. "It's fine."

"It's not too repulsive for you?"

I take a sip to prove to her that it isn't, and then hand the glass back. She watches me, grinning, and then has another sip for herself.

I'd never tell her this, but that's the first time someone has done that. Is that how normal people treat each other? I watch as Jo puts the glass down on the kitchen counter and pulls her shirt on. She picks up my underwear and pants, tossing them at me.

"Put some clothes on, Your Highness. What would people think?"

"Probably the same they already think about me," I grin. I dress myself, and look up to see Jo watching me.

"What?" I ask.

"Do you enjoy it?"

"Enjoy what?"

"Riling up the media like you do? Being the bad guy?"

I avoid her eye by focusing on zipping up my fly, and then rake my fingers through my hair. I shrug. "No, I wouldn't say I like it."

"So why do you do it?"

"I don't do it on purpose."

"Are you sure?" She tilts her head, searching my eyes.

I shift my weight from foot to foot and clear my throat. Reaching down to grab my shirt, I throw it on and start buttoning it up. "You think that just because we had sex, you know me now?"

I know I'm being harsh, but I don't like the way she's speaking to me. I'm the Prince of Farcliff, and who is she? The gardener's daughter.

A nobody.

Hurt flits across Jolie's face, and she hides it quickly. She shrugs, turning back to her glass of water.

"I should go," I say, gathering the last of my things.

"Yeah." Her back is still turned to me. I hesitate for a moment, wanting to go to her. I want to wrap my arms around her waist and whisper something sweet in her ear. I want to make her look me in the eye again, and see that smile brighten her face.

But I don't do any of those things. I just sigh and let myself out, and the devil on my shoulder laughs. I know I shouldn't have done that—but who is she to dictate how *I* should act?

All I did was have sex with the girl. I don't owe her anything. She should be happy she got an orgasm from me.

I pause on the lawn and glance back at the Gardener's Cottage, shaking my head. This is me—I ruin things. Good things, mediocre things, bad things—it doesn't matter. I ruin them all.

What if I tried not to? What if I went back and apologized? What if I was kind to her?

The distance between the cottage and me seems impossibly far, though. The steps that would take me back there are too difficult to take. What would I even say?

I close my eyes and take a deep breath, and then turn back toward the castle. Trudging back to my chambers, I keep my head down and I ignore everyone in my path. After a long, hot shower, I've washed all of Jolie off my body and out of my mind.

She's just a girl that I wanted, and I had her. That's all.

Still, my feet carry me to the window. I glance out and look for her in the rose garden. When I don't see her, my shoulders slump and I turn away from the glass. I let out a heavy sigh and press my hands to my temple.

This is exactly what happened with Paulette. I got involved, and I got addicted, and then I ruined it all. I couldn't resist her, and then it all went to shit.

Here I am, six years later, doing it all over again.

How stupid could I be?

I stalk over to my desk and sweep my arm across it. A roar erupts through my chest as papers, and glasses, and pens go flying across the room. Slamming my hands on the desk, I exhale sharply and lean over it, panting.

"Daddy? Are you okay?"

I jump at the sound of my daughter's voice. Turning toward the door, I see her in the doorway with wide eyes. She looks at the carnage on the floor and back to my face. Her eyes water and she shrinks away from me.

My chest tightens and I reach for her, crouching down.

"I'm fine, kiddo," I say, forcing a smile. I swallow, grimacing as Flora's eyes look at the mess on the floor again. "I'm okay."

"Why did you do that?" She doesn't come near me, and my heart breaks at the thought that she might be scared of me.

I inhale through gritted teeth, then walk toward her. "Come here," I say. "Don't worry about it. How was your day?"

She's wearing flannel pajamas, and her hair is wet from a bath. She takes one hesitant step, and then relaxes as I wrap my arms around her. I carry my daughter to the sofa on the opposite side of the room and sit her down next to me.

"Now," I say. "Tell me all about it."

"Well," Flora says, turning her eyes away from the mess on the other end of the room and smiling at me. "Mrs. Grey said my subtraction quiz was perfect today."

"What's six minus two?"

"Four," Flora answers with an exaggerated eye roll. "That question is for babies, Dad."

"Of course," I laugh, ruffling her hair. "I forgot you're a math whiz."

"Jo says she'll get me new books when she goes to Farcliff. She said she knows an old bookstore with all her favorites."

"Jo?" I try to sound casual, but a lump forms in my throat.

"The rose gardener. She's Mr. Marcel's daughter, and she's writing a book. I asked if I could read it, but she said only when I was older. How old do you think I'll have to be to read it?"

"I'm not sure, honey." I force a smile. "You don't need to go to a bookstore to get new books. We'll just order them."

"Jo says that a bookstore has a special smell—one that's like nothing else in the world. What does it smell like, Daddy?"

"It smells... sleepy and comfortable. Just like you're going to feel in five minutes, because it's bedtime. Come on, I'll read you a story."

Flora jumps off the couch, her fear forgotten as she slips her hand into mine. As usual, my daughter's calming influence soothes my heart, and I follow her down the hallway to her chambers.

"How well did you know Mr. Marcel, Flora?" I glance at my daughter, wondering how exactly it is that my six-year-old has a secret life that I don't know about.

"He was my favorite," Flora answer simply. "Last year, he gave me the most beautiful roses in the garden—he said so himself. He had lots and lots of books—just like me. I hope he's feeling better now."

"Mm," I answer, frowning. My daughter even knew that he's sick?

I tuck her into bed and read her favorite story, which she interrupts with a thousand and one questions about the rose garden, Marcel, Violet, and Jolie. I do my best to steer her away from them, because every time she says Jolie's name, a pang passes through my heart.

"Jolie is so beautiful," Flora sighs when I close the book. I doubt she's heard a word I've said. She glances at me. "Don't you think, Daddy?"

"I think you're beautiful." I lean down to kiss her forehead.

"I hope I grow up to be like her. She's so brave. Did you know she lived in New York City all by herself?"

"No, I didn't." There's a lot I don't know about my rose gardener, apparently. I just wish my daughter would stop talking about her. "Time for bed now."

Flora smiles at me, and points to her cheek with her finger. "One more kiss, please."

I chuckle and do as she says. When I straighten up, Flora looks up at me.

"Daddy, why don't I have a mom?"

It's hard to keep a straight face when your heart shatters in your chest. I swallow thickly, and stroke my daughter's cheek. "You have a mother, kiddo. She just lives somewhere else."

"Doesn't she love me? Is it because I'm sick?

"Of course she loves you." I sit down again, frowning. "It

has nothing to do with you, and everything to do with her. She just... She couldn't take care of you."

"Is she sick?"

"In a way, yes. Where is this coming from?"

Flora sighs, shrugging. "I don't know. Goodnight, Daddy." She closes her eyes as if to tell me the conversation is over.

I walk to the door and glance back at my daughter once more before slipping out. When I walk back to my own chambers, my chest aches. I rub my fingers over my temples, trying to get rid of the headache that's gathering behind my eyes. The scar on my face pulses.

For the first time since I left Farcliff Castle, I wonder if raising Flora on my own was the right decision. Has she missed having a mother her whole life—just like me?

17

JO

THE PRINCE LEAVES my cottage and I stare after him, feeling deflated and a little embarrassed. Apparently, my taste in men hasn't changed. It's still terrible. I lean against the kitchen counter and take a deep breath, raking my hand through my hair.

My body is still buzzing from my orgasms, but my mind is a mess and my chest feels hollow. Biting my lip, I head for the bathroom to wash the sex off my body.

We didn't even use protection, which is stupid and irresponsible. It's not like me.

Or maybe, it's exactly like me—stupid and irresponsible seems to be my modus operandi. Maybe that's why everything in my life always falls apart.

Standing under the stream, I replay the evening's events in my mind. The Prince is hard to read, and has his defenses up almost all the time. The only moment that I saw a flash of something real inside him was when I tossed him his clothing. He had this look on his face—a little smile, and a brightness in his eye.

I wash myself slowly, unsure of exactly how I feel. A big

part of me regrets what happened. I shouldn't have slept with him—that much is obvious. I let my desire jeopardize my position in the castle. My heart squeezes at the thought of leaving Westhill. I'd be leaving Sam and all my new family behind. I'd have to leave Flora, too. I'd ruin my father's hopes of ever coming back here.

As I dry myself off and put my pajamas on, I steel myself against the guilt and shame that try to wriggle their way into my heart. I refuse to feel bad about what happened. Prince Gabriel followed *me* to the cottage. I didn't pursue him. If he's unhappy about the fact that we had sex, that's on him.

I'm drying my hair with a towel when someone knocks on the cottage door. I freeze, my heart thumping. Is Prince Gabriel back? Is he fucking serious? That man needs to make up his damn mind.

Barefoot, I walk toward the front door. My mouth goes dry and a lump forms in my throat. I'm still holding my damp towel in my hand as I take a deep breath and pull the door open.

"Oh," I say when I see Sam on the other side.

"Disappointed to see me?" She grins. "Who were you expecting?"

"Of course I'm not disappointed," I respond, stepping aside for her to come in.

She holds up a plate covered in tin foil. "Brought you some dessert. George made *mille feuille*. I grabbed you a piece before it disappeared. The staff are like starving animals in that kitchen."

I smile, accepting the plate. I take the foil off the top of it and bring the plate up to my nose, inhaling the scent of pastry and cream. I sigh.

"George is a magician. Here, let me cut this in half."

"I already had my share." Sam shakes her head.

I cut it in half anyway, and Sam accepts the slice of dessert with a guilty grin.

"Twist my arm, why don't you."

I laugh, and the two of us sit down.

Sam nods to my discarded bra on the floor. "Messy! What would Mrs. Grey say at that kind of slovenly behavior?"

My cheeks flush, and I focus on the pastry in front of me. I can still feel Sam's eyes on me, though, and I know the question is coming. It only takes a few more seconds for her to prod me.

"So?" She asks. "What did the Prince say?"

"You weren't just coming over here to bring me dessert after all," I laugh.

"Maybe it was a bit of a bribe," Sam says with a giggle. "So, spill it! What did he say?"

I take a deep breath. How do I answer this? "He asked me what I was doing in the East Wing."

"And?"

"And I told him that Princess Flora had brought me up there."

"He was happy with that?"

"I don't know if I'd go so far as to say *happy*," I reply, remembering the way the anger rolled off the Prince in waves, "but he accepted it."

"So, you still have a job?"

I laugh, nodding. "I still have a job—for now."

I glance away from Sam, afraid that if I look at her too long, more secrets will come out of me. The last thing I want to do is tell anyone about what happened in the cottage tonight—or how it ended. I may have a job now... but what about tomorrow?

Sam stays with me for an hour or so, and we giggle and gossip about everything happening at Westhill. When she leaves, my heart feels calmer than it did before, and I'm able to get to sleep.

I WAKE up ready to work. Pulling on my gardening clothes, I know that I'll have a long day of weeding ahead of me. It's only a matter of days before the first roses bloom and I want to make sure that they're well taken care of. The Annual Rose Festival judges will be coming to Westhill to judge this year's blooms, so the pressure is on.

I have some instant oats in the cupboard, and I eat some quickly to avoid going to the castle kitchens this morning. It might cause gossip among the staff, but all I want to do is go and see my flowers.

When I open my front door, a golden envelope catches my eye. It rests on my welcome mat, with my name on it in big, round letters.

I bend over and pick it up, glancing around the lawns to see if I can spot its messenger. Seeing no one, I turn back to the envelope. It's sealed shut, and the golden paper is so beautiful that it feels wrong to rip it open. I tear it as carefully as I can and pull out a card.

I frown as I read it. Gulping, I try to make sense of the words I'm seeing.

Dine with me tonight.
—G.

I glance up at the huge building as my heart hammers against my ribcage. Retreating back inside my cottage, I slump down onto the nearest chair and read the words again.

There's no doubt in my mind who 'G' is. The invitation— if you can call it that—sounds like it was written by the

Prince. He's as commanding as always. I look up from the card, staring off into nothing.

Is this a joke? Some sort of sick power play? Is the Prince toying with me?

Or, does he actually want to see me again?

Inhaling sharply, I drop the card and envelope onto the table and head back for the garden.

That man makes no sense. One minute, he wants to screw my brains out, and the next he's storming off. Then, he wants to see me again? I can't keep up.

Who invites their gardener to dinner? My parents weren't even sure the Prince knew their names until the day they left.

My steps are hurried as I make my way to the rose garden. I've oiled the hinges on the gate and it swings open noiselessly. My eyes drift up to the windows above me, looking for any movement.

They stay empty, and I get to work.

I weed viciously, pulling out the pesky plants until sweat drips off my forehead and my shirt is soaked. When the sun is high in the sky, my stomach grumbles and I finally look up from my work.

Sighing, I wipe my brow with my forearm and stand up. My back aches, and my shoulders feel tight. I stretch my neck from side to side and make my way to the palace kitchens.

As I step inside the castle, I brace myself for the onslaught of questions that will surely come my way. Everyone will be wondering why I was called to see the Prince last night. What would they say if they knew I was having dinner with him?

I wipe my shoes off on the mat in the servant's foyer and when I look up, Bertrand is staring at me from the doorway.

"His Highness would like to know if you'll be accepting his invitation?"

The butler's face stays perfectly still, and his eyes are

unreadable. If he's surprised by the invitation, he doesn't show it.

I clear my throat. "Uh... Yeah, I guess. What time?"

"Seven o'clock."

Bertrand bows to me—which, to be honest, feels weird—and disappears down the hallway. I stare after him, and the only thought that crosses my mind is: *What the hell am I going to wear?*

The only dress I have is the yellow sundress I wore to the Westhill Town Fair. Otherwise, I only own ripped jeans and gardening clothes. When I left New York, I didn't exactly think I'd be attending any royal dinners.

I glance down the hallway, hoping to see Bertrand to ask him more questions. What do I wear? What fork do I eat with? *Why is this happening?*

But he's gone, and I'm alone with my thoughts, which I already know will plague me until seven o'clock tonight.

18

GABRIEL

I STRAIGHTEN MY TIE, wondering if I've made a mistake. I should be getting rid of Jolie—not inviting her to dinner. I didn't sleep a wink last night, though, and all I've thought about is her. Well, her and Flora. Jo is the only person besides Flora that I've met in the past six years who's made me feel like a regular person. She's the only person who's prompted Flora to ask about her own mother.

It's hard to ignore the connection. Maybe having Jolie around will be good for Flora.

That's worth something, isn't it?

Scoffing at myself, I shake my head. I can't pretend that my intentions are pure. I'm not having dinner with Jo just to vet her as a mother figure for my daughter.

I want to see her again. I want to have her again.

When I get to the dining room, she hasn't arrived yet. Bertrand pulls my chair out for me, and flicks my napkin over my lap after I've sat down.

I sip fine wine and wait for Jolie to arrive. The seconds tick by, and I start to sweat. I pull at my collar, loosening my tie before taking another sip of wine. Staring at the crystal glass throwing light across the table, I wonder if she's stood me up.

It wouldn't surprise me—she seems like the headstrong type who would refuse me, just to prove a point. As time stretches onward, it becomes harder and harder to ignore her absence. My knee bounces up and down, and I stare at the door as if my gaze will make her appear.

Finally, she does. The door opens and Jolie steps through, wearing the same yellow sundress she wore to the Westhill Town Fair. The sight of her in that dress does the same thing it did to me when I was perched on the dunk tank platform. My body starts to heat up, and my pants get tighter.

Jolie's hair is curled into soft waves, pinned back from her face. She smiles at me as I stand up to greet her, and Bertrand pulls out a chair to my right.

Her eyes drift down the long, polished table and then they slide over to me. She smiles tentatively.

"Your Highness," she nods.

"Thank you for joining me—finally."

Her eyebrows draw together. "First of all, the invitation didn't have a time. Bertrand said seven, and it's," she glances at the grandfather clock against the wall, "six fifty-eight. So, don't give me that 'finally' bullshit."

Bertrand inhales sharply, and I stare at Jolie. Heat teases my insides as a smile curls over my lips. Jolie's soft curls tremble as she stares at me. I gesture to her seat again.

With a huff, she sits down.

I like pushing her buttons, I realize. The tip of her nose gets really red when she's angry, and she pinches her full lips together so tightly they look like a thin line. I get some sort of sick enjoyment out of seeing the frustration ooze out of her every pore.

As the first course is served, Jolie steals a few glances my way. Her shoulders relax, and the anger leaves her face. That's another thing I like about her—she doesn't seem to hold a grudge.

"I have to say, Your Highness, I was a little surprised to receive your invitation."

"Were you?"

She glances at the waiter as he fills her wine and a blush creeps over her cheeks. "I was."

"Why's that?"

The waiter hovers, topping off my glass and taking his time to clear the table. Jo shifts in her seat, and I grin. Is it wrong that I like seeing her like this? She's usually so self-assured. Seeing her off-balance gives me a dark kind of pleasure.

Does that make me an asshole?

Yes. Definitely.

Do I care?

Not really.

Jo clears her throat and steals another glance at the waiter. I wave my hand to dismiss him, putting Jo out of her misery. As soon as the door closes and we're alone, Jolie's eyes lift up to mine.

"I was surprised you invited me here because I didn't think you enjoyed my company."

"I'm not sure I do, either."

Jo's eyes flash, and she turns back to her food. Her shoulders vibrate, as if the anger inside her is trying to break free.

I feed off her anger. It builds me up, making me bigger than I was before. Jolie takes her wine glass between delicate fingers, bringing it to touch her luscious lips. I watch her throat bob as she swallows, entranced by the movement.

She puts the glass down and turns to face me. "Is there a reason you're such an asshole?"

"Maybe it's just my nature," I shrug.

She rolls her eyes, looking away from me. Her body angles the other way, and she focuses on the food on her plate. I'm losing her, I can tell. This isn't playful anger anymore, I can sense her opinion of me changing by the second, and I don't like it.

"I have a hard time trusting women," I blurt out.

"Because of your ex?" She lifts her eyes back up to mine.

I nod. "Yeah."

"I was out of the Kingdom when that went down." She nods to my scar. "What happened?"

"You mean you don't know?" I arch an eyebrow skeptically.

Jolie shakes her head. "You know, you may be a Prince of Farcliff and everything, but the entire world doesn't revolve around you. No, I didn't hear about it, because I was living in another country. There were maybe one or two news reports on it, but I didn't watch the news because I was busy working sixteen hours a day to try to get my writing career off the ground."

"And how did that go for you?"

"Terrible, thanks for asking. I failed, and had to come back to Farcliff with my tail between my legs—under the guise of helping my parents out with this stupid garden." Her fork clatters against her plate, and she pushes her chair back.

Her cheeks are red now, as well as the tip of her nose. She nods her head to me, and panic shoots through my chest.

"Wait," I say, standing up with her.

"Why? You're just going to sit there and lord over me, making me feel like I'm a piece of shit. I'm over this." She starts walking to the door, and my heart starts to thump. I open my mouth, but I don't know what to say. I'm not the kind of man who begs.

"I know I'm an ass," I blurt out.

"That's very self-actualized of you," Jolie answers, turning to look at me from the door. "How many years did it take you to realize that?"

"Too many," I say softly. Jolie keeps staring at me, and a thin thread of hope starts weaving its way through my heart. I clear my throat. "Things changed when Flora was born."

Jo turns her body a fraction of an inch toward me, and the thread of hope in my heart gets thicker.

"I never wanted to be a father. Things between Paulette and I were... explosive, for lack of a better word. We were too similar. We'd fight all the time. She got pregnant, and I thought it would change things, but it just made them worse."

I take a deep breath, raking my fingers through my hair. Jolie waits quietly for me to continue.

So, I do.

"I broke up with her when she was six months pregnant, which I'm not proud of. She was drinking while pregnant with Flora, and we just—it was messy. Let's leave it at that. After we broke up, she released that book. Did you hear about the book?"

"Only recently."

"Well, it was packed full of lies. Made me out to be this animal, and made her out to be a saint trapped in a toxic relationship. It *was* toxic, but it wasn't all because of me. We were both to blame for that."

"And Flora?"

"Flora has cystic fibrosis. It's hereditary." My voice catches. "Paulette left her without anyone looking after her to go promote her book on a breakfast television show. She left a three month old baby home alone."

Jolie takes a step toward me, but my mind is elsewhere. The memories of that day start crashing through my mind. The floodgates that I've worked so hard to erect have opened, and the pain from those days is tumbling through my body. I slump back down in my chair.

"I'm not proud of what I did. I should have just taken Flora and done things legally. Gained custody, had my lawyers deal with Paulette—that kind of thing."

"It would be hard to think clearly in that situation." Jolie walks back to her seat and sits down, but her eyes are full of pity and I can't bear to look at them.

"I was thinking more clearly than I've ever thought before," I answer flatly, staring at my half-eaten plate. "I wanted to kill her. I've never been that mad. Flora is my world, and my ex didn't give a damn about her. I went to the set where Paulette was filming, and I snapped. I started yelling. She had a knife."

I gesture to my face, where my scar feels like it's hot to the touch. Jolie reaches toward me tentatively, running her fingers along my jaw. I close my eyes and let her feel the evidence of my greatest shame.

I used to think that I wasn't myself in those days. I was so out of control, so out of my mind. But the worst part is—I was still me. I know that part of my soul still exists inside me. The black part. The beastly part. The angry part.

Jolie lets out a sigh. She chews her lip and grabs her fork, pushing the food around her plate. I watch her for a few moments.

"So, what do you think?" I ask.

"About what?"

"About me. You think I'm a monster?"

Jolie takes a deep breath. She lets it out slowly, moving her head from side to side. "I don't think you're a monster..."

"...but?"

"But I think you need therapy." She doesn't say it in a derisive way. Jolie says it matter-of-factly, as if it's the same thing as saying I need to buy some milk because I've run out.

"You think that would do anything to help?" I shake my head. "I'm beyond therapy."

"That's probably the perfect indication that you could benefit from it," Jolie grins. She shrugs. "It's hard to ask for help, though."

"Have you ever been to a therapist?"

Jolie shakes her head. "I should have, but I didn't. I struggled in college. Couldn't keep up with my classes. I had this horrible relationship, I was drinking a lot, my father was diagnosed with cancer for the first time. I was a mess—depression, suicidal thoughts. The works."

"But you worked it out on your own?"

"I dropped out and moved to New York. Pretended like I was this free spirit, but I was just scared. I used up all my money and spent the next six years struggling to survive, telling myself that it's what real writers did. Therapy probably would have been a better option."

I stare at Jolie's delicate features, seeing the pain flash across them. She tucks a strand of hair behind her ear, and for the first time in a long time, I feel close to another human. I feel like we share a piece of the same pain—like she's built of the same material that made me.

"Can I show you what I do to deal with it?" My heartbeat starts to speed up. I can't believe I just said that, but Jolie makes me feel comfortable. She makes me want to open up to her, makes me want to tell her exactly what's on my mind.

Jo chews her lip. "As long as it doesn't involve anything violent or dangerous, then yeah, sure."

I chuckle, shaking my head. "I promise it's safe... mostly."

Standing up, I hold out my hand. When Jolie slips her palm into mine, it feels like something clicks into place in my chest. Her eyes shine as she smiles at me, and I lead her out of the dining room and up toward the East Wing.

19

JO

My heart thumps when the Prince fits the key into the lock. It slides noiselessly, and Prince Gabriel pushes the door open. He glances at me, his eyes dark and unreadable. He's brought me up to the East Wing, to a door at the far end of the corridor from Flora's room. This door has been closed every time I've been up here. I've heard of this room—Sam told me it's the off-limits room in the off-limits East Wing. I've heard whispers that the Prince does all kinds of things in here. He locks himself in here for days at a time, and emerges looking like a shell of a human.

I don't know what I expect. Something sinister, maybe? A depraved torture chamber? A weird fetish room?

Instead, what greets me is a mostly bare space. It's stark white, with a long couch along one wall, and a desk and chair at the far end. An easel sits in a corner, with a fresh page pinned to it. Opposite the couch, a fireplace is recessed into the wall.

It's not what I would expect from an artist's studio—it's clean and clinical. It looks like an art studio before an artist touches it. It doesn't have the energy, and chaos, and color of art. It's cold. White. Orderly. Bare.

Nothing like the Prince.

Prince Gabriel closes the door behind me, and I hear the lock click. I glance back at him, frowning.

"Habit." He nods to the lock. "I never want to be disturbed when I'm in here."

I take a tentative step forward, feeling the Prince's eyes following every movement. I stare at the few pieces of furniture and then back at him.

"Is this it? This is the room that everyone is afraid of? This is what's off-limits?"

Instead of answering, the Prince walks to the easel and places it in the center of the room, facing the couch.

"Sit," he commands.

I hate that I want to obey. I hate that my feet carry me to the sofa, and that I sit without even uttering a word. I lift my eyes to the Prince, and the air between us crackles.

He watches me, tilting his head slightly. Then, he moves to the desk and pulls open a drawer. He takes out a single piece of charcoal and walks back to the easel. Every movement is purposeful. He doesn't waste a twitch, or a glance, or a breath on anything except doing exactly what needs to be done.

Leaning over to lie down on the sofa, I turn my head to look at the Prince.

He inclines his head. "Don't move."

I watch him, mesmerized. His hand moves with assurance, slicing the page with strokes of charcoal. When I see him smudge the page and then smooth his fingers through his hair, leaving a small dot of black on his forehead, a smile stretches across my lips.

Prince Gabriel's eyebrows draw together, and a slight

crease appears in his forehead. His eyes move from me to the page, and my body burns. Wherever he looks, liquid, hot honey flows inside my veins. My heart thuds against my ribcage, like a giant's fist pounding against a door. My whole body thrums with every beat.

Thump, thump, thump.

I close my eyes for a moment, and when I open them again, Prince Gabriel is staring at my face. His eyes meet mine, and lava pours into my belly, teasing between my thighs and making me forget that I ever hated him.

His gaze is indifferent, and it flicks back to the page. With a few quick strokes of the charcoal, he finishes the drawing. Stepping back, Prince Gabriel looks over his work.

I expect him to turn the easel, or invite me to come look. I expect him to show me what he's done.

Instead, he turns to the fireplace and presses a small button on the wall. I hear the hiss of gas and the click of an ignitor, and a fire roars to life. The Prince takes the sheet of paper on the easel, and drops it straight into the fire.

"Wait!" I say, jumping up. I rush to the fireplace in time to see the edges of the paper curling, and my likeness dissolving into ash.

The Prince drops the charcoal back into the drawer, wipes his hand on a rag, and places the easel back in the corner. I watch him, nailed to the same spot on the ground. Outrage flames to life inside me.

"Why did you burn it?"

"Because I like to ruin beautiful things," he answers darkly, stalking toward me. His arm slips around my back and he pulls me close, searing his lips to mine.

I don't understand him. The Prince's beautiful, tortured soul is knocking against mine, and I want to let him in—but he terrifies me.

What is fear in the face of desire, though?

The Prince slips his hand beneath my dress, feeling the heat of my sex. He drags his fingers along the outside of my panties as molten desire surges through my center. My knees knock together as he pins me against him with the arm around my back, his lips devouring mine.

We don't make it to the sofa. The floor will do. I collapse at his feet and he follows me down, running his hands under my dress to rip my underwear down my legs. He slides his fingers inside me then and my back arches in response. A gasp catches in my throat as the Prince's fingers fuck me once again.

When his mouth covers my clit, warm wetness gushes out of me. His tongue dances over me and I claw at his hair, grinding against him until I come. Prince Gabriel laps up my orgasm with a groan, and then lifts his eyes to mine.

"You're beautiful, Jolie," he growls as his eyes burn through me. Reaching up to my chest, he slips my dress down to expose my breast, and brushes his wet fingers over my puckered nipple.

"Do you want to ruin me, too?"

The Prince's lips curl into a black smile and he crawls over me. His tongue traces a line up my neck that sends shivers tickling down my spine. His hot breath melts into me, and he drops his lips to my ear.

"I already have."

I don't even know when the Prince unbuckled his pants and kicked them off. I don't realize he's hard and waiting at my entrance—but when he speaks the words, the Prince spears me with his length. He splits me in half, drawing a cry from me as his cock fills me up.

It's not painful. Never painful.

It's perfect.

Dragging himself out of me, Prince Gabriel leans his forearms on either side of my head. His eyes stare into mine—inky, and dangerous, and alive.

"I want to see your face when you come all over my cock," he growls, his lips brushing mine. He thrusts inside me again, and a whimper escapes my lips.

I don't want to be like this—weak and broken as he fucks me on the floor. Mustering all my strength, I flip us over. Either I catch him by surprise, or he lets me, because I land with my legs straddling him and my hands braced against his chest.

I'll come on his cock if he wants me to—but I'm doing it my way. A growl rumbles from his chest to mine, and I roll my hips against his. His lips part, and the darkness in his eyes drops for an instant. My fingers curl around the collar of his shirt as he gathers my dress up above my waist and pulls it off over my head.

The Prince's fingers sink into my ass as he guides me with his hands, thrusting into me as I grind against him. He spreads my ass wide and white heat flashes through my body.

My breasts bounce. The Prince reaches up to tug at my nipple, sending heat crashing from my chest down to my groin. Sensing the tension inside me, Prince Gabriel pinches harder, and his other hand comes down on my ass with a loud crack.

I've never been into rough sex before—not like this, anyway. Not in a way where anger, and lust, and hatred collide. Not where the blackness of a man's heart pours into mine, and I drink it up with gluttony.

I tear his shirt open and leave red scratch marks on his chest. His handprints mark my body, and his eyes scream *mine, mine, mine.*

"Come on my cock," the Prince growls.

"I don't come on command," I spit back.

"You do with me."

The Prince grabs my hips and plunges himself inside me. He reaches down between us and slips his thumb over my clit, and I come—just like he told me to. Molten heat spills through my stomach and splashes through my veins. My head falls back as a scream slips through my lips.

I give myself over to the pleasure—to him. I let myself fall into my orgasm head-first, not caring what the Prince thinks of me, or why he can do this to me. I'm done resisting. I'm done hating.

I just come.

When the Prince feels my walls contract around him, he lets out a low grunt as his cock grows even harder. I feel it pump hot seed into me, and another wave of pleasure washes over me.

In the deep recesses of my mind—the ones that haven't been clouded by my orgasm—I register that we haven't used protection this time, either. But the thought flits away, and I give myself over to the pleasure of his touch.

Falling onto his chest, my body twitches and trembles as he wraps his arms around me. A soft whimper escapes me, and the Prince lets out a growl in return.

We have no words. They've been stolen from our lips by the heat of the moment. All we have are soft noises, gentle touches, and subtle movements.

Prince Gabriel's fingers trail up my spine and I melt into his chest. I listen to his heartbeat with my eyes closed as he softens inside me.

The Prince is wrong. He hasn't ruined me. Something has shifted inside me, but it's not for the worse. I'm open... and I'm happy.

20

GABRIEL

THE TILE FLOOR is cold and hard underneath me, but I don't want to move. Jo's skin is too warm and silky to want it anywhere except pressed against mine. We lay there, unmoving, until my phone goes off.

I stiffen. I know that alarm.

Jo senses the shift and crawls off me. I get up, swearing under my breath, and grab my phone.

"What is it?" She asks, reaching for her dress.

"Flora."

I don't have time to explain. I just throw my clothes on as a lump forms in my throat. Flora has a distress button near her bed, and if she's pressed it, it means something is seriously wrong. Her lungs are infection-prone, and any sort of bacteria can leave her bedridden for weeks.

I've gotten sloppy. I used to be so careful with Flora, and she hasn't had an infection in almost eighteen months. Now, I'm fucking my gardener and not taking care of my daughter. What kind of monster am I? I knew I was bad, but really?

This is a new low.

I can't bring myself to look at Jo. The second my pants are

fastened, I rip the studio door open. My shirt is still open, my tie lost somewhere on the floor. It doesn't matter. I sprint down the hall toward Flora's room.

Vaguely, I hear footsteps behind me, but my mind is spinning so fast I don't have time to think about it. Blood rushes in my ears as I make it to Flora's door.

I strain my ears for the coughing that I know I'm going to hear. Sometimes, she coughs non-stop for hours and hours. Seeing your baby girl cough up blood is one of the most harrowing things a father can go through.

But I can't hear anything. My own heartbeat is too loud. I fall through the door as my stomach churns. The room spins...

...and Flora sleeps peacefully in her bed. I rush to her side, double- and triple-checking that she's still breathing. My hand goes to my head and I let out a heavy sigh. On the edge of my daughter's bed, a book rests on top of the distress button. I move it out of the way, glancing at the title—*Charlie and the Chocolate Factory*.

I frown, putting the book down on the floor next to Flora's bed. I stroke her cheek—just to make sure she's okay.

A noise at the door makes me turn my head, and I see Jolie standing there.

"Is she okay?" She whispers.

"She's fine," I nod. For a second, I want to tell her to leave —to get out, and never come back. What right does my gardener have to be in my daughter's bedroom?

I don't say anything, though, and Jolie takes a step toward the bed. In a way, it feels good to have her here. Flora stirs, blinking her eyes open and making a soft noise.

"Daddy? Jo?"

"Go back to sleep, kiddo," I say, stroking her forehead. "Sorry to wake you."

My daughter frowns sleepily, rubbing her eyes. She looks over at Jo, and the creases in her forehead disappear. She smiles.

"I'm almost done with the book," she says, reaching up to the top of her bed. When she doesn't find her novel, she lifts herself up. I pick it up off the floor where I left it, and Flora smiles wider.

She glances at Jo. "I really like it."

"It was one of my favorites," Jolie responds softly. "I can't believe you've read it so quickly!"

Flora shrugs. "I have a lot of time to read."

My heart squeezes. Is my daughter starved for human contact? Is that why she's befriended Jolie? Have I been wrong to isolate her like this?

"You're lucky," Jo winks. She steps closer to the bed and strokes Flora's legs through the blankets. "Now you should get to sleep. Didn't you tell me your governess is giving you an exam tomorrow?"

Flora sighs. "It's just math—it's easy."

I glance between Jolie and my daughter, snapping my mouth shut and frowning. How does Jo know so much about my daughter's life? Even I didn't know she had an exam tomorrow. And *Charlie and the Chocolate Factory*? I had no idea Flora would have been able to read something like that. My baby girl is reading books faster than I can.

Flora smiles at the two of us and closes her eyes, falling asleep in an instant. Jolie and I tiptoe out of the room. I glance at my gardener.

"I didn't know you were spending so much time with my daughter," I say.

Jolie blushes, averting her eyes. "I'm sorry."

"About what?" My throat tightens.

159

"Jolie and I read together sometimes in the evenings. Apparently, she used to do it with my father."

"You what?"

Jolie's eyebrows draw together. She looks at me with those big, brown eyes of hers, and I can't be mad. Jolie takes a deep breath. "I think she's lonely."

I glance at my daughter's door, and my shoulders slump. "I know—but she's vulnerable. Her lungs..." I trail off. Jo doesn't answer.

Instead, she lets out a soft sigh, twisting her hands together in front of her.

"I should get going."

"You don't have to."

Her eyes widen, and she shakes her head. "I think I should." Jolie takes a step toward me and places her hand on my shoulder before kissing me gently on the lips. "Thank you for dinner... and everything else."

Before I can stop her, she's heading down the hallway and I'm left alone. I watch her until she disappears around a corner, and then I head toward my chambers.

When I strip down and lay in bed, I'm surprised to find that my mind is quiet. There's no devil whispering into my ear—no insomnia tugging at my mind. I close my eyes and fall asleep.

THE SUN IS high in the sky by the time I wake up. My body is stiff from sleeping so long—it's more than I've slept in many months. I rub my fingers over my eyes and crawl out of bed. I wake up under a hot shower, and then pull on some clothing.

I'm supposed to meet with the Mayor of Westhill today to talk to him about the community garden, but all I want to do is find Jolie and carry her back to bed.

I glance at my watch. I still have two hours before I need to meet the Mayor, so I decide to find my rose gardener.

My attraction to her overrides everything else—sense, decorum, responsibility. It all flies out the window when I think about Jolie. I've taken her to my inner sanctum—the studio where even the maids aren't allowed to go. I've let her into my daughter's room, and I don't feel angry.

Having Jolie's bright smile and musical laugh fill these spaces is more refreshing than I could ever have anticipated.

Bertrand has left a croissant on my desk along with a cup of coffee that, somehow, is still warm. I gulp the coffee and take a bite of croissant before heading downstairs.

My face relaxes into a smile. That, in and of itself, is unusual. Smiles aren't relaxing to me. They're forced or cruel. Never natural.

But when I step outside, I smile. I walk around to the rose garden at the back of the castle, noting that the first flowers have started to bloom. Most of the buds have turned from solid green to having their colors poking out. Soon, they'll burst open with color and scent, and my soul will be calm.

Walking toward the gates of the rose garden, I hear voices. Then, I hear that laugh of Jolie's that I've started to love so much.

When I hear a man's voice respond, I frown. Jealousy grips my stomach like a bright green claw, squeezing me from the inside.

Jolie is with another gardener—the tall, handsome man that always seems to have a maid or a female cook hanging off his arm. The one who had his arm around Jolie at the Westhill Town Fair.

Today, he's making her laugh.

My eyes blaze. I push the gate open a little too forcefully, and the two of them turn toward me. Jolie's eyebrows fly up toward her hairline. The male gardener inclines his head in a slight bow as his expression sours.

"Leave us," I tell him, nodding my head to the gate.

The man's eyes flash, but he does as I say. They always do as I say. No one questions me...

...except Jolie.

"What was that about?" Jolie asks when the other man leaves.

"What was what about?"

"Why are you so rude to people?"

"That wasn't rude."

She scoffs, rolling her eyes before turning back toward the roses. Turning the hose back on, she angles her body away from me and gives me her back.

Rage flares inside me.

"You'd turn your back to your Prince?"

"Do you get off on acting like a total prick?" She looks over her shoulder, spitting the words at me.

"What? Do you like that guy?"

Exasperated, Jolie turns the hose off again and stares at me. "Like him? Harry Brooks? Are you serious right now?"

"Completely."

"Your Highness, if you really must know, that guy kind of gives me the creeps. He's not my type, all right? So you can forget about this whole macho, alpha-male act you've got going on."

"You didn't mind the macho, alpha-male act last night— or the night before."

A blush blossoms on Jolie's cheeks as she pushes her sleeves up. She bares her teeth, glaring at me.

"Are you going to hold that against me, then?"

This is what I do. I push people's buttons until they push

me away. I make myself so unlovable that rejection is inevitable. I make people hate me.

Jolie's chest heaves, and I realize that I don't want her to hate me. My heart grows in my chest, and I know that this is the first thing in my life that I don't want to ruin.

"I don't want you to leave," I say quietly.

"Well, don't make it so unbearable for me to stay here."

I close the distance between us and sweep my hand into her hair, crushing my lips to hers.

21

JO

When the Prince and I walk out of the rose garden together, Harry is hanging around the lawns, pretending to weed. Did he hear any of that?

Does it matter?

The Prince guides me around to the garages. He's asked me to go along with him to meet the Mayor about a community project in Westhill.

"Are you sure you want to take me?" I ask. "Wouldn't one of the more experienced gardeners be more use? I really just take care of the roses."

"I want you." His tone is final, and a quiver of delight passes through my stomach. Am I so weak that a simple, possessive display makes my knees knock together? Am I that pathetic?

When the Prince opens the car door for me, I decide that yes, I am that pathetic—and I don't care. Every time he's around me, my heart skips a beat. Every time I feel his gaze on me, heat sparks in the pit of my stomach.

When was the last time I felt this good? When was the last time I had something to look forward to? My life used to be one big rejection after another. Now, I have friends, a newfound family, and someone who makes me feel like the sexiest person in the world. Is it so wrong that I enjoy it for a little while?

I watch the Prince as he walks around the car and gets behind the steering wheel, and I realize that he makes me feel more than just sexy. Prince Gabriel has an intensity about him that makes me feel alive. Being around him is like sticking my finger in a light socket.

The Prince glances at me, arching his eyebrows as if to ask, 'You okay?'

I smile. "Where's your entourage? Shouldn't you have a slew of bodyguards when you leave the castle?"

Prince Gabriel chuckles. "Why do you think I moved to Westhill in the first place? Can't stand having people around me."

"I guess you and I aren't so different after all," I grin.

We take off down the long driveway and the Prince places his hand on my thigh. My heart skips a beat—just as it always does whenever he touches me, or looks at me, or exists in my general vicinity.

His hand slides up my thigh, and shivers of pleasure run up my leg. We drive slowly, and I savor the delicious tension in the air between us.

We drive out of the castle gates and down Westhill's Main Street—well, Westhill's *only* street. The Prince's hand stays on my thigh, and my heart continues to beat erratically.

The council office is a small building with a simple sign in front of it, sandwiched between the library and the barber. Prince Gabriel parks in front of the office in a No Parking Zone, and I'm reminded that I'm not with a regular man.

"You sure you want to park here?" I ask when we exit the car.

Prince Gabriel frowns. "Yeah, why?"

"It's a No Parking Zone."

The Prince's eyebrows arch as his eyes flick to the sign before us. Surprise registers on his face, as if he's never even considered that he's not allowed to park somewhere.

"I'm sure it'll be fine," he says, nodding toward the council offices.

We're greeted by the receptionist, a kindly old lady with curly, snow-white hair. Her cheeks are bright red, and she fusses over us from the moment we enter to the moment we step into Mayor Thornley's office.

"Thank you, Margaret," the Mayor says with a nod as she offers us coffee for the seventh time. "We're fine."

The woman bows, and then curtsies, and then bows again —before backing out of the room. Mayor Thornley greets us both with a warm handshake.

"Your Highness," he smiles, before moving to me, "and you are?"

"Jolie," I respond. "I'm a gardener at the castle. Nice to meet you, Mr. Mayor."

"Wonderful!" He beams, glancing between us. "But please, call me Bob. Follow me."

The Mayor has long, grey hair. It's tied back in a low ponytail with curled ends. He has a thick, reddish-grey beard, and bright blue eyes. He looks like the type of guy who went to Woodstock. He leads us down the hallway and out through the front of the building, and I realize he's wearing cargo pants and sandals.

Not exactly what I was expecting from the Mayor, but somehow fitting for a town like Westhill.

"His Majesty the King told me that you were interested in volunteering," the Mayor says, smiling at the Prince. I glance at Prince Gabriel, surprised. He didn't seem interested in volunteering when he asked me to come with him.

"Yes," the Prince responds. "I've been wanting to give back to the town for a while now. You've been very good neighbors to me."

The Mayor laughs, waving us forward toward a small patch of land on the other side of the library. He's wearing a leather necklace around his neck, with what looks like a shark tooth hanging in the center of his chest. Wiry, grey chest hair pokes out of his linen shirt. Every step Bob takes seems casual but somehow purposeful at the same time. The gate around the community garden creaks as he pushes it open.

"Here we are," he proclaims, smiling at us.

I look around at the rotting planks of wood that edge every garden bed, and the overgrown weeds that have taken over the space. The remnants of a collapsed shed are in the corner of the lot, with half a roof and three walls remaining. A rusty wheelbarrow is tipped over beside us.

I let out a heavy sigh, arching my eyebrows.

"It's not much," Bob agrees, "but it's got potential. Kind of like me." He laughs at his own joke, and waves us forward. "Now, over here in this corner, we get a lot of sun."

The Mayor points to different features—if you can call them that—around the garden, smiling like a proud father. As we step through to the back corner of the garden, he grunts and touches a plant.

"Well, what's this doing here," Bob says under his breath.

As soon as the mayor touches the leaves, I know it's a cannabis plant. My eyebrows jump up and I steal a glance at Gabriel, who's expression is stuck somewhere between boredom and politeness.

"I need to talk to Neil about this," the Mayor says to

himself as he shakes his head. "I told him to get this out of here before today."

I clear my throat, and the Mayor glances up. He lets out a laugh and waves his hand. "Just some local horticulturalists," he winks.

The Prince says nothing, but the edge of his lips twitch. I wonder why he works so hard to hide his emotions. Does he know it makes people uncomfortable? Maybe that's the reason he does it.

Bob puts his hand on his hips, shrugging. "So, that's it." He looks at the Prince with hopeful enthusiasm in his eyes and a faint smile floating over his lips.

"What do you think?" Prince Gabriel asks me.

I look around the overgrown, weed-infested, collapsing garden, and I smile.

"I think it's perfect."

Bob chuckles, clapping his hands together. "I knew you'd like it. The town has been crying out for a little TLC."

I nudge the Prince with my shoulder. He responds by sweeping his hand over my lower back, and heat floods my belly.

"We'll start next week," the Prince says, always serious. "I'll get my gardeners to source some materials, and that should give you enough time to enlist the help of some residents."

"We're getting a bit of a late start—it's the middle of June," I say, looking around. "There's lots of work to do. If we get lots of help from the people of Westhill, we could probably start planting in four weeks or so. We could plant a few veggies that might yield a crop before it gets too cold. Maybe some broccoli, spinach, radishes—that kind of thing."

"Sounds fantastic," the Mayor grins. "I like you already, Jolie."

We walk back out to the street, and the Mayor's sandals slap on the concrete sidewalk. He tucks a stray piece of hair behind his ear, and I notice that he has a small, golden earring.

The Prince stiffens beside me, making a small noise. I follow his gaze to a car as it takes off from the other side of the street. The Prince watches it leave, and then relaxes.

Mayor Bob doesn't notice anything. He walks with us to the royal car with a smile on his face, his sandals whacking the concrete with every step.

"Oops," the Mayor says, pulling a parking ticket from under the Prince's windshield wiper. "I'll get this taken care of." He winks at us, and I laugh again.

We say our goodbyes and get back in the car. I watch the Mayor wave at us, and then turn back to the council building behind him.

I chuckle, shaking my head. "I like him."

"I thought you might."

"Is that why you brought me? To meet the kooky mayor of Westhill?"

"That—and the fact that you're going to be spearheading the community garden project."

"Me?"

"Well, who else am I going to want to spend time with?

I blush, and the Prince pulls out of his illegal parking spot. He doesn't drive back to the castle though. I glance back the way we came, and the Prince's hand slides over my thigh again. "I also brought you because I wanted to show you something."

22

GABRIEL

I STOP the car beside the castle fence, on the far side of the grounds. We're just off the gravel road that loops around the castle.

"We have to go the rest of the way on foot," I say.

Jo grins at me. "Good thing I'm dressed in gardening clothes."

"Do you own anything else?"

Her mouth drops open in mock outrage. "I own *one* dress, thank you very much." She grins, stepping out of the car. The nature reserve at the back of the castle grounds extends beyond the boundary fence, all the way to the edge of Farcliff Kingdom. I find the trailhead that I'm looking for, and we take off through the trees.

"I used to come here when I was a kid," I say. "There's a gap in the castle fence, and I'd sneak out here to be alone."

"Always been a loner, hey?"

"Careful," I growl.

"Why? I like making you angry." She laughs, nudging me with her arm. Dappled sunlight filters through the trees, making her look like a wood nymph. I want nothing more than to lay her in the mossy forest floor and claim her right now.

Instead, I nod to the trail ahead of us. "Come on."

"Yes, Your Highness—whatever you say."

"At least you're learning."

Jolie laughs, and the sound soothes my aching heart. I never knew how much I needed her laugh in my life until I met her, and now it's like oxygen to me. I don't know if I'll be able to go another day without hearing it.

I haven't walked along this path in years. I used to come here a lot when I was younger, but once I had Flora, I stopped. My life started revolving around making sure she was safe and taken care of, and the small pleasures that I once enjoyed became painful, until I forgot what it was like to live. I locked myself in Westhill Castle and suffered by myself.

Jolie slides her hand in mine and glances up at me. Her cheeks flush and my heart warms. I glance down at our intertwined fingers as my heart thumps against my ribcage. I don't pull away.

We walk in comfortable silence for a few minutes, until the path in the trees bends to the left and opens up onto a small clearing. It's just as I remember it.

Since it's early June, the ground in the clearing is covered with wildflowers, spilling across the area like a multi-colored carpet. Jolie gasps, pausing at the edge of the glade. Her eyes shine, and I can't help but smile at the rapt expression on her face.

"Your Highness," she breathes, "it's gorgeous."

"I know," I answer, staring at her.

Jo takes a tentative step forward on the path, wiping a bead of sweat off her forehead. She's still wearing a dazzling smile. Sunlight angles into the dell, shining its light on Jo's soft face. She glows, smiling back at me and extending her hand.

"This is incredible! Flora loves it here, doesn't she?"

I shake my head. "She's never been here."

Jolie's jaw drops open. "This sort of beauty exists right beside the palace grounds and Flora's never seen it? That's *wrong*, Your Highness."

"She's sick."

"She's smart, and gorgeous, and strong," Jolie retorts. "She can't live her life locked away on her own in Westhill. You need to learn to let go of control."

"That's not one of my strengths."

She grins. "I noticed."

I slip my palm against hers and let her carry me forward through the path. Wildflowers brush against our legs as they spill onto the path, swaying softly in the breeze. At the far edge of the clearing is an old, ruined fort. Toppled boulders lay where walls once stood. It was my playground when I was a child, and I never through I'd bring anyone here.

Jolie runs her hand over the stones, shivering. "I love ruins, don't you? They always feel like history is soaked into them—like there are thousands of stories just screaming to be squeezed out."

"You're definitely a writer, then," I grin.

Jolie laughs, shaking her head. "You don't think?"

"Looks like a pile of old rocks to me. They were fun to play in when I was a kid."

Jolie turns toward me, shaking her head. "I think you're lying."

"Oh, yeah?"

She nods, her face serious. "Yes. I don't think that's true at all. I think you have a wild imagination and a romantic heart, but you hide it behind that mask of yours."

"You think you know me so well? We've only slept together twice." I take a step toward her, sweeping my hand over her hip.

Jolie blinks, and a soft smile curls over her lips. She slides her hands over my chest, angling her head as she looks at me. "It's not about the sex. It's everything else. I see the way you talk to people, and how you hide yourself away. Even your studio is bare. That should be where you're able to be vulnerable and completely yourself—but you burn every drawing you create, and you keep the room as sterile as an operating room. You hide all the softness you have, because you think it makes you weak—but it doesn't."

Her words make me still for a moment.

I shake my head. "What if you're wrong? What if there's nothing more to me? Maybe this is it, and you're imagining that I'm someone that I'm not."

Jolie's fingers curl into my shirt as she molds her body against mine. She shrugs. "Wouldn't be the first time I saw something in a man that didn't exist." She shakes her head. "But I don't think so. You wouldn't have brought me here. You wouldn't care about Flora the way you do. You wouldn't agree to take care of the community garden."

I kiss her—maybe only because I can't bear her probing gaze any longer. She might be right about me, though, because my kiss is soft, and my touch is gentle. I brush my fingers over her jaw and tangle them into her hair, pulling her close to me. She moans softly, wrapping her arms around my neck. Jolie's body fits perfectly against mine.

Yesterday, I would have destroyed her here. I would have spun her around and fucked her against the ruins, splashing my cum all over her body. I would have left her breathless and dazed, knowing she belonged to me.

Today, though, it's different. My touch is tender as I cup

Jolie's face and swipe my tongue across her lower lip. She trembles in my arms, pressing her body into mine. I sweep her hair into my hand and pull her close to me. I feel the thumping of her heart against my own, and I drink up every sound that she utters.

Sinking down among the wildflowers, I hold Jolie close to me as I make love to her. I soak up her body, committing every curve to memory as my fingers sweep over them. I smile when she comes, enthralled by the rapture on her face. For a few moments, I forget who I am. I forget who she is. I forget everything except the pleasure flooding through my veins, and the ecstasy painted on Jolie's features.

When it's over, we lay amongst the wildflowers at the foot of the dilapidated ruins, and we stare up at the clouds in the sky. Jo rests her head on my chest, letting out soft sighs every few minutes. I trail my fingers across her scalp and kiss the top of her head.

There's no sound except the birds in the forest and the wind rustling the leaves. Jolie breathes quietly, and my heart beats peacefully. There's no devil on my shoulder, and no beast inside my heart.

I'm happy.

23

JO

I'm still picking grass out of my hair when the Prince drops me off at the castle. With one last furtive smile at each other, we head off in opposite directions. Me, toward the rose garden. Him, toward the palace.

I float all the way to the roses, inhaling their scent as I walk through the gate. I run my fingers over a few petals, smiling as a few friendly bees buzz from one flower to another. It's only a matter of days before the whole garden will be in full bloom. My father planted my favorite flowers— Pierre de Ronsard climbing roses—on a trellis against the castle wall. I walk over to them, inspecting the budding flowers.

Within days, they'll burst open, and their blooms will be so heavy they'll hang off the trellis like apples. I smile as I go near them, knowing my father was thinking of me when he planted them.

I'm pulled from my dreamy mood by a gruff voice.

"Where did you run off to with the Prince?" Harry is standing near the gate, staring at me with an arched eyebrow.

His gaze sweeps up and down my body, and I shift uncomfortably.

"We went into town," I answer, even though I know I don't owe him an explanation. "He's helping the Mayor with the community garden."

Harry pushes the gate open, and I stiffen. He's intruding into my space when he comes into the rose garden. He feels too big, too rough to be around these delicate flowers. He looks the roses over with disdain, and I clench my fists. Who does this guy think he is?

"Why did he ask you, and not me? I'm the head gardener."

I shrug, turning back to the plants. I bend over to pluck a weed from the ground. "Maybe he was impressed by the rose garden."

"Your father did most of the work. You just got the glory," Harry scoffs.

I stand up again, spinning to face the big man. "Can I help you with something? Jealousy doesn't suit you, Harry. Whatever this whole intimidation schtick is, I'm not into it. So, if you don't need anything, you can leave."

"You know, when you first came to Westhill, I actually considered fucking you—but you're just an uppity little bitch, and I wouldn't touch you even if you paid me."

My whole body vibrates with anger. The tips of my ears burn, and every breath I take sends pins and needles through my tightening chest. Harry stands there, puffing his chest out and snarling at me.

I watch him turn around and walk out of the garden. When I'm sure I'm alone, my shoulders slump. What is he jealous of, exactly? Is it the community garden project, or is it the fact that I'm not interested in him? He seems like the type of guy who doesn't take rejection well.

I don't have time to cater to his ego. I march around the garden, taking my anger and outrage out on stray weeds .

My phone rings, pulling me from my thoughts. My father's name flashes on the screen, and I take a deep breath to calm myself.

It's a video call, and as I press the 'answer' button, I rearrange my features into a smile. "Hey, Dad."

"Hi Jo," he says. "Good! You're in the garden."

"Here I was thinking you were calling to talk to me," I grin. "All you wanted to see were your roses."

My father chuckles, and then starts coughing. My heart squeezes. Is it just the video, or does he look more pale than the last time we spoke?

I give him a tour of the garden and then sit down to talk to him. My mother comes onto the screen, and the two of them glow with pride as I tell them about the community garden project.

"And how's your writing coming along?" My mother asks.

I smile. "It's really good, actually. I've started a new project —a children's book. I found your old copy of *Charlie and the Chocolate Factory* in the cottage, and I thought I'd try to just have fun with my writing."

"No more thrillers full of psychos and murderers?" My father grins.

"Not right now. The Princess inspired me."

My parents both smile, glancing at each other. My mother beams. "She's a wonderful little girl. I can't wait to read your new book.

"I've still got a lot of work to do on it, so you'll need to be patient."

When I hang up the phone, I take a deep breath. I've been in Westhill for almost two months now, and I'd like to see my parents. My father doesn't look great, and I'd like to visit him sooner rather than later. One of the reasons I came back to Farcliff Kingdom in the first place was to be closer to them so I could visit.

I glance up at the palace behind me and my heart squeezes. I've been so caught up with the Prince, his daughter, and everything going on here in Westhill that I've forgotten what's important—my family.

Pushing myself off the bench again, I decide to ask Mrs. Grey for some time off to go see my parents.

After dinner, I do just that. In a month's time, near the end of July, I'll have two weeks off to spend time with them. By then, the roses will be past their bloom and I'll have a bit of respite from the garden.

Mrs. Grey approves my time off without hesitation, and when I walk back to the cottage after dinner, my heart beats easier. I'll see my parents, and maybe even bring them a bouquet of roses from the garden. Then, I'll work hard to finish my new book and make them proud.

When I reach the cottage, I'm surprised to find Prince Gabriel waiting outside. He's holding a bouquet of wildflowers in his hand, which he presents to me with a slight smile. I think I even see him blush, but it's hard to tell in the fading evening light.

"Thank you," I smile.

"I went back to the clearing to get them," he says, "and I think you're right—I want to take Flora there. I'd like it if you came, too."

"I'd be honored," I smile, reaching up to kiss his cheek. He follows me into the cottage, and we fall into bed together.

. . .

THE PRINCE LEAVES SOMETIME before dawn, and I roll over to his side of the bed and inhale the scent of him that clings to the pillow.

For the next two weeks, this becomes our routine. Sometimes, we steal a kiss in the rose garden. The Prince seems to relax whenever he's there, the lines in his face melting away. He smiles more often. At night, he sleeps next to me. The weight of him in bed beside me is comforting, and within a few days, I forget what it was like to sleep alone.

Princess Flora visits me in the garden most mornings. She has a bright smile and a quick wit, and I find myself becoming more attached to her, too. I mold the protagonist of my book after the Princess, and I find myself looking forward to our time together each morning.

The rose garden explodes. Prince Gabriel smiles whenever he's in it, and I spend hours and hours around the flowers. Sometimes, I just stare at them, and breathe in their perfume. Even with the repeat bloomers that my father planted, I know that these few weeks in the garden will be the most exquisite. Photographers from the Annual Rose Festival of Farcliff come to the garden, oohing and ahhing as they walk through the blooms.

I'm proud of my parents, and proud of myself. The Prince beams.

In the afternoons, I go into town and help with the community garden. Mayor Bob always has a smile on his face. Sometimes the Prince comes with me, and sometimes he doesn't. When he does, Prince Gabriel always leaves the garden with a bright smile on his face, and it makes my heart melt.

My love for Westhill grows. The castle truly becomes my home. Not only is it somewhere for me to live and work— when I was almost on the street before I came here—but there are so many people here that I care for. Mrs. Grey is a mother hen with a streak of tough love for us all, and Sam becomes like a sister to me.

But it's the Prince who really makes me fall in love with this place. Every evening we spend together, he peels away another layer of his tough exterior to show me the man he is underneath. He keeps my vase of wildflowers well-stocked, and his touch becomes more and more tender.

I don't know if anyone notices our budding relationship. No one says anything to me, but I know that it's hard to keep secrets in the castle. Harry keeps his distance, and Sam doesn't make any comments, so I assume that no one knows.

Not that I care, anyway. I'm so caught up with the Prince that I wouldn't mind if the whole of Farcliff was talking about us. I look forward to our evenings together, and I miss him when he leaves my bed in the morning. Every time he walks into the rose garden as I work, my heart stutters and my face breaks into a smile.

As the roses bloom, so does our romance—and I never want it to end.

Sometimes, though—late at night—I feel the Prince shift beside me in bed. I can tell by his breathing that he's still awake, and I know that he's hiding parts of himself from me.

Of course he is—I'm just his rose gardener, and we shouldn't be together anyway. I have no right to the Prince's heart, or to his deepest thoughts.

He keeps part of himself hidden away from me, and I pretend that I'm okay with it.

24

GABRIEL

FLORA IS BOUNCING up and down in the back seat of the car. Jolie glances at her from the passenger's seat, smiling.

"Excited?"

"I can't wait! Daddy never takes me anywhere."

"Hey now," I growl. "I take you lots of places."

"I mean you never take me anywhere outside the castle," Flora responds with a grin.

I drive extra slowly, taking every turn carefully as I glance at my daughter in the back seat. Her cheeks are rosy and her eyes are shining. She looks healthier than she has in weeks. I've seen her in the rose garden with Jolie some mornings. Watching them work alongside each other has made me realize that my daughter isn't as weak as I'd thought.

Quite the opposite, actually. She's strong. She's been fighting this illness her whole life—been told that she's sick her whole life—and yet, she still persists. She attends to her studies and reads a lot. She works in the garden and she's kind to the entire castle staff.

She thrives.

How could I have missed her strength? How had I not

noticed it before? It wasn't until Jolie pointed it out to me that I realized that my daughter isn't an invalid.

When I stop the car, Flora rushes out. I reach for her, but she brushes past my hand to take Jolie's.

"It smells so fresh out here! I can taste the air," Flora says, licking her lips. She holds onto Jolie and smiles.

Jo glances at me, her face glowing. I can't believe my own daughter would choose Jolie over me—but seeing them together makes my heart swell in my chest. They walk ahead of me along the trail, hand in hand, and Flora says a thousand and one things about the forest, and the trees, and the birds, and the butterflies.

"I read that moss mostly grows on the north side of trees. Is that true?" She glances up at Jolie.

"I think so—and in the Southern Hemisphere, it mostly grows on the south side of trees."

Flora stops to look at a tree, frowning. "This tree has moss all around it."

"I think it's more of a guideline, type of thing," Jolie grins. "Not a hard and fast rule."

"Oh." Flora skips ahead, waving us onward. "Come on!" She bounces along, hopping from one foot to the other and dragging Jolie along the path.

When we make it to the glade of wildflowers, Flora squeals. She jumps up and down and spins in a circle before leaning down to smell a flower. I slide my arm around Jolie's back and we watch my daughter. Flora looks happier than I've ever seen her.

I lean into Jo's ear. "You were right."

"Sorry? Say that again? I didn't catch that." She laughs, winking at me.

"You were right about bringing her here. I've never seen her like this."

"What, happy?" She nudges me, laughing. "You should try to let go a little. Let her live her life."

Flora dances to music that only she can hear, spinning in a slow circle. She skips to the far end of the clearing and climbs up onto one of the collapsed walls of the ruin. I stiffen, wanting to run over and pull her down. Every part of my body is screaming to get her down from there. What if she fell?

Jolie senses the tension inside me, and wraps her arm around my waist. "Let her play," she says softly.

Flora sits down on a rock and swings her legs, grinning from ear to ear. She waves at the two of us and laughs. In that moment, I realize Jolie is right. She's right about everything. I need to let go of all the fears that I have in relation to my daughter. I need to treat her like the smart, precocious child that she is, and I need to let her explore the world like only a six-year-old can. I need to let her play, and run, and jump, and have friends.

She'll take her medication, and do her breathing therapy, and we'll take every precaution—but I can't keep her locked away in Westhill Castle if I want her to grow into a truly healthy young woman.

"I think we should bring her to the community garden," Jolie says, leaning her head on her shoulder. "Bob's kids were there last time—they're about her age."

"That old pothead? You want Flora to play with the hippie Mayor's children?"

"Why not?" Jolie smiles at me. "Look at her, Your Highness. She's happy."

"You make it sound like she's unhappy at the castle."

"I'm sorry. That's not what I meant." Jolie pulls away from me slightly, and my heart tugs.

185

I shake my head. "No, you're right. I know you're right. I'm just…" I sigh. "I'm just scared."

We spend a few hours in the glade. Jolie brought a picnic, and the three of us eat sandwiches and drink water in the sunshine. After lunch, Flora's eyelids droop, and I lift her up onto my back to carry her back to the car. She falls asleep as we walk back, and Jolie helps me load her into the back seat.

After I close the car door, I turn to Jolie. I cup her cheek in my hand and kiss her with all the strength of my feelings. Jolie has shown me everything that's been missing in my life —softness, love, and courage. She's shown me that I've let my fears for Flora overshadow everything—maybe even my fears for myself, too. I've lived the past six years afraid that I'd lose Flora, afraid that someone would trick me like Paulette did, afraid that I'd be alone and pathetic and foolish.

Now, I think I might have missed out on a richer kind of life.

So, I listen to Jolie's advice. I take Flora with me next time I go to the Westhill Community Garden. Flora shakes with excitement, and I scan the streets. For what, I'm not sure. Maybe for a sign of the dark-haired woman I saw a few weeks ago—for the shadow of the woman who haunts my dreams.

Mayor Bob greets us with open arms, and Flora immediately befriends his sons. She digs her hands straight into the dirt and laughs more boisterously than I've heard in a long time. Jolie grins at me, and I relax.

After a time, I glance across the street and I think I catch a glimpse of the raven-haired woman. I freeze as my blood turns to ice, stifling my desire to grab Flora and take her back to the safety of the castle. The woman ducks behind a door without looking my way, but my pulse still hammers.

"You okay?" Jolie glances up at me, holding a shovel in her hand.

I clear my throat, nodding. "Fine."

"Here." Jolie hands me the shovel unceremoniously, once again forgetting that I'm her Prince—or maybe she does it on purpose. "Dig up this garden bed. I'll get some fresh topsoil."

Glancing once more at the door where the woman disappeared, I shake my head and get to work. When Jo returns with the rich, black soil, she looks over my work and nods, satisfied.

"Not bad for a Prince."

"You know, I could have you thrown in jail for speaking to me like that."

"I think you like it when I talk back. Gives you an excuse to punish me later." Her eyes darken, and a smile teases over her lips.

"I will—and I'll enjoy every second of it."

Jolie grins, dumping her topsoil into the new garden bed.

I look around, making sure no one can hear us. Everyone is at work, and Flora is laughing with Bob's sons. Mayor Bob himself is pushing a wheelbarrow toward the new compost bin in the corner

With just a few words, Jolie calms me down. She makes me forget about my ex—the one I still see visions of everywhere. She makes me forget that my daughter is sick, and that I'm afraid of losing her.

That night, I punish her in the best possible way, just like I promised her I would. Our lovemaking is frantic and wild, and when it's over, we collapse into each other's arms.

"Thank you for today," I whisper into Jolie's thick mane of hair. "Flora was happier than I've seen her in a long time."

"Good," Jolie sighs, snuggling into my chest. "She deserves to be happy—and you do, too."

Jolie tells me that she's leaving at the end of the week to go see her father, and I try to ignore the sinking feeling in my stomach. Am I so selfish that I feel bad she's going to see her sick father? She'll only be gone for two weeks.

But when she says that she's leaving, for the first time in months, the demon reappears on my shoulder and starts whispering in my ear.

She's not coming back, he says. *She's leaving because of you. Everything that happened over the past six weeks was a lie. She doesn't care about you. She was using you.*

Jolie falls asleep in my arms, and I stare at the ceiling until the sun comes up.

25

JO

THE DAY before I leave to visit my parents, the Prince comes to the Gardener's Cottage, as usual. I get up from my desk to open the door for him. My heart does that funny little flip it always does when I see him, and I wrap my arms around him.

I love Prince Gabriel's kiss. It's as complicated as he is—sometimes soft, sometimes hard, and always all-consuming. As soon as his lips touch mine, everything else in the world disappears.

Pulling away from him, I smile. "I'm going to miss you."

"Don't go." He nuzzles his nose against mine.

"I have to." I smile sadly. "Dad isn't doing so good."

"I know—I'm just a selfish asshole."

I disentangle myself from the Prince's arms, shaking my head. "You shouldn't say those things about yourself. You'll start to believe them."

The Prince smiles, but it doesn't quite reach his eyes. He looks over my shoulder and nods to my computer. "Writing?"

"Oh, yeah." I walk over to my computer and close the screen. "Just a new book I've been working on."

I don't know why I hide it from him. Maybe because it's so

different from anything I've written. Maybe I'm embarrassed that Flora inspired me, or I'm worried he'll think I'm crossing a line. It's not that it's *about* Flora, but the main character is undeniably inspired by her.

"Don't want me to read it?" His eyebrows arch. There's an edge to his voice.

I frown, shrugging. "It's just the first draft, you know? I'd be embarrassed."

"You're not writing about me, are you?"

I laugh, shaking my head. "Don't be so vain, Your Highness."

The Prince stares at me for a moment, and then sits down on the couch. I've been waiting for the Prince to tell me to call him Gabriel, but he hasn't. It feels weird to be sleeping next to him for almost two months now, and still call him by his formal title.

He doesn't correct me, though, and I don't push it. I sit down next to him, but he feels stiff. I try to kiss him, but his lips are cold. After a few minutes, the Prince stands up again.

"I'm going to let you pack tonight. I have some things to do at the castle."

I frown. "Oh, okay. I was hoping..."

"See you when you get back." He glances at my computer once more, and then disappears through the door. I look after him, confused.

What just happened? Did I say something? Is this because I wouldn't let him read my book? Is he mad that I'm leaving?

I stand at the window, watching him walk back toward the palace. His shoulders are slumped and his arms look stiff. I take a deep breath and shut the curtains.

I always fall for the broken, complicated men.

I'll deal with it when I get back. That thought makes me

scoff. *What* am I dealing with? My casual relationship with the Prince? With my *boss*? Where do I think it's going?

The only way this will end is in heartbreak. *My* heart breaking, to be exact.

I can feel myself shuttering my heart away from him. For a few blissful weeks, I've ignored the inevitable disaster of this little relationship.

Isn't that my specialty? Turning any situation into a disaster? Failing at everything? Never finishing what I start?

I stopped my college degree halfway through. I failed at my writing career. I've never had a successful relationship. The only thing I finished was a book that was rejected by every single publisher I've ever sent it to. I have half a dozen unfinished manuscripts wasting away on my hard drive.

Why am I surprised that my relationship with the *Prince* is going to shit?

The Prince once told me that he ruins things. Well, that makes two of us.

I take a deep, shaking breath to try to steady myself, looking around my cottage. Sighing, I settle onto the couch and turn on the television to spend the night on my own.

When I get to Farcliff, my mother meets me at the bus station and wraps me in a bone-crushing hug. I grunt, trying my best to survive her embrace until she pulls away.

"It's good to see you, Jolie. You look beautiful. Are those for your father?" She points to a bouquet of roses that I snagged from the garden.

I smile. "And you."

"But mostly him," she winks. "Come on."

"How's he doing?" I ask as we head to the car.

My mother sighs, angling her head from side to side. "Oh, you know."

I don't know, but I don't push it. We make it back to their tiny apartment, and the blow-up mattress is already set up for me. My father is in his room, lying in bed. He looks pale and tired, and most of his hair has fallen out.

"Oh, Dad," I sigh.

"I don't look that bad, do I?" He laughs weakly.

"Your father just had a chemo appointment this morning, so he's feeling a bit nauseous."

"Is that from the garden?" My father asks, nodding to the bouquet in my hands.

I nod, sitting on the bed beside him and handing them over. My father inspects the blooms and lets out a satisfied grunt.

"I knew I could count on you." He clucks my cheek with his fingers, and I hand the flowers to my mother to put in a vase. Kissing my father's forehead, I leave him in the bedroom to rest.

I find my mother in the tiny kitchen and lean against the wall. "He looks weak."

"Just two more chemo appointments, and then we're done with this round," she says, not looking at me. "The doctor said he's responding well."

"That's responding well?" I ask skeptically, nodding to the bedroom. "He can hardly lift his own arm."

"It's just the nausea, honey. His bloodwork has been good."

Sinking down into a chair, I let out a sigh. My mother wraps her arms around me and kisses my temple. "It's good you're here, Jolie. Your presence will give him strength."

"I hope so." I force a smile, trying to ignore the sinking feeling in my stomach. I knew he was weak—I could see it every time we had a video call. Videos don't tell the whole story, though, and I wasn't prepared for seeing him like this. My strong, boisterous father has been ravaged by his cancer. It breaks my heart.

That night, I lay on the air mattress and listen to the sounds of the city. It's so much louder here than it is in Westhill. I've gotten used to sleeping in absolute silence, with the weight of the Prince's arm across my body. The Prince doesn't even have a phone, so I have no way of contacting him. I don't even know if he'd want me to.

I fall asleep thinking of the Prince, and I wake up after dreaming of him. My mother is making eggs in the kitchen, and my father sits at the kitchen table, reading the paper. I roll off the partially deflated air mattress and groan as I pick myself up.

My father chuckles. "You're not old enough to be making those kinds of noises."

"That air mattress makes me feel like I am."

"There's always the couch," my mother quips. I laugh.

Dad grins and pats a chair beside him. "I have a surprise for you—a thank you, for taking care of the garden for me."

"I don't need anything for that, Dad. It's been great —really."

"Still," he smiles, pulling a sheet of paper out of his shirt pocket. "Here."

I take the little folded piece of paper from him, flipping it over to see a name and a phone number.

"Jeremy Vickers?"

"An agent," my father responds. He coughs into a handkerchief and then wipes his lips. "I knew his father through a book club years ago. Ran into old Marty at the hospital—he's got the same oncologist as me. Bowel cancer," my father sighs, shaking his head. "I said you wrote books and he said his son would meet you."

"You're joking." My eyes widen, flicking from my father to the crumpled piece of paper. My hands tremble, and I try to swallow past a lump in my throat. Suddenly, my heart is hammering.

"Nope," my father smiles. "Call him today. He said he'd make time for you this week."

"No way." I stare at the name on the paper. "Really? This is serious? An agent wants to meet me?"

"I hope you don't mind, but I sent him the chapters you emailed to us. That new fantasy book you're working on with the young girl protagonist. He said he loved it. It was exactly what he was looking for—those were his exact words."

"He didn't say that!"

My mother laughs, putting her hand on my father's shoulder. He pats her hand and nods at me. "You're a good writer, Jolie. You should believe in yourself more."

I gulp again, and then laugh and throw my arms around the two of them. Tears fill my eyes and when I pull away from them, the first thing I think about is the Prince.

I want to tell him about it. I want him to read the book I've written—I want him to see Flora in the main character and be proud of his daughter. Maybe, I want him to be proud of me, too.

My cheeks already ache from smiling so hard. I clutch the phone number to my chest and jump up and down as my parents laugh.

"You deserve it, Jolie. Now call him, and get that book published."

My father beams, and I realize that even though he's weakened by the treatments, he's still the same man he was. He's strong, and resilient—just like his roses...

...and maybe, just like me.

If I'm made of the same stuff as my parents, maybe I'm not as weak and destined to failure as I've always thought. Maybe I haven't had the right conditions to flourish.

Maybe *this* is my chance.

I MEET with Jeremy Vickers two days later, at a restaurant in Farcliff's city center. My stomach is in knots the whole way there. As I near the restaurant, I take a deep breath and try to steady myself.

My future is about to be decided.

Jeremy is a big man with an open, friendly face. He stands up when he sees me, taking my extended hand in both of his. He pumps my arm up and down two or three times, and then gestures to a chair.

"How's old Marcel?" He asks, waving for the waitress. "Last time I saw him, he was just starting chemo."

"He's okay. His spirits are high, which is the main thing."

"Good to hear. Cancer's a bitch, isn't it? My old man's struggling. Never thought I'd see him like that. It humbles you."

"It does." I smile sadly.

Jeremy orders a bottle of wine from the waitress and then turns to me, folding his hands on the table in front of him. "So, I'm not going to beat around the bush. I want to represent you."

My eyes widen. "Really?"

"Really. I've read the sample your father sent, and I think there's a real gap in the market for your type of writing. I know for a fact that at least two publishers will be interested in your work."

"Are you sure my father sent you *my* work?"

Jeremy laughs, opening his mouth wide and throwing his head back. Every movement of his is larger than life. He smooths his big palm over his thinning hair and grins at me.

"You and I are going to work well together, I can already tell."

The waitress brings the wine Jeremy ordered, and we get some food. Jeremy Vickers is made to entertain. He makes me feel like I can take on the world, and for the first time in a long time, I feel like I might not be a total failure.

Moving to Westhill was the best thing I ever did. Not only did it give me a bit of stability, it gave me the inspiration to write my best work—something I never would have written otherwise.

When our meal is over, Jeremy shakes my hand again. "I'll send you the contract via email. Look it over and let me know if you have any comments. Then, we can get that book sold. I see big things in your future, Miss Beaumont. Big things."

When I say goodbye to him, I can't keep the smile from my face.

The one thing that really strikes me, though, is that the only person I really want to share my success with is Prince Gabriel. I wish he had a phone, so that I could tell him how happy I am. I wish he was beside me, and that we could celebrate this together.

It'll be ten days before I see him again, though. Maybe by then, my contract will be signed and my manuscript sold to a big publishing house. Maybe, when I see him again, we'll have even more to celebrate together.

26

GABRIEL

I DIDN'T THINK it was possible to get so attached to someone in such a short period of time. As soon as Jolie leaves, the castle is more depressing than it was before. I sit in the library, staring at the painted ceiling.

She's been gone four days, and I haven't heard from her. How would I? I don't have a phone. Maybe I can ask that redheaded maid if she's heard from her—but that would be admitting to the entire staff that there's something going on between Jolie and me.

Do I care?

No, I decide. I don't care if anyone knows.

It might put Jolie in an awkward situation, though, and the rest of the staff might start treating her differently. I know it would make her uncomfortable—and I *do* care about her comfort in the castle.

I let out a breath, squeezing my eyes shut. I *care*. How the fuck could I get to the point where I care? I'm not supposed to care. I'm supposed to fuck her and leave her. I'm supposed to forget her name. I'm supposed to ruin her reputation and not give a damn.

But I care—a lot.

Too much.

It bothers me that she wouldn't let me read her work. A niggling voice in my head tells me that it's because she's writing about me. Soon, there'll be another novel full of trash about me, another book for people to latch onto when they want to call me an animal.

It's not the public's opinion that bothers me—it's that Jolie would do something like that to me.

Because I fucking *care*. About her, about us, about Flora's love of her, about my own fucking feelings. I like her so much that it's making me weak.

Shaking my head, I push myself off the sofa and leave the library. I need to get out of here. Flora is in breathing therapy, and she'll be in bed early. I can't bear to look at the rose garden without Jo in it. The flowers are already starting to wilt, and seeing them die breaks my heart.

So, I head to the glade. Maybe in the shadow of the ruined fort, I'll be able to clear my head.

I decide not to drive. Instead, I take a golf cart to the nature reserve at the back of the palace grounds, and I head to the boundary on foot. My feet carry me across the gurgling creek and through mossy undergrowth until I get to the wall. Pushing aside some overgrown vines, I find the small opening in the fence.

It's still here, all these years later.

I'm bigger than I was before, though, and I rip my shirt on the way through. The sleeve hangs off my shoulder and I shake a leaf from my hair. Glancing behind me, I sigh.

It feels good to be alone—not as good as it feels to be with Jo, but still good. As I walk through the woods and find the trail to the fort, my steps get lighter and lighter.

Jolie wasn't writing about me. She was probably protective of her work because she's an artist, and she doesn't want anyone to see it until it's done. I laugh to myself, in the silence of the forest.

She's exactly the same as me. I don't show people my work, either—not always because I want to ruin it, but sometimes, because I doubt its quality.

How could I fault her?

I wouldn't even show her the sketch I drew of her, that night in my studio.

My smile widens and I shake my head. I inhale the clean forest air, and I stare up at the leaves above me. A bird sings in a nearby tree, and a squirrel rustles in a bush. I watch it shoot up the trunk of a tree and disappear in its branches, and I laugh.

Jolie's not writing a book about me. She's not going to destroy my reputation. She's not going to betray Flora's trust —or mine.

Jolie is better than that. Better than *I* am.

When I get to the clearing, most of the wildflowers have already died. Now, the opening is just a grassy dell with the fort looming at the far end. I step into the sunshine and enjoy the warmth of its rays on my skin, smiling from ear to ear.

I care about Jolie. Maybe... I love her?

Closing my eyes, I tilt my head up toward the sun and take another cleansing breath.

I love her.

Another laugh bubbles up my chest and tumbles through my lips. I rake my fingers through my hair and laugh to myself, relishing the feeling in my heart.

Love.

It's intoxicating, addictive, and so fucking terrifying—but I like it. I drink it up, wanting to scream it at the top of my lungs. I love Jolie Beaumont!

Then, movement catches my eye. Someone steps out from the shadow of the fort.

"Your Highness."

It's Paulette, sinking down into a deep curtsy.

The laughter dies on my lips. My face falls, and my blood turns to ice. I stare at the woman in front of me, trying to make sense of this. Why is she here? How did she get here? How did she know where I was?

This woman ruined my life. She abandoned our daughter. She used me for her own personal gain, and then aired out all my dirty laundry for the world to read. She wrote a book about our sex life, and spilled my deepest secrets. She used the birth of our daughter—no, *my* daughter—to make money for herself. She neglected Flora when she was an infant, choosing instead to go on a fucking book tour. She slashed me across the face with a knife when I gained custody of my daughter, and accused me of taking her beloved child away.

She never cared about Flora, and she never cared about me.

"What the fuck are you doing here?" I spit.

"Is that any way to greet the mother of your child?"

"It's the way I'm greeting you." The tension in my body is increasing by the second. My blood is burning hotter with every second that passes with Paulette in my presence. "I would never call you her mother."

She looks like she's enjoying my hatred. My ex takes a step toward me, tilting her head and staring at me with the same eyes that used to bewitch me.

Now, I hate them.

"You took my daughter away, and now you're gallivanting around with a fucking gardener."

My eyes narrow. She knows about Jolie?

It's not outside the realm of possibilities. Jolie and I haven't exactly been super secretive. We've tried to be discreet, but someone could have seen us together. Maybe that other gardener, Harry?

"She's not who you think she is," Paulette continues. She comes closer, and I catch a whiff of her perfume. She still wears the same scent as she did when we were together. Back then, I loved it. Now, it's cloyingly sweet and it clings to the inside of my nostrils. I want to take a step back, but I force myself not to.

I stiffen. "What are you talking about?"

"Here." Paulette takes out an envelope from her bag and presents it to me. I hesitate, not wanting to know what poison she'll inject into my life this time.

"Fuck off with your lies. I don't trust anything you touch."

"You don't have to trust me, Your Highness. You just have to look at the photos. They'll be easy enough to believe—even if you don't want to believe me."

When I take the envelope from her hand, my fingers brush against hers. A shiver of revulsion runs up my spine, and I do my best to keep the snarl off my face.

"Why are you here?"

"I've been in Westhill since the ten-year celebration in Farcliff. I saw Flora in the procession..."

"...and your motherly instincts kicked in?" I scoff, shaking my head. "You don't have a motherly bone in your body. When Flora was inside you, you called her a cancerous tumor. Do you remember that? Because I do."

"I was hormonal."

"Fuck off."

"Look at the pictures. Your rose gardener isn't so different from me. At least we know you have a type." She arches a graceful eyebrow, and I hate that she's still beautiful. Looking at her face is like staring at all the mistakes I made all those years ago:

Believing her. Loving her. Trusting her.

My hands shake as I open the envelope. I don't want to look inside. I know that this is just a ploy on Paulette's part to wriggle her way back into my life. Everything she touches dies a painful death, and now she's reaching for me. For Jolie. For Flora.

I stop, shaking my head. "I don't care what's in the envelope."

"Even if it's your new girlfriend meeting with the same agent who represented me?"

As soon as Paulette stepped out from behind the ruins of the fort, I knew she was going to drop a bombshell on me. I knew she was back because she wanted to ruin my life again. I *knew*.

Yet still, I'm surprised. Shocked. *Angry.*

More than angry. Liquid rage floods through my chest as I pull the photos from the envelope. I see Jolie having wine with a man I recognize all too well. Shaking his hand. Smiling at him. Laughing with him. Laughing at *me*.

Jolie's smile sends a dagger straight through my heart. I stare at the photo, trying to make sense of what I'm seeing.

"This is fake."

"I promise it's not," Paulette responds, triumphant. "I wouldn't do that."

"Wouldn't you? Last time I checked, you assaulted me and tried to kidnap my daughter when she was an infant. You neglected her and called her a cancerous tumor—and yet you still couldn't bear the thought of not using her for your fucking publicity stunt. Photoshopping a couple photos to get back at me seems like it would be right in your wheelhouse."

Paulette waves a hand, as if the traumas of our past are an annoying fly buzzing around her head. "I'm not evil."

I snort. "Right."

Turning on my heels, I walk away from her. I leave her standing in the clearing in the woods as my worst fears come true.

The beast inside me stirs as my anger grows. It's been quiet, these past weeks, but it's still inside me. White-hot anger pumps through my veins as I make my way back to the castle. The envelope of photos burns a hole through my breast pocket as I hurry toward my studio.

When I lock myself inside, I pull the photos out with a trembling hand.

Jolie betrayed me. She's been using me all this time. She's been using Flora.

My whole body shakes as I try to contain the anger brimming inside me. An urge is building in my heart—an urge to hurt. To ruin. To destroy.

MY FATHER BEAMS, and my mother wraps her arms around me in a tight hug. I just sent off my signed contract to work with Jeremy, and he's already in contact with publishers. My new novel might become a reality, and I can hardly contain my excitement.

"I've got good news, too," Dad says, exchanging a glance with my mother.

"What is it?"

"Well, I had a blood test today, and my results were the best they've been so far. The doctor says that if they stay at this level for a month after my last round of chemo next week, I might officially be in remission."

I nearly explode from happiness, rushing to my father and practically bowling him over as I wrap my arms around him.

"We still have to wait and see," he says, his voice muffled against my shoulder. "The cancer could come back. I still have to get checked out every couple of weeks."

"I know, but this is good, right?"

"It's good." He smiles as he pulls away. "Couldn't have done it without you and your mother."

"I haven't done anything," I say, shaking my head.

"You took care of the roses," Mom says, winking at me. "That did more than the chemo, I think. Your father actually started to relax when he saw they were in good hands."

"Hopefully, you can come back and see for yourself soon. The repeat bloomers should be flowering in September, in about six weeks or so. You could be in Westhill by then, right?"

"I could be, if everything keeps going the way it is." My father smiles, and I sit down in a chair beside him.

Mom decides to go to the butcher and get a roast for dinner to celebrate. I spend the afternoon with my father, leaning my head on his shoulder as we watch television.

"Thanks for coming to see me," he says during a commercial break.

I chuckle. "Of course, Dad. I missed you and Mom."

"You look healthy and happy, Jo. You're glowing. Maybe you should keep taking care of the garden—even when I'm better."

"I don't know, Dad," I say, glancing away. I know I'm blushing. "I have a meeting with Jeremy tomorrow, so we'll see if this manuscript will actually get picked up, and then go from there."

"Have a little hope, Jolie," my father winks. "You'll get your book deal, I'll get better, and then we'll all go back to Westhill together. It'll all work out."

I bite my lip as my heart thumps. I want to believe my father. I so, *so* want it to be true. If he's healthy, and I'm writing, and the Prince is near—I'd have everything I could ever want.

But how would it work with my parents back? Would the

Prince still want to see me? Still, a smile tugs at my lips. Maybe we could all move back together. My father could teach me everything he knows about rose gardening, and I could work on my book. I could spend time with the Prince, and with Flora...

...and I could be happy. I could have a successful career and a healthy relationship. I could move on from being a constant failure, and I could grow into something more.

When my mother comes back, I help her to make dinner. My stomach grumbles loudly, and when the food is ready, I descend on my plate like a hungry seagull. Scarfing my food down, I nod at my mother and go back for seconds.

"I'm glad to see you eating, Jolie," she laughs, "I was worried about you when you got back from New York. You look better with a bit of meat on your bones, but you should slow down. You'll choke yourself."

"You look like your mother did when she was pregnant with you," my father grins.

I stop, my fork frozen midway to my mouth. My parents are laughing, as if it's the funniest thing my father has ever said.

Seeing the look of horror on my face, my mother laughs at me. "You're not pregnant, are you?"

"No. I couldn't be." I shake my head, knowing that it's not true. It *could* be true. The first three times Prince Gabriel and I had sex, we didn't use any kind of protection. It wasn't until I walked into Westhill and bought some condoms that we started being safe.

I could *definitely* be pregnant.

My parents laugh, and an uncomfortable feeling gurgles in my stomach. I stare at my heaping plate of foods—my second plate of the evening—and my heart falls.

No. I'm not pregnant. There's no way.

I finish my meal in silence, doing my best to avoid my parents' looks. They're too busy being happy for me and happy for each other to notice anything amiss.

After dinner, I go to the bathroom and strip naked. I stand in front of the mirror, staring at my stomach. I stand sideways, running my hand over my abdomen.

Is it bigger?

Of course it's bigger—I just had a massive meal. Even if I wasn't pregnant right now—which I'm not, of course—I'd look like I was.

I jump at a knock on the door. "Are you okay, honey?" My mother asks. "You looked a bit worried after dinner. You don't have indigestion, do you?"

"I'm fine, just having a shower before I go to bed."

"Okay, Jolie." Her footsteps fade, and I stare at myself in the mirror again.

Shaking my head, I turn on the shower. There's no use freaking out about it right now. My stomach is bloated from food, and it would be too soon for it to be showing if I were pregnant.

Which I'm not. Obviously.

WHEN I WAKE up in the morning, I do the same routine of checking myself out in the mirror. I turn sideways, staring at myself and frowning. Do I look different?

Would it be so bad if I did have a baby growing inside me?

I stare at my stomach, putting my hand just below my belly button. I could be a mother. Flora could be a big sister.

I've seen how much the Prince loves his daughter... Does he have enough love to give to another child?

Yes, I decide, he does. I've seen the softness inside him. I know his capacity to love is almost infinite, even though he'd deny it if anyone said it.

He's not the savage everyone says he is. He's loving, and gentle, and protective. He's a wonderful father and a generous lover.

Maybe he *would* want another baby.

Maybe *I* want a baby.

My hands tremble as I put my clothes back on. I hurry to the nearest pharmacy, pulling a hood over my head as I slink to the aisle with the pregnancy tests. I glance around me when I grab one, worried someone is watching.

Why am I being so secretive? No one knows me in Farcliff. No one knows I've been sleeping with Prince Gabriel. So, with a deep breath, I walk to the cashier with my head held high.

I use my false confidence to carry me all the way home and up to the bathroom. I take slow, deep breaths as I read the instructions on the pregnancy test, trying to ignore the panic that starts to creep into every heartbeat. I pee on the end of a test, and set the timer on my phone…

…and then I wait.

Who knew three minutes could last so long? The seconds tick by, one eternity at a time. I sit on the bathroom floor and bite my nails. When my timer goes off, I'm almost too scared to see the results.

I take a deep breath, and then grab the pregnancy test and look at the little window that holds my future. I gasp, and then let out a sigh.

Then, I cry.

THAT AFTERNOON, Jeremy ushers me into his office with a big smile on his face.

"I've been talking to the publishers," he starts.

"Already?"

"I don't waste any time, darling," Jeremy winks. "They're very interested. Your story is fresh, it's new, and it's exactly what the middle-grade market needs."

My head is spinning. Jeremy explains that a deal is imminent, and he expects an offer before I leave for Westhill.

"I'm going to have a book deal?"

"I'm trying to get them to buy into a series," Jeremy says, tenting his fingers across his chest. "I think we could get three, maybe four books out of this. You in?"

I laugh, nodding. "Yeah. I'm in."

Jeremy's phone rings, and his eyebrow arches. "This is them," he says. "Let me take this call in the conference room."

I nod, watching him slip into the next room. My heart thumps. My future is about to be decided. My knee bounces up and down and I wring my hands together. Standing up, I start pacing the room. I go to the bookshelves that line Jeremy's office and start reading the spines of the books, just to distract myself.

One title catches my eye: *Loving Prince Gabriel: The Tell-All Memoir*.

My eyes widen. I've never seen an actual physical copy of this book. It was banned from the Kingdom when I was away, and all the known copies were destroyed. Glancing over my shoulder, I check to see if Jeremy is still on the phone.

I'm alone, so I pull the book out of its slot on the shelf. My eyes widen as I open the first page. My heart thumps, and my hands start to shake. This is the book that started it all. This is the book that broke Prince Gabriel, that turned him into the reclusive, brooding person that he is now.

Prince Gabriel's ex-lover's words are addictive. The book starts with an anecdote of Paulette and the Prince's meeting at a state event. She describes the look in the Prince's eyes, and how it made her feel alive.

It feels wrong to read this. I feel jealous and embarrassed, and like I'm betraying his trust somehow...

...but I can't stop myself.

I don't hear Jeremy coming back in the room until he starts chuckling. "Curious about your boss, are you?"

I slam the book shut, shaking my head. "I thought this book was illegal."

Jeremy shrugs. "Kind of."

"Kind of?"

"Well, not illegal, exactly. Just out of print, and usually destroyed when found."

I stare at him, wide-eyed.

"Keep it," he says, waving a hand. "I don't need it anymore."

"Why do you have it in the first place?"

My agent sighs. "Well, it's a reminder of another life. When I started my career, I was just chasing money. Everything I did was in service to my bank account. That book was my rock bottom. Made a lot of money, but I realized that spinning lies wasn't what I wanted to represent. When shit hit the fan, I dropped the author as a client, and I vowed to only pursue projects that I truly believe in."

I frown.

"What, you don't believe people can change?" Jeremy asks, grinning. He flops back onto his chair and tosses his phone on his desk. "Look at my client list since then, and tell me I haven't redeemed myself."

"I think people can change, but I'm just surprised." I point to the book in my hand. "So, all of this is a big lie?"

"Mostly. Let's say it's more fiction than non-fiction. I'm not proud of it."

"Why do you still have it, then?"

Jeremy sighs. His jovial expression fades, and for the first time since I've met him, I see creases appear on his forehead. "I kept the book in my office as a reminder of what's important to me."

"And that is...?"

"Truth, integrity, respect. I didn't want to be caught in that kind of controversy again. I didn't want to see anyone else's face slashed open because of something I'd helped create. So, yes. I represented Paulette—and yes, I regret it." He stares at me, his face open. "Does that bother you?"

I stare at the controversial book, chewing my lip. I'm trying to reinvent myself, too. I'm trying to change from my eternal failure to something more. My writing is becoming more honest, and I'm realizing what's important to me—the Prince. Flora. My family.

I shake my head. "I respect you for changing your ways."

Lifting the book up, I move to put it back in the bookcase.

Jeremy stops me. "You should read it," he says.

"Why would I do that?"

"I can tell you want to. Plus, I don't want us to work together if there's this book hanging between us. Honesty and integrity, right? So, read it, and then throw it out, or burn it, or give it to the pigeons to build a nest with—I don't care. Take it as a sign that I'm here for you, and that I believe in your book a hell of a lot more than I believed in that drivel."

I stare at the tome, chewing my lip. I shouldn't read this—especially not if I'm back in Westhill. I shouldn't bring it anywhere near Prince Gabriel.

But what does it say? Why did it explode the way it did, and why does it hold so much power over the Prince? Maybe, if I read it, I'll understand where his pain comes from. Whether it's sick curiosity, or a more noble desire to understand the man I'm falling in love with—either way, I want to read this book.

I nod. "Okay, thanks."

"Good." Jeremy claps his hands together. "Now, do you want to hear about that phone call, or not?"

28

GABRIEL

THE DAYS DRAG on as I wait for Jolie to come back. I don't sleep. I'm trapped. I claw at the walls of my own mind until my fingernails are cracked and bloody. I stare at the photos Paulette gave me, trying to come up with any explanation that would make sense.

The facts are the facts, though. Jolie wormed her way into my household. She gained my trust and my daughter's affection, and saw everything that I try to hide away. Then, she wouldn't let me read her work—and she left me to meet with the same agent who helped destroy my life.

All signs point to betrayal.

Still, I resist. The devil on my shoulder laughs, and laughs, and laughs. He whispers everything I'm trying not to believe.

And I resist.

I don't believe it. Not fully. Jolie is different. She's *good*. To her core, I believe that she's good. I wouldn't be that wrong about someone.

When I was with Paulette, it was mostly self-destructive. I was drinking a lot and partying all the time. She was beautiful, and available, and rich. Our relationship was tumultuous and explosive, and it ended with me snapping and her slashing my face open.

Jolie isn't like that. She didn't come to Westhill to be with me. She came here because her father needed her help. She didn't seduce me—I pursued *her*.

Right?

The other gardener—Harry something—takes care of the roses while Jolie's gone. It feels wrong to see him in there. He walks around like he owns the place, and I miss Jolie's gentle touch. I miss hearing her sing to the flowers at night.

I miss her. All of her.

And all the while, I wonder... Was any of it real?

I pretend not to notice when I see her walking across the lawn to the Gardener's Cottage. I pretend that my heart doesn't thump out of my chest, and force myself to stay sitting in my chambers, even though my eyes are glued to her.

She comes back to the garden and finds Harry. I crack the window open and strain my ears to listen to them. Jolie laughs at something he says, and hot, green envy poisons my blood. They come into view of my window, and her eyes dart up toward mine, as if she can sense my presence.

A smile tugs at the corner of her lips, and my mouth tastes like ash.

Is this all a lie?

She works in the garden all afternoon, and I sense that she's waiting for me to come see her.

I don't.

I can't bring myself to face her—not yet. Even after staying up for nights on end. Even after thinking about her non-stop for the past two weeks. Even after staring at the pictures Paulette gave me until my head pounded and my heart ached.

I still can't go to the rose garden.

From my window, I watch her gather fallen rose petals as the sun goes down. She wipes her forehead with her arm, and my stomach sours.

The roses are wilting, just like our relationship. I turn away from the window, disgusted.

I PACE up and down my room until Bert knocks on my door. "Dinner, sir?"

I wave him away. I can't eat. How could I eat, when my whole world is falling apart? And the woman to blame is walking around my castle like she owns the place?

How dare she? The fucking nerve of her, to come back here like nothing is wrong. To walk through *my* garden and live in *my* cottage, as if she hasn't already betrayed me.

To glance up my window and smile, as if she actually wants to see me.

How. Fucking. Dare. She.

Ripping my bedroom door open, I tear down the hall. Flora calls after me from her bedroom.

"Not now, Flora," I snap. Somewhere deep in my heart, I regret speaking to my daughter like that—but right now, at the forefront of my mind, I'm consumed by sweet, intoxicating anger. It pumps through me like hot metal, urging me forward and making me feel invincible.

My hands are shaking. My breath is ragged. I can't think about anything except the audacity of the woman in the cottage.

With every step I take toward her, my rage intensifies. I'll kick her out. I'll have her jailed. I'll shame her and ruin her family name until she's forced to leave the Kingdom.

I *will not* be disgraced again by a goddamn writer. I won't be made a fool, and I won't put Flora through that again.

When I make it to the Gardener's Cottage, my blood is pumping thick and hot through my veins. My vision is cloudy, and I can't hear anything except my thundering heartbeat.

I pound on the door so hard it shakes.

Within seconds, Jolie opens the door. For a moment—just a split second—my anger evaporates. She looks radiant, with her hair falling around her shoulders, and a silky, white nightgown hugging her body. She smiles at me so genuinely, so openly, that I hesitate.

But I am who I am, and when faced with a choice between anger and grace, I choose anger. Always anger.

Jolie's face falls. "Are you okay?"

"Anything to tell me?" I growl, pushing past her. My eyes scan the room, as if I'm going to see some hidden camera or other evidence of her transgressions.

Jo closes the door and faces me, her brow creased. "What do you mean?"

"Your trip to Farcliff. Is there something you wanted to tell me about?"

"I..." She pauses, staring at me. "I got a book deal. And my father's tests are getting better. And..." She gulps, shaking her head.

"And what?"

"Nothing. Why are you speaking to me like this?" Her spine stiffens.

We face off opposite each other. I squeeze my hands into fists, digging my fingernails into my palms to try in vain to contain my anger. Jolie stares at me openly, her emotions flitting on her face in quick succession. Confusion. Hurt. Outrage.

218

Fear.

When her eyes fill with tears, I realize she's afraid of me, and something inside me breaks. My shoulders sink, and the anger inside me comes crumbling down. I sink down onto a chair and drop my head in my hands.

I realize what she just told me—she got a book deal, and her father is getting better. She didn't hide the fact that she met with an agent. She didn't lie to me.

I groan as the guilt and shame come surging up inside me. Squeezing my eyes shut, I try to contain the bitter taste that starts to fill my mouth.

"Holy fuck, Jolie, I'm sorry."

She doesn't answer, so I force myself to look at her. Jolie brushes a tear from her face and gulps. She won't look at me.

I stand up and take a step toward her, but she flinches.

"I'm sorry," I whisper.

"You come charging in here like you're going to kill me... Why? What have I done? I was so excited to see you, so happy about everything that happened in Farcliff. Do you realize that when I got that book deal, the first person I thought about was you? I wanted to share that moment with you. I wanted to be happy *with* you. I thought you'd be happy for me. My father and I talked about coming back here together. I couldn't wait to bring him back!"

She shakes her head, staring at me like she doesn't understand what's going on.

"I shouldn't have spoken to you like that," I say quietly.

"No, you shouldn't have." She turns away from me, and panic starts to grip my throat. I can't lose her. Not like this! Not because I'm fucked in the head and I didn't trust her! Not because of something my ex made up.

"I thought you were writing a book about me. I thought you were another Paulette," I blurt out.

Jolie's eyes widen and she stares at me. "What?"

"I got pictures of you with her agent. My mind went crazy..."

"Are you spying on me? You had me followed? You took *pictures* of me?"

"No!"

Her eyebrows arch, and she takes another step back.

"I didn't do it. They were given to me."

"By who?"

I inhale sharply.

"By *who*, Your Highness?"

I close my eyes. "By Paulette. She followed me to Westhill after the Farcliff celebration. When you left, she gave them to me..."

"... and you assumed that I was just the same as she is?"

I nod, ashamed.

"I wrote a *children's* book, Your Highness," Jo spits at me. "I didn't write tabloid fodder about our affair."

"Our affair?"

What we have is so much more than an affair—but is that all she thinks of me? I'm just a lover that she'll forget about one day?

"What would *you* call it?"

I open my mouth and close it again. What *would* I call this thing between us?

Everything is falling apart in front of me. Jolie is so close, so perfect, so beautiful...and she's slipping through my fingers. I'm ruining everything, just like I always do.

She'll walk away, and I'll lose the only woman who's ever treated me like a real person. Flora will lose her. My face twists as my heart breaks. I'm a fucking idiot.

I cover my face with my hands, wanting to hide my shame. Hide my guilt. Hide myself.

A second later, I feel a finger on my forearm. Jolie pulls my hands away from my face, and cups my cheeks in her palms. Her eyebrows arch as she strokes my face.

She shakes her head. "What am I going to do with you?"

I'm too scared to speak. If I say the wrong thing, Jolie will back away again. She'll leave, and I'll lose her. Instead, I put my hands on her hips, tentatively pulling her toward me.

She melts into me, angling her lips against mine. The moment our mouths press together, my heart melts. Relief floods through me, and I wrap my arms around her more tightly than ever before. I deepen the kiss, singing my fingers into her skin and inhaling her scent.

I've been a fool. I've listened to all the wrong thoughts, and I've given false truth to my darkest fears.

I almost lost her—and for what? Over a misunderstanding?

Jolie doesn't say another word. She lifts my shirt off over my head and kisses my chest. Her touch is gentle, loving, tender. Taking my hand, she leads me to the bed. I watch her undress and lay down, spreading her arms toward me.

There's no fear in her eyes now, only affection.

Only love.

I was wrong to doubt her, and I vow to never do it again. And in those few moments together, it feels like it's possible. With my head buried between Jolie's thighs, I don't see the storm brewing on the horizon.

29

JO

MY BEAUTIFUL, fragile Prince. I don't know what happened when I was gone, but I know that he suffered at the hands of his own mind. I want to look in his eyes and steal the pain from them. I want to shoulder his burdens as if they were my own, because I want him to be free. I want to drink the hurt he carries with him, and suffer in his place.

Instead, I just lay next to him and trail my fingers over his skin. I reach up to touch the scar that runs from his ear to his jaw. Prince Gabriel doesn't flinch away from my touch. He turns his head to look at me as I caress his scar, trying to take some of his pain away.

He catches my fingers in his hand and kisses them. His eyes shine, and he shifts his body closer to mine in the bed.

"I love you," he says in a hoarse voice.

My eyes widen. "What?"

"I said I love you, Jolie Beaumont. I'm sorry I scared you, and I'm sorry I acted like that. I don't want to make you feel badly, ever."

A lump forms in my throat. I smile. "I love you too, Your Highness."

"Are you ever going to call me Gabriel, or are we sticking with formal titles for the rest of our lives?"

"I was waiting for you to give me permission," I laugh, my heart thumping at the thought of forever with him.

"When have you ever asked for permission for anything?"

I laugh, rolling on top of the Prince to cover him in hot kisses from his neck to his navel. I've spent the past week in fear—fear of what he would say when he found out I was pregnant. But he loves me! Maybe that means he'd be happy about another child, too.

I want to tell him, but the words stick in my throat. Instead, we make love in the Gardener's Cottage, with stars in our eyes and our hearts beating as one.

You know that feeling when everything is going well and you know—you just *know*—that it's all going to fall apart?

That's the feeling I wake up with.

The Prince leaves my bed to go back to the castle before dawn, and I lay there, staring up at the ceiling. I put my hand over my stomach, trying to shake the persistent tiredness that seems to be clinging to my marrow. I try to sleep, but I can't get comfortable.

What if he doesn't want the baby?

When I took the pregnancy test, I was terrified. When Gabriel stormed into the cottage last night, I was hurt. But now?

Now, I feel hopeful.

Hope is the beginning of the end. Hope leads to disappointment.

I get up with the sun and make my way to the kitchens for breakfast. I feel a bit groggy, like I have the remnants of a hangover that stays with me all the time. Pushing through the discomfort, I eat a bit of dry toast and make my way to the garden.

Throughout the morning, my movements are labored, and the roses smell so damn *sweet*. After an hour or so, I end up puking behind a rose bush. Wiping my mouth, I lean on my knees and sigh. This is going to be a tough nine months—well, seven and a half months, now.

A noise at the gate makes me turn my head, and Flora's smiling head appears. She coughs into her hand, and then smiles at me again.

"Jo!"

"Hey, kiddo."

"I'm not a kid," she says, rolling her eyes. She coughs again, her whole body contracting.

I frown. "You okay?"

"It's nothing." She forces another smile. "Can I help you with anything?"

"Are you sure that's a good idea? Maybe you should get some rest."

"I've been waiting for *ever* for you to come back, and now you want to send me away?" She has the same big, blue eyes as her father. Right now, they're wide and pleading, and I can't say no.

"All right," I sigh. "Grab that bag, I'm picking up the fallen petals."

"Mr. Marcel said the roses bloomed again in September. Is that true?"

"These ones will." I point to the roses along the southern fence. We get to work. Flora coughs a lot as we gather the wilted rose petals. She has to sit down after a few minutes, and coughs so hard I'm afraid her little body will break into pieces.

"Let's go find Mrs. Grey, Flora." My voice is a bit sterner, now. The Princess shouldn't be out here. Maybe it's because I have my own child growing inside me, but my motherly instincts are starting to kick in.

The Princess doesn't protest. I slip my hand into hers, and we walk back toward the castle. Mrs. Grey meets us at the door—she always has a sixth sense when it comes to Flora. The old woman's lips pinch together as her brow furrows, and she takes the coughing girl over to the East Wing.

I watch them leave, and worry knots my stomach.

The Prince told me cystic fibrosis is hereditary... Will my baby have it, too?

Shaking my head, I get back to work. My mind keeps flicking back to the Princess, though, and my stomach keeps twisting. She didn't look well. I haven't known her very long, but seeing her so pale, and weak, and coughing so much. It's scary.

I head back to the Gardener's Cottage around two o'clock in the afternoon. My feet and back are aching, and I can't get rid of the nausea that seems to churn my stomach every time I move. So, instead, I go back to my little abode, put my feet up, and pull out Paulette's book.

I can't help it. It's addictive. A lot of her stories, I dismiss immediately as lies. Still, she's woven in enough truths for her book to sound plausible. I can see Gabriel in her stories —the wildness in him, the walls that he put up, the chaos that he seems to attract.

WHEN A KNOCK COMES on the door, I jolt awake on the couch. The sun has gone down, and I have no idea how long I've been asleep. Paulette's book has tumbled to the floor, and I stuff it between the couch cushions. Heading to the door, I try to smooth my hair and make myself look presentable. There's only one person that knocks on my door at this hour—Prince Gabriel.

Yet when I open the door, it's not him standing on my stoop. It's his butler, Bertrand. The eagle-eyed man inclines his head.

"His Highness regrets that he can't join you tonight," Bertrand says, his face unreadable. "The Princess has fallen ill."

A cascade of emotions rushes through me. First, embarrassment—Bertrand knows about us? Second, disappointment that Gabriel won't be coming over. Third—worry.

"She's sick?"

Bertrand nods. "She hasn't been this bad in almost a year."

"She was coughing a lot in the garden today." I open the door wider. Bertrand hesitates, but steps inside. I offer him some tea or coffee, but he shakes his head.

"Is she okay?" I ask, putting the kettle on anyway.

"She started coughing blood. You know that with her condition, she gets lung infections easily."

I nod.

Bertrand shakes his head. "It's bad. The Prince is worried."

Typically, Bertrand is the image of professionalism. He's fiercely loyal to the Prince, and never lets his own feelings show. Today, though, he sinks into a chair and drops his head in his hand. My heart starts to thump.

"It's bad, Jolie," he says quietly. "She's very sick."

"How could it get so much worse so quickly?"

Bertrand shakes his head. "She's very vulnerable to infections." He lifts his eyes up to mine. "The medical staff were talking about airlifting her to Farcliff. They've set up good medical facilities in the castle, but nothing compared to the Farcliff Royal Hospital."

"Airlifting her out of here?"

Bertrand nods, sighing.

"And the Prince—is he okay?"

"I haven't seen His Highness like this in a long time. I think..." He hesitates, lifting his eyes up to me. "I think he might benefit from your company."

"You want me to go up to the castle uninvited?" I ask, biting my lip.

A small, selfish part of me worries about my unborn child, too. If Flora has some sort of bacterial infection, couldn't I get it, too? What if I got sick?

Bertrand lets out a heavy sigh. "Maybe not." He pushes himself up to his feet and heads for the door. When he gets there, he pauses and glances over his shoulder. "The Prince has been happier since you've been here."

Our eyes meet, and for a brief moment, I see how much Bertrand cares about Gabriel. It looks like the love of a father, worried about his son.

I nod my head as if I understand, but I still don't know what to do.

Bertrand leave the cottage, and I stare off into nothing. The butler may think that I should go up there, but I'm not sure I can. I glance down at my stomach and let out a heavy sigh.

I just can't bring myself to put my own child into any kind of danger—however slight it may be. So, instead, I sit down at the desk and try to write. The words I put down are complete garbage, and I know I'll have to scrap them all, but at least by typing them, I'm not thinking about Flora, and the Prince, and me.

. . .

I DON'T SEE Gabriel at all that night, or the next day. There are whispers in the castle that Princess Flora's condition is deteriorating, and the possibility of her being transported to Farcliff by helicopter becomes more and more likely.

I desperately want to go see her. I want to wrap my arms around the Prince and make sure he's coping. I want to kiss Flora's forehead and hold her hand...

...but I don't.

I stay away, and I wait for Gabriel to come to me. He needs his space, I tell myself. He needs to be with his daughter, and it's not my place to interrupt. When he said he loved me, he didn't say that I could use the castle as my own home. He's never invited me to his own chambers—what right do I have to go up there at all?

That evening, I go back to the cottage and I wait for him, unsure that he'll come at all. He doesn't—not until dawn the next morning.

I wake up to a soft knock on the door. I fell asleep on the couch again, waiting for him. I rub the sleep from my eyes and open it up, and my heart breaks.

The Prince is broken. He has big, dark bags under his eyes, and he looks like he's aged ten years overnight.

"Oh, Gabriel," I whisper, wrapping my arms around him.

He sobs, trembling in my arms. I drag him inside and hold the Prince as he breaks in front of me. Standing there, in my tiny cottage, I hold him in my arms as if it'll do anything to keep him together. He pulls away from me, his eyes rimmed red and tears still streaming down his face.

"She's sick, Jo. Really sick."

"Will they airlift her out of here?"

He nods. "By this afternoon at the latest. I'm going to

Farcliff with her." He opens his mouth, and for a moment I wonder if he'll ask me to come with him.

Yes, I'll come. I'll do anything.

Instead, he drags himself to the sofa. Leaning back and staring at the ceiling, he lets out a heartbreaking sigh.

"I can't lose her."

"You won't." I sit next to him, leaning my head on his shoulder.

The Prince shifts his weight to put his arm around me. I rest my head against his chest, listening to his heartbeat as it slows down. He takes a few deep breaths, tangling his fingers into my hair. His lips press against my forehead, and I hold him close.

"Thank you," he whispers. "It's good to be able to not be strong for a little while."

"You're still strong, even if you're hurting." I brush my fingers over his cheeks. I kiss him tenderly, wanting to draw the pain out of him and into myself.

Then, a sequence of events makes my entire life unravel like an old sweater. The Prince shifts his weight on the couch, putting his hand down on the edge of the cushion. He makes a noise, feeling something hard with his fingers.

My heart starts to race as I realize what he's just touched between the cushions.

People say that things happen in slow motion, that they can see everything happen in vivid detail, and that their life flashes before their eyes.

That's not what happens to me. Things occur very, very fast. First, Prince Gabriel shifts his weight. Then, he reaches between the couch cushions. It takes approximately four nanoseconds for him to recognize the book that he pulls out of the sofa, and two more nanoseconds for him to explode.

I can *feel* the rage vibrating within him as he swings his gaze toward me.

"Gabriel..." I silence myself as he stands up, his eyes wide with fury as he glances at the book, and then back at me.

Nothing flashes before my eyes. Time doesn't slow down. It crashes around me all at once, and I know it's all over.

30

GABRIEL

ANGER IS TOO KIND a word for what I feel. Rage is too gentle. Fury is too soft. Poisonous, gangrenous betrayal is injected straight into the center of my heart, and I die. In those few seconds, I die over, and over, and over.

The woman that I love—*loved*—stares at me with those unforgettable eyes. I look at her, and then at the book, and my body starts to shake. My heart turns black, and my vision clouds. A deep, unending well of wrath is opened in my soul. It spills venom into my veins and kills everything inside me. In that moment, I realize there's no beast inside me.

I *am* the beast.

Then, everything goes dark.

I BLINK, and I'm in a helicopter. There's a dull thumping in my head. Someone is prodding at my palm. I look down, dazed.

Blood everywhere. *My* blood.

Is it mine? Or is it Jolie's?

I close my eyes, and flashes of memory go through my mind.

Flora's illness. Jolie's kindness.

The book.

The betrayal.

I remember Jolie's cries as I smashed the door to the cottage. The sound pierces through my head like a thousand daggers. I bring my hands up to my face to try to drown out the memory of her voice. Something scratches against my cheek as pain shoots through my hand.

"Easy, your Highness," a medic says. "I'm trying to get the thorns out. Try to sit still."

I squint, trying to make sense of the blood on my hands. It runs between my fingers and soaks into my sleeves. It stains my shirt, my pants, my socks.

The chopper's blades go *whomp-whomp-whomp* against my skull, and I close my eyes again.

I remember my breath, ragged and heavy as I dragged myself away from the cottage. Away from Jolie. Away from what I might do to her if I stayed.

I remember stumbling, as if drunk, on my way to the rose garden.

Exhaling, I open my eyes. Memories return to my mind like the flick of a light switch, illuminating the putridness of my rotten soul.

I destroyed everything.

I ruined it all.

My knees sink further down into the dirt as my tears soak the soil. I'm in the same spot where I collapsed in the rose garden when Gabriel's monster was unleashed.

I watched him rip the plants from the earth with super-human strength. I heard him roar like a man unhinged. His screams were wordless, but I know what they meant.

This is your fault, he told me, ripping the bushes from the earth. *You killed these flowers, just like you killed me. You did this.*

I watched him tear his hands to shreds on thorny bushes, snarling and snapping his teeth as he tore from one end of the garden to the other.

I knelt, crying.

When his vengeance had been extracted from the plants we once loved, he walked past me without a word. He left a trail of blood in the dirt beside me, and I wept. I wept until the helicopter landed on the grass, and the medical staff took Flora and the Prince away. I wept until the sound of the aircraft faded, until I was alone.

I still weep.

I can't stop crying. I can't move, or think, or do anything except kneel among the butchered roses.

My chest splits open as if the Prince took an axe to it, cracking it asunder with all the strength of his fury. I bleed into the soil with him, dying on the patch of dirt that I tended in his honor.

When the chill of the air starts to freeze my body, I force myself to stand up. Everything aches. My knees are covered in dirt, and it's hard to walk. I stumble, catching myself on the fence.

I have to turn away from the carnage. I lean into the intricate iron fence, resting my forehead against one of its spikes as I take a deep breath. I can't bear to look at it, but I have to.

Straightening myself up, I turn to look at the destruction in the garden. No plants have been left untouched. Every single rose bush is uprooted, broken, and destroyed. When I get to the trellis of climbing roses, my heart breaks all over again. The Prince pulled the trellis off the wall and ripped the delicate plant from the earth. He tore the bush apart, bit by bit, knowing it was my favorite.

My lip trembles, and I take one of the few remaining roses between my fingers. I cradle it in my arms like a wounded bird, my tears dripping onto its soft petals.

"I'm sorry," I whisper to the rose. "I'm so sorry it ended like this."

I say it to the rose, and I say it to myself, too. I weep for the relationship that could have been between Gabriel and me. I know it's over now.

Even if he apologizes, it doesn't change the fact that he did this. I've seen this side of him, and I'm not sure I can ever be okay with it.

I bring the wilting rose up to my nose and I inhale, burying my face in its petals. My other hand drifts to my stomach, and the pieces of my shattered heart melt into my flesh.

Yes, I was wrong to bring the book to Westhill. Yes, the Prince has a right to be upset about that.

But this destruction is wrong. This kind of anger is unacceptable.

I have to think of my child—and that's not the kind of person I want as a partner.

Tucking the rose into my pocket, I take a deep breath. I walk to the small shed at the corner of the garden and pull on some gardening gloves. I'm still wearing my pajamas, but it doesn't matter. I can't go back to the cottage. I can't look at the broken door, the smashed chairs, or the book he tore to pieces.

There's too much destruction around me, and I need to fix some of it.

So, I get to work. I'm barefoot, and within minutes, the soles of my feet are cut and bleeding. All the better—we'll both bleed in this dirt, and maybe it will nourish the roses in the future.

A light flicks on, and I ignore it.

"Jo?" Sam's voice calls out. "Are you okay?"

I turn to see her with Mrs. Grey, their faces painted with concern.

"Got to clean this up." I grab a shovel, turning away from them.

"Go to bed, dear," Mrs. Grey says softly. "We can work on this tomorrow."

I shake my head. "No. It has to be now."

Sam tries to take the shovel from me, and I growl at her. I literally *growl* at my friend.

Maybe the Prince and I aren't that different, after all?

"I have to," I whisper, as if that explains anything. Mrs.

Grey puts her arm around Sam's shoulders, but Sam shakes it off. She walks to the shed and puts some gloves on, and starts working beside me. Mrs. Grey lets out a heavy sigh and walks away.

The older woman comes back with a tray of coffee, bread, and butter, which she leaves by the edge of the garden. "Don't stay up too late," she says, sadness creeping into the edges of her voice. I nod to her, and then turn back to the roses.

At one point, maybe around two or three in the morning, I notice Sam is crying. Silent tears stream down her cheeks, and I wrap my arms around her. We cry in each other's arms, not needing to say a word to each other. Nothing can bring comfort right now, so we just cry for a few minutes. Then, we keep working.

When the sun comes up, Sam stumbles to bed, and I keep working. There's a feverish sort of need inside me—a panic, as if I'll die if I don't fix this. We've cleared about half the garden, and I've salvaged a handful of plants. Less than ten percent of the exquisite roses will survive, but my tears have dried up. I don't have anything else to give. My body is sore, my eyes are stinging, and my feet are bleeding.

Once I finish this cleanup, I'm not sure what will be left of me.

A few minutes after Sam leaves, Harry shows up with two other gardeners. He nods at me without saying a word, and for the first time, I'm grateful for his presence. I see a softness in his eyes, and I think I might have judged him too harshly before. We work until about noon, clearing the garden of its murdered flowers. We're able to salvage about twenty plants whose root balls were still intact. The rest of the garden, though, is gone.

A massive pile of brambles and dead flowers lays in the center of the rose garden like a funeral pyre.

"Burn it," I say to no one in particular.

Harry glances at me, and then nods. I stand on the far side of the fence and watch the garden burn away to nothing. The heat of the blaze dries the tears on my cheeks. Its warmth sends a whisper of a feeling into my numbness.

Then, I walk back to the cottage. I shower, pack my bags, and drag them up to the castle. Before I leave, though, there's one last thing I need to do.

32

GABRIEL

I FEEL HUNGOVER, but I haven't had anything to drink. I have a skull-splitting headache and a persistent churning in my gut. Charlie and Damon come to the hospital. They say things to me, telling me Flora will be fine, but I hear nothing.

All I do is relive the past twenty-four hours, feeding off my pain.

I was right to snap. Jolie deserved it. She should never have brought the book to Westhill. She shouldn't have been reading it at all.

She's just like Paulette. Like every woman.

She was wrong, wrong, wrong.

I say it to myself again and again, as if it'll help me believe it. I try to convince myself that my reaction was correct, that I was justified.

That I'm not an animal.

I do Cirque du Soleil-worthy mental contortions, telling myself that I'm right. I've always been right. My only mistake was trusting Jolie.

All the while, Flora lays in a hospital bed.

. . .

I SPEND two weeks like that, floating somewhere between life and death. Flora is strong, and the doctors are confident about her recovery.

I'm not strong, though. I'm weak. Damaged. Broken.

Charlie drags me back to Farcliff Castle every couple of days to sleep and eat. I'm not sure I'd need it—I'm fairly certain I can survive off of pain alone.

Insomnia sits on my chest like a laughing hyena, snarling its teeth at me whenever I get too close to sleep, so I just lay in bed and stare at the ceiling.

I eat a couple of bites of something as Charlie and Damon watch me. Then, I go back to the hospital.

On the morning of the fifteenth day in Farcliff, Flora wakes up looking rosier than before. She smiles at me, reaching her hand out to me. Her palm feels so tiny and frail in mine, but her voice is strong.

"Are you okay, Daddy?"

I chuckle. "I'm fine, kiddo. You're the one I'm worried about."

"You shouldn't be worried," she says.

My daughter reaches for the side table, where her bag rests. I hand it over to her, and Flora digs through it. When she finds what she's looking for, her face brightens.

"See?" Flora opens her palm to reveal her good luck rock. "I knew I'd be okay."

"Is that my rock?"

"I had Mrs. Grey take it from your desk," Flora smiles. "I knew if I brought it with me, I'd be okay."

I chuckle, kissing my daughter's forehead. The tension in my chest eases the tiniest bit, and I lean my forehead against my daughter's arm. She pats my head.

"It's okay, Daddy."

I squeeze her hand and nod, but I'm not sure I believe her.

THE DOCTORS URGE us to stay in Farcliff for a little while—at least until Flora is fully healed. I reluctantly agree. We spend two months there while Flora recovers.

I, on the other hand, don't recover.

My heart has a hole in it the size of Farcliff. Jo's essence is etched into my bones, and I see her face every time I close my eyes. I think of her all day, every day.

I miss her.

As pathetic as it is, I miss everything about her. I miss smelling her skin, and touching her hair. I miss the face she makes when she comes. I miss her laugh, and the softness in her eyes.

I miss her kindness, and how she made me a better person.

I miss her even though she betrayed me by bringing that book into my home. She wanted to read those lies about me—she was just as fascinated by my downfall as the rest of Farcliff.

My mind tears itself to pieces, one painful strip of flesh at a time.

One voice in my head tells me that I'm wrong—that she cared about me just as much as I cared about her. She told me she was writing a children's book and she told me about the agent. She never lied to me. Not once.

The other voice—the louder one—tells me to burn. Kill. Destroy. Spread salt in the earth of my heart and make sure nothing ever grows there again. Shatter my love for Jolie into a million pieces and let the wind carry the shards to the end of the earth.

Even Flora's smile doesn't cheer me. Even when the flush returns to her cheeks, and when her laugh grows stronger while she heals.

I still miss Jolie.

I TAKE my daughter back to Westhill at the end of September. The weather is starting to turn, and both of us are happy to be home. Even though Flora's eyes were bright with the sights and sounds of the big city, I can tell she's glad to be back in Westhill. She sleeps longer and smiles more. She takes deeper breaths.

I try my best to survive, but the first time I see the remnants of the rose garden, the last piece of my heart dies. There's a big, charred patch of ground in the middle of the fenced area. The rest of the earth has been cleared. Not a single rose bush remains.

For the first time since I left, I realize that I was wrong. Completely, utterly, irredeemably wrong.

Jolie brought the book to Westhill, sure, but I was the one who ruined everything.

Me.

What's a book, anyway? A collection of words. A few hundred thousand letters, arranged in a particular order. The only power those letters have is the power we give them— and I gave that book all of my power. I let Paulette's words be the key to my anger. I let her lord it over me, years after they were written.

Pushing the Royal Rose Garden gate open, I bend over to take the ashy soil into my fingers. I let the earth run between them, swirling around my legs in the wind.

It's gone, and it's all my fault. It'll take years to plant a garden like the one that was here before.

Jolie is gone, too, and that's my fault as well. As I survey the rose garden, I know that it won't take years for me to find another Jolie. It won't take a lifetime. It won't even take an eternity.

It'll never happen. There's only one of her, and one of me —and I killed what we had.

Kicking my feet in the dirt, I turn away from the rose garden and make my way up to my studio. I know what I'll draw when I get there. It's the only thing I've drawn for the past five months, ever since that day at the beginning of May, when my new rose gardener walked through the front gate.

I'll draw the face that's burned forever into my memory. The smile that makes my heart break every time I think about it. The body that still makes me wake up with a cock as hard as steel.

Jolie. Jolie. Jolie.

33

JO

WITH MY ADVANCE from the publisher, I'm able to rent a small two-bedroomed house in Grimdale. Apparently, it's across the road from the house where Queen Elle lived when she met the King. Rumor has it, the King walked through the yard of my new home when he was looking for her.

Good for him, and his fucking happily-ever-after.

I'm not bitter, I swear.

I do my best not to look at the house across the street, and try my hardest to forget about the royal family.

My parents move out of the tiny apartment they were in and stay with me. When I tell my parents about the rose garden, the heartbreak on my father's face mirrors my own.

"I'm sorry," I whisper.

My mother shakes her head. "It's not your fault. We shouldn't have sent you there."

Then, I tell them I'm carrying the Prince's baby, and their shoulders droop even further. I chuckle bitterly, shaking my head. I don't know what else to say.

Apparently, the Prince spends a few months in Farcliff,

but I never see him or hear from him. I tell myself it's for the best.

I mostly just struggle to write through my nausea and bone-crushing tiredness. When I hit my thirteenth week of pregnancy, I wake up refreshed for the first time in months. My father gets back from his latest appointment with the oncologist, and he tells me he's officially in remission.

My face rearranges itself into a smile, and my muscles ache from the effort. I haven't smiled in a long time.

"Let's garden," Dad says, rubbing his hands together. "I want to stick my fingers in some dirt and make something grow."

I laugh, nodding. "Okay."

Over the next few weeks, we build a compost bin together, deadhead some flowers, and water some of the plants that were already growing in the run-down yard. We plant a small veggie garden with some cold-weather crops. Color returns to my father's cheeks—and to my own—and we both work on the garden as our bodies heal.

Him, from his cancer. Me, from my heartbreak.

In the afternoons, I write. I send off the first draft of my manuscript to the publisher, and start the second book the next day.

I still think of Gabriel all the time. I still miss his touch, and his words, his beautiful, broken soul.

Love is a wild animal—it can't be tamed. Even though I know I can't be with Gabriel, I still love him as fiercely as I did in the rose garden. Heartbreak is a gash in the heart that never heals. It doesn't cauterize. Contrary to what everyone says, the pain doesn't dull. You just get used to it.

I carry my heartbreak everywhere, just as I carry my child. They both simultaneously make me stronger and weaker than I was before.

After endless rounds of edits with half a dozen editors, the release date of my book is finally set. Jeremy smiles constantly whenever I see him. I try to match his excitement, but I can't. It's not his fault. It's just that the brightness of the world has been dimmed. The volume is turned down low. True happiness is just out of reach.

It's not until my baby moves for the first time that something shifts inside me. I'm outside, with my father, checking on our crops. I pause, hand on stomach, my eyes wide.

My baby moves against my hand, as if it knows I'm there.

I'm listening. I'm feeling—and a part of my heart stitches itself back together.

My eyes mist up, and a lump forms in my throat. I may be heartbroken over Gabriel. I may have led to the destruction of the rose garden at Westhill. I may be living with my parents, pregnant and partner-less, but I'm not doomed.

This whole time, I've felt like I've failed. I failed to keep the garden safe. I failed to make my way in New York. I failed to maintain my relationship with the Prince.

But when my baby moves, I realize that none of that is true. I'm not a failure. I can't be, because I have a child who depends on me. Failure might have been my modus operandi a few months ago, but it's not even an option now. I won't let myself give up on the baby, or on my family, or on my writing.

A laugh bubbles up from my lips as I stand in the garden. My father glances up at me, frowning.

"Never mind," I say, shaking my head. How could I explain that I've just had an earth-shattering realization? How can I tell him that I know, now, that I don't need the Prince?

I don't need his heart. I don't need his bewitching smile or his shattered soul.

I just need my baby. My love. My writing.

I may never be complete without Gabriel, but it doesn't mean I have to live wounded and crippled. I can still succeed.

My mother appears in the doorway, lifting up a package. "It's for you, Jolie. Feels heavy."

I make my way to the house, and rip open a package to find a little bundle of books—*my* books. I smile wider, taking the novels in my hand and flicking through them.

My words, printed and bound. My mother hugs me, and a tear slides down my cheek. I take one of the novels, lifting it up to my nose. It smells like paper and glue—like love and inspiration and ideas all in one.

Taking one of the books, I head to my room and sit down on my bed, grabbing a pen.

I hesitate, my hand hovering over the page. Then, I take a deep breath and write what's in my heart—for Flora. The pen trembles, but I need to put it in writing. Maybe, a small part of me wants Gabriel to read this and see the meaning in the words.

The next day, I go to the post office and address the package to Sam. I write her a letter telling her how much I miss her jokes and her late-night dessert runs to the kitchen. I ask her to give the book to Flora, and beg her not to tell anyone.

Then, I post the package and let out a sigh. In a way, it feels like writing the final chapter.

I still care about Flora, and about her father, but I know that fixing him isn't my responsibility. My heart will always be broken, and I know that my days in Westhill will stick in my mind like peanut butter on the roof of my mouth. I'll always taste the memories on my tongue, no matter how much I try to get rid of them.

When I post that book to Flora, though, I accept the

finality of it. I run my hand over my stomach and feel a wave of strength come over me that I've never felt before. I won't break. I won't crumble. I won't fail.

I won't burn like the mound of uprooted roses in Westhill. I'll live, and I'll love, and I'll thrive.

34

GABRIEL

I work up the courage to look for Jo only once in the six months that follow the destruction of the rose garden.

Flora and I go back to Farcliff for the holidays. For the first time in my daughter's life, we're surrounded by family for Christmas. To my surprise, I don't hate it.

We're in the week between Christmas and New Year's Eve, when shops are mostly shut and there's a weird lull in everyone's lives. The chaos of gift-giving is over, and the whole city groans with a collective holiday hangover.

I can sense Jo's presence like a drug in the air. In Westhill, I could ignore her absence. In the city, though, I know she's near enough to see. To smell. To touch.

Like an addict, I can't resist.

It's not difficult to find out where she lives. I wait until the palace is quiet, and Flora is in bed, and I take one of the dark-tinted royal cars out to Grimdale.

My mouth is dry when I pull up outside of her house. Jolie's house is brightly lit. I stop my car on the opposite side of the street, trying to work up the courage to walk up to the door and knock.

I shouldn't be hesitating. I'm royalty. I'm the third Prince of Farcliff. My family own this land and everyone who walks on it bends the knee to us.

Still, I hesitate. I watch the house like a starving dog, looking for any glimpse that I might get the sustenance I need to survive. That I might see her. Smell her. Touch her.

A van pulls up outside her house, and people pour out of it—people I recognize. There's the red-headed maid from Westhill, and that fucking tall, GQ-model gardener that wouldn't keep his eyes off Jolie. There are two other garden hands, and even Mrs. Grey appears. They're all carrying presents.

The maid has a balloon—baby blue, with the words 'congratulations' written on it. Everyone is smiling. The red-head sprints up to the front door and mashes her finger on the doorbell. My mouth is so close to the car window that my breath fogs it up. I wipe it away hastily, my eyes still glued on the little group.

Behind them, I can see the door open.

I sense her.

Jolie.

So close. So, so far.

I see her arms. Did you know that when you love someone, you recognize their arms? Those arms wrap each of the guests in a hug—even fucking Harry the GQ gardener. When her arms wrap around his neck, hot jealousy spears my stomach. I sink my fingers into the seat of the car to stop myself from launching at him and tearing his head off.

Jolie has her back to me now, ushering everyone through the door. I can hear the laughter and exclamations from them, and my loneliness crushes me from the inside.

Jolie's hand is on her lower back, rubbing it gently as if it's sore. I frown. Is she okay? Maybe I should send a doctor over.

At the very last moment before the door closes, I see Jolie's profile.

More specifically, I see her stomach.

It bulges out slightly, and she lets her hand drift over it protectively. My mouth goes dry and my heart starts beating wildly. Jolie smiles, glancing once more through the door.

It closes, and I let out a strangled gasp.

The balloon, the presents, the party.

Is she...

...pregnant?

So soon? Did it take her no time at all for her to move on? Not only move on, but get knocked up by someone else?

Hot, angry blood starts pumping through my body. I count the months on my fingers, confused. Could it be...?

No, I decide. It couldn't be mine. We were hooking up in, what, June? She doesn't look six months pregnant...

But what do I know what a six-month pregnant woman looks like?

I open the car door, flinging myself towards her house. My feet carry me all the way to the stoop...

...and then I stop.

It's not mine. She would have told me. She would have called, or sent a letter, or done *something* to let me know. It can't be mine.

My mouth sours. If it's not mine, then it's even worse—it's someone else's. Another man had his cock inside her. Had his *cum* inside her. Another man tasted Jolie's lips, her skin, her cunt. Another man wrapped his arms around her.

My body is vibrating with rage, and hurt, and confusion. I stand in front of her door, willing myself to knock. To find out the truth.

To see her. Smell her. Touch her.

Maybe it's cowardice that makes me turn away. Maybe it's pride. Maybe it's jealousy.

Whatever it is, it forces me back into my car. It compels me to drive away, even though the last piece of my dead heart stays lying on Jolie's front stoop.

I go back to Farcliff Castle and endure the rest of the holidays until I can hole myself back up in Westhill for the rest of eternity.

ETERNITY IS A LONG TIME, it turns out—especially when you're an insomniac and there's a certain doe-eyed woman who invades your thoughts like an army of ants.

I buy a smartphone, just so that I can make fake social media profiles and look up pictures of her. Then, I jerk off to every single one of them.

I draw Jolie's face from memory every day, every night, every hour. I burn every sketch I create, feeling the singe of the flames in my chest, and tasting the ash on my tongue.

Winter is long, cold, and dreary.

When the snow melts, and the first buds start appearing on the trees, I feel worse. The rose garden, instead of being a hum of energy and life, is dead and empty. Like my chest.

Even Flora avoids the garden.

In February, Jolie gives birth. I know this, because she posts about it online, and because I check her profiles multiple times a day. I trawl through her social media profiles, trying to see any hint as to who the father is. I find nothing.

My chest is tight, and I feel like I haven't taken a full breath in months. Leaning my head against my bedroom window, I look at the black patch of earth where the rose garden once was, and blink back tears.

I won't cry. I can't cry.

At the far end of the rose garden, near the shed, fucking Harry walks into view. He grabs a few things, throwing them in a golf cart, a phone to his ear. He rummages through the shed, nodding to the person on the phone, and then drives off.

Suddenly, I'm angry. I need to know where he's going. I need to know if there was ever anything between him and Jolie. If he ever laid a finger on her, I might have to rip his arms off.

My vision is tinted red as my heart starts racing. I tear my bedroom door open, and sprint down the hallway. I make my way to the garages and get into a car. I can see the golf cart at the end of the long driveway, and I press on the accelerator to catch up.

I follow Harry down the street into Westhill, frowning when he stops outside the community garden. Parking outside the council chambers, I get out of the car and follow him.

"So, how much do I prune them? Right. Okay. Yeah. I'll send you a picture of the first one, and you tell me if it's all right." Harry says. "Okay, bye, Jo."

The sound of her name makes my pulse thump. I can't even hear my footsteps over the sound of the blood rushing in my ears. All I know is that fucking Harry was on the phone with the woman I love, and it's time for him to lose an arm or two.

I stomp into the community garden, ready to raise hell. Ready to kill. Destroy. Ruin.

Except I can't, because the gardener is bending over a rose bush, carefully pruning its branches. He takes a photo and sends it to Jo, just like he said he would. My eyes widen, sweeping across the side of the community garden.

The rose bushes. *My* rose bushes. Jolie and Marcel and Violet's rose bushes. They're here, bare and unpruned, devoid of leaves and flowers...

...but they're here.

They didn't die. Jolie didn't let them perish. She saved them.

A noise escapes my lips, as if a hand squeezes all the air out of my lungs. It's halfway between a wheeze and a grunt, and it makes Harry turn his head.

"Oh, Your Highness," he stammers. "I didn't know you were here."

"What are you doing?"

Harry stares at me, his eyes flashing dangerously. It only lasts a second, though, and then the man inclines his head. "I'm pruning the roses, Your Highness."

"The roses... The royal roses?" My voice is low. Menacing. Dangerous.

Harry nods. He straightens his shoulders. "We brought them here after..."

His voice trails off.

"...after I ruined them." I don't even know why I'm angry. I should be elated. I should be happy that Jolie chose to save whichever plants that she could, instead of letting them die.

Doesn't that mean she'd want to save whatever she could of *us,* too? Doesn't that mean there's hope? That I have a chance?

But instead of hope and happiness, my mind chooses anger—always anger. It rips through me, and I welcome it with open arms.

"Did you fuck her?" My voice is black.

Harry's eyebrows arch. "Excuse me?"

"Jolie. Did you put your cock anywhere near her?"

"What if I did?" He puffs his chest out, his eyes narrowing into dangerous slits.

It doesn't matter that I'm a Prince, and he's a groundskeeper. It doesn't matter that I'm his boss, and I could ruin his life with the wave of a hand.

Right now, we're equals. Equally angry. Equally fucked up. Equally in love with a woman who's painfully out of reach.

Harry's lip twitches, and he lets out a scoff. "No. Never. Even though I wanted to. Even though I tried. All she ever wanted was to make you happy—to fix you, or fuck you, I don't know. I don't get it—I never will. The only thing I know for sure is that you never deserved her."

My nostrils flare. My foot scratches the dirt like a bull about to charge.

Harry doesn't seem threatened, though. He shakes his head. "You didn't deserve her love, or her body, or any piece of her heart that she gave you. None of it."

He drops the pruning shears, his hands balling into fists. I watch him gulp, and every fiber of my being is screaming at me to *kill, kill, kill.*

Maim him. Punch him. Destroy him.

But his words hold me back. The truth of them hits me in the face, and I know I can't hit him. If I hit him, I'm denying it —but isn't it the awful, plain truth? I *didn't* deserve her. Not then, not now—not at all.

I turn on my heels and head for the exit.

"She won't take you back," Harry calls out behind me. I pause, not turning my head. I hear the snap of the shears as he prunes a branch. "Not as you are, anyway—angry. Violent. Not since she had the baby."

I start walking again, his words peppering my back like bullets. When I get to my car, a parking ticket is slipped under my windshield wiper. I tear it into pieces and let them flutter to the ground.

WHEN I'M BACK in the castle, I find myself walking toward the rose garden. I frown when I see my daughter sitting in the middle of the ashy, charred circle, reading a book.

She looks up when she sees me, smiling. "Hi, Daddy."

"What are you doing out here?"

"Reading."

"I can see that," I sigh, my heart easing slightly. "Why here? Why in the dirt?"

Flora's face reddens, as if she doesn't want to tell me. Then, she takes a deep breath and hands the book over to me. When I see the author's name on the front cover, heat flashes through my body, from my chest outward to every extremity.

My hands shake. I try to swallow, but I can't.

"Jolie Beaumont," I say in a strangled voice. I flip the book open, my eyes landing on a short, handwritten note:

Flora,

I wrote this book while thinking of you. Your bravery, your smile, and your unwavering confidence.

I hope you'll see yourself in these pages.

You'd be a wonderful big sister—just like the girl in this book.

Take care of your father.

Jo

I'm TREMBLING SO HARD I struggle to read. Then, I read the note over again.

Big sister.

Those words stick in my mind, and my whole body feels hot.

Big sister.

I glance at my daughter with tears in my eyes, because I know the truth. Jolie's baby is mine—and she doesn't want me anywhere near him.

Flora slips her hand over my arm, her big blue eyes staring up at me.

"You want to read the book? I've already read it twice. It's really good."

"Twice? When did she send it?"

Flora shrugs. "A few months ago."

"*Months?*"

My daughter grins, shrugging, and then steps around me and skips away. I stare after her, speechless, and then drop my gaze to the book.

After half a page, I take my daughter's place and sit on the charred patch of land that used to be the rose garden, and I read.

35

JO

I DIDN'T KNOW it was possible to be this tired. Thorne is a fussy baby, and he's always keeping me awake. The only time he falls asleep is in my arms, which makes it almost impossible to do anything—including sleep myself.

Right now, though, my mother is rocking him back and forth and he's babbling happily to his grandmother. I slink out of the room, rubbing my temples. There's baby vomit on my shirt, and I haven't changed my underwear in three days.

I'm not proud of my appearance—I'm just explaining what I look like when I hear a knock on the door.

Sighing, I drag myself to the front door.

I immediately regret not at least wiping the vomit off my shirt when I see Prince Gabriel standing in the doorway. Not only does he *not* have a single speckle of bodily fluid anywhere on his impeccable body, but he's also clean-shaven and dressed in a tailored suit.

His eyes soften when he sees me, and his full, kissable lips part ever so gently.

I'm weak. So, so weak.

I've spent the better part of a year convincing myself that I was over him, that I didn't want anything to do with him, that I was stronger without him—but as soon as I see the Prince, I know I've been lying to myself.

"Jolie," he breathes. "You look beautiful."

I bark out a laugh, and then start giggling. That's the funniest shit I've heard in months. Beautiful? *Beautiful?*

"Okay," I snort between chuckles. "Right. What are you doing here?"

"Can I come in?"

"I'd rather you didn't."

The pain in his eyes shoots an arrow straight through my chest. He gulps, and I watch his Adam's apple bob up and down.

"I read your book," he says quietly.

Why does that make me nervous? I didn't write it for him. It shouldn't matter what he thinks—but it does.

It always matters what he thinks. Even if I try to tell myself it doesn't.

"Yeah?" I say, sweeping my gaze over his shoulders, his jaw, then down to his hands. I close my eyes for a second, afraid that if I look at him too much, I'll invite him in.

"It's good."

Opening my eyes again, I nod. "Thanks."

The air is pregnant between us. It hangs heavy with everything we haven't said to each other. The day he tore apart the rose garden stands between us like an impenetrable wall, and neither of us moves to tear it down.

The Prince takes a deep breath. When he speaks, his voice is quiet. "Can I meet him? Our son?"

Heat flares through my chest, all the way up to my hairline. My eyes narrow. "*My* son."

"Jolie..."

264

"You're violent, Gabriel. I'm a mother now. I have to think about what's best for my baby. I can't have him around someone who'd act the way you do. I'm sorry."

In the second before I close the door, I see Gabriel's face crumple. Then, I fall to my knees and cry.

36

GABRIEL

FOR THE FIRST TIME... ever, probably... I don't choose anger. I don't fly off the handle and rip Jo's door off her hinges. I don't put my fist through a wall.

Instead, I get in my car and drive to Farcliff Castle. I find my brother, Damon, and I do the one thing I've been terrified of doing since I was a child.

I ask for help.

"I need to talk to your therapist," I say.

"Why?'

"Because I'm fucked up, Damon, and I need to un-fuck myself so that the woman I love will love me back."

Damon chuckles, nodding. "I know that feeling." He walks to his desk and pulls out a business card. It's pale green and has the name 'Agnes Fournier' written on it with a phone number.

"Just be warned," Damon says. "She won't take any of your shit."

. . .

MY HANDS SHAKE when I make the call, and my stomach is in my throat when I go to her office that afternoon. She's an old woman with a shock of white hair and bright, blue-rimmed glasses. She wears chunky jewelry and socks that don't match. She stares at me through her big glasses, tilting her head to the side.

"What can I do for you?"

I take a deep breath, not quite sure what to say. How can I explain how fucked up I am? Where do I start? What am I even trying to fix? My problems are like one long piece of string, knotted a million times over. They're a big ball of painful knots, sitting in my stomach, and I don't even know where to start pulling to unravel them.

So, I don't start at the beginning. I don't start with the death of my mother, or my anger as a teenager, or my father being a murderer. I start in the middle—or maybe the end. I start with Jolie.

AGNES SEES ME EVERY DAY. She challenges me on everything. I quit therapy a thousand times, and then show up a thousand more. I break down, build myself back up, break down again.

I work harder than I've worked in my life, and I have nothing to show for it. I look the same. I sound the same. I feel different.

Flora moves to Farcliff with me, and she's the first one to notice a change.

"Your eyes look different, Dad," she says to me one day, taking my cheeks in her hand. She inspects my eyes one at a time before releasing me, satisfied. "They look brighter."

"That's good, right?"

My daughter grins. "Yeah, it's good."

I'm changing. I know I am. How can I prove it to Jolie, though?

When I ask my therapist, Agnes just shakes her head. "Don't worry about that now. Work on yourself first, and then we'll worry about her."

"I don't want to wait." I'm breathless, impatient, needy.

"You have to."

Slowly, torturously, Agnes helps me loosen the ball of knots. It's still there, but it's looser. I don't turn to anger quite so quickly. Now, there's a pause. There's a choice.

A lot of times, I still choose rage—but not *every* time.

I draw more sketches, and I force myself not to burn them.

Jo releases another book, and I devour it the day it launches. I call her a few times a week, but she never answers. I don't blame her—I wouldn't answer either.

It kills me, though.

BY THE END OF JUNE, I feel like a new man. It's been a year since Jolie and I were laying in the wildflowers. A year since she stole my heart. A year since I knew I'd never be the same.

On a warm evening, I decide to walk down the streets of Farcliff. I've been doing it more and more lately, just walking by myself—well, me and a couple of bodyguards, but they stay far enough back that I sometimes forget they're even there.

Usually, I take the same route through the bustling center district of the city. I put a hat and sunglasses on, hoping that it'll be enough for me to go unnoticed. I stroll down the side-walks, heading nowhere in particular. People are eating and drinking on patios, laughing together. I soak up the happiness, breathing in the scent of flower boxes and letting my heart dance in my chest.

My feet take me to the botanical gardens that wrap around part of Farcliff Lake. I make my way to the rose garden there, floating along the gravel path. I inhale the scent of late spring, of flowers, freshness, and earth, and my heart is at ease.

So, when I see a woman with a stroller, sitting beside a trellis of climbing roses, I don't panic. I pause for a moment, staring at her.

Jolie still makes my heart flip. She still makes my mouth go dry. I rake my fingers through my hair and watch her pick the child out of the stroller and rock him in her arms. Taking a couple of steps forward, I clear my throat.

As Jolie turns her head, the sun angles across her face and makes her look like a queen among the roses.

"May I?" I ask, motioning to the bench.

She nods. I glance at the baby, noting it has bright blue eyes—my eyes. The baby waves his chubby arms at me, gurgling and smiling as he drools all over himself.

Jolie puts a protective hand over the baby's stomach, and then stares at me. She looks deep into my eyes, reading everything that I've ever written in them.

"You're not angry," she says. It's a statement, not a question.

I nod. "I've been going to therapy."

Her eyebrows arch, and then she smiles. "I'm proud of you."

As her smile fades, panic wells inside my chest. I need to see that smile again. I need to hear her voice again.

Say something. Do something. Make her see.

She's air, she's oxygen, she's food and water and everything I need to live. My heart starts thumping, and I turn my head away to try to compose myself. Closing my eyes and inhaling the scent of the flowers, I gather my courage to say the words I still haven't said to her.

"I'm sorry, Jolie. I was wrong to react like I did when I saw the book in your cottage. You have every right to be mad at me until the end of time, but just know that I'm trying to change. I'm going to therapy. I'm trying to be better. I *am* better"

I'm doing it for you. All for you. Because I love you now and forever, and I'd do anything to have you again. I love you. I love you. I love you.

The words stay stuck somewhere in my esophagus.

Jolie's throat bobs as she swallows, and she turns her eyes to the baby. Our baby.

"Thank you," she says. "I'm sorry I brought the book back to Westhill." She takes a deep breath, and lifts her eyes to me. "You want to hold him?"

Holy mother of Farcliff, I think my heart just exploded. I can't speak, I just nod. She transfers the baby into my arms, and all my organs melt. Thorne wraps his tiny little fingers around my thumb and babbles happily at me. I lean down and kiss his forehead, just brushing my lips over his soft skin. He smells like only babies do, and I kiss his skin again.

I don't even realize I'm crying until Jo brushes a tear away.

She smiles. "I called him Thorne. I hope you don't mind."

"He's perfect."

Jo snorts. "Maybe he'll be perfect when he sleeps through the night."

We sit in silence for a while, and I just stare at my son. My perfect, tiny, glorious son.

"Jo," I whisper, my eyes still glued to Thorne's round face.

"What?"

"I can't let you go." I'm still whispering, still not looking at her. "I'll do anything. Counselling, therapy, I'll get a lobotomy if I need to. I can't live without you."

Finally, I lift my eyes to hers. Her brows are drawn together, and I can see the pulse thundering in her neck.

"Gabe..."

I exhale, relishing the sound of my name on her tongue. "Don't say no. Please, please don't say no. I can change. I *have* changed. I want to be a father to our son—a husband to you, if you'll let me. I want you in my life, in my bed, under my skin. I'll let you rip my fingernails off with rusty pliers if it means I get to spend the day with you."

Instead of jumping into my embrace, Jolie's lip starts trembling. She reaches for Thorne, taking him out of my arms. My heart starts to thump violently in my chest. I'm losing her all over again. I can see it in her face that she doesn't want me. Maybe she never wanted me. She doesn't think I can change.

I open my mouth to say something—but I'm interrupted by the snap of a camera shutter.

IT TAKES me a couple of seconds to recognize the woman cat walking up the path. Her long, sleek, black hair shines in the sunlight and a cruel smile twists her lips.

Paulette.

I frown, clutching my baby to my chest. Gabriel puts his hand on my thigh protectively, and, damnit, I love his touch.

I was just about to tell him that I can't be with him. I just can't. He's too violent. Too angry. He's a pile of gunpowder, and the world is a match. Anything will set him off. Thorne and I can't be there when it happens.

His ex-girlfriend sashays her way up the path, with a row of paparazzi trailing after her.

Bodyguards materialize on either side of Gabriel and me, but he holds up a hand. They stop in their tracks.

"Well, well, well," Paulette says, angling her face toward the cameras. "If it isn't Prince Gabriel and his new baby mama. Are you going to steal her baby away, too?"

Gabriel's hand tightens on my thigh. That's it—this is the match. Paulette is striking it on her curvy, perfect body, flicking it toward the bomb beside me.

Tick, tick, tick.

I wait for him to explode.

Instead, his grip on my thigh loosens. I bounce my baby in my arms, eyes scanning the people around me warily. Gabriel's hand sends waves of calm through me.

Paulette arches a thin eyebrow. "Well? It would make a great epilogue to my new book."

"New book?" Gabriel's voice is a razor blade slicing through the air.

Tick, tick, tick.

"It releases next month," she proclaims to the cameras. "It's called 'Surviving Prince Gabriel'. Maybe you could write the introduction," Paulette says to me.

I brace myself for detonation. I know Gabriel. To his core, I know him, and I know that this is the end. The big boom. The snap that breaks him in half, and ends up with me and Thorne as nothing more than collateral damage.

But it never happens.

Instead, Gabriel puts his arm around my shoulders, lifting his other hand to shield our baby from the cameras.

"Your words have no power over me, Paulette. Not anymore. Do whatever you need to do to survive—even if it means spreading lies about me." His voice is even, calm, and soothing.

Paulette's eyes narrow, and she cocks her hip to the side. "It'll be bigger than my first book," she threatens.

"Sequels are never as good," Gabriel says. I look over to see his lip tugging up at the corner.

I repeat: His lip. Tugging up. At the corner.

He's *smiling.*

Not exploding. Not tearing down rose bushes and scaring my baby. Not being violent or menacing. Not covered in blood.

He's smiling at the woman who ruined his life.

Gabriel waves a hand, and his bodyguards descend upon the paparazzi. They usher them out of the garden, and suddenly we're alone again. I realize I'm trembling, so I put Thorne back in his stroller. I grip onto the edge of it, sucking in a deep breath.

Finally, I look over at Gabriel. With a shaking hand, I slide my fingers over his scar. I feel the smooth skin, slicing up toward his ear.

It's cool to the touch. He leans into my hand, letting out a soft growl. Gabriel leans into me, resting his forehead against mine.

"What do you say, Jolie? Will you give me another chance?"

Instead of answering, I angle my lips against his. I kiss him, softly at first, until his tongue swipes at the seam of my mouth and I let him in. His hands crawl up my legs, gripping my hips, my waist, tangling into my hair. He inhales, moaning softly as we kiss each other.

My fingers curl into his shirt and I pull him close. Tears slide down my cheeks as I let myself give in to love, to lust, to need, to want.

To *him*.

I keep one hand on the stroller while the other one claws at Gabriel. He scoops me onto his lap, crushing his lips against mine. He holds me there, and I cry and laugh in his arms.

When we come up for air, I lean my forehead against his. Tears soak my cheeks. He brushes them away with a soft finger.

"Don't cry, Jo."

"I love you," I whisper. "I love you so much it hurts to breathe."

"The past year has been torture without you." His voice is breathy and raw. "I felt like tearing my own heart out of my chest, but you'd already taken it with you when you left. I can't live without you, Jo. Never. Not again. Not one day. Not one hour."

"Not one hour?" I pull away, tilting my head. "Bit psycho, no?"

He laughs, kissing my tears away. "Okay, as many hours and days as you want, as long as you promise that I'm yours, and you're mine."

His lips find mine again, and he kisses my pain away. I wrap my hands to the nape of his neck, staring into his bright, blue eyes.

"I'm yours, and you're mine," I repeat, brushing my lips against his. I rest my head against his chest, and watch as Gabriel reaches into the stroller. Thorne wraps his hand around his father's thumb, and I let out one last sigh. I exhale all the hurt that I've held onto for so, so long, and I melt into Gabriel's arms.

EPILOGUE
JO

GABRIEL and I are married on a Saturday in the new Royal Rose Garden at Westhill. We have temporary staff brought in, because I insist in having our usual staff attend the wedding as guests. Sam is my maid of honor, and she cries during the entire ceremony. Mrs. Grey is a bridesmaid, and to her credit, she only starts crying *after* the ceremony.

When I walk—or waddle—down the aisle, I'm already eight months pregnant with our second baby. Gabriel beams, leaning over to kiss my belly before straightening up for the ceremony.

The wedding is quick, mostly because my feet hurt and I can't stand for too long. Gabriel stays by my side all day, and we mostly just stare at each other. It's sickening—and perfect.

FLORA IS STILL small for her age but quickly showing how much of a genius she is. Since her bad infection two years ago, she hasn't had to be at the hospital a single time. Managing her illness takes time and patience, but she does it with remarkable bravery.

I end up writing three more novels inspired by her, and all of them have gone on to find commercial success. Since I no longer need the money, I donate all the proceeds to a cystic fibrosis organization in Flora's name.

Thorne is sixteen months old when Gabriel and I get married, and he spends the wedding day being bounced on my mother's knee. He's a happy kid, talkative and active, and when he gets a little older, I discover he's not at all interested in reading.

We had him tested for cystic fibrosis as an infant and were relieved to find out he didn't have it. I got a blood test and found I wasn't a carrier, and Gabriel let out a big sigh of relief, knowing that any other children we have wouldn't be at risk of having the illness.

GABRIEL CONTINUES THERAPY, but decreases from daily appointments to one a week, and then once a month. He starts visiting Farcliff more often, but we spend most of our time in Westhill. I think it's the solitude and serenity that keeps us out here—or maybe it's the annual Westhill Town Fair.

Whatever it is, we try to balance family with everything else in our life. Thorne and Flora, and our youngest, Gabriela, spend lots of time with their cousins in Farcliff Castle. I want them to grow up with no fear of the capital, and with a healthy attitude toward being in the public eye.

The rose garden soon outgrows the community space where I first planted it, and soon becomes a vibrant tourist attraction for the sleepy town. Gabriel also sets up an art gallery in Westhill, and holds a yearly charity fundraiser. He sells his sketches. It grows in popularity every year, and I think he reluctantly accepts the praise that his drawings generate. He sticks to charcoal as his preferred medium, and most of the time he's drawing me, or the kids, or roses.

My parents move back into the Gardener's Cottage and take care of the roses—both the ones at the castle and the ones in Westhill.

We get four good years together before my father's cancer comes back. When I start to cry, he smiles at me and shakes his head. "I had four more years with you since the last time. I saw you married. I got to meet my grandchildren. No tears. I'm one of the lucky ones."

I snort and cry in his arms, and he pats my head like a child. When he passes away, I vow to plant a rose bush in his honor every year—even if it means all of Westhill is covered in them.

As for Gabriel and me—we live as happily ever after as is possible, given the constraints of real life. Sometimes we're sad, and sometimes we argue, but we're never truly angry. Never volatile. Never violent.

He kisses me every chance he gets, and still makes my stomach clench when he runs his hands over my body. He calls me the love of his life, and every day, he kisses me like we're lying in a bed of wildflowers again.

I realize that my love for him isn't a wild animal or a wound that never cauterizes—it's more of a weed that just won't go away. It grows and grows until I'm overrun, and I finally just accept that my heart belongs to him, always and forever.

∾

Thank you for reading!

Want a free extended epilogue to find out what happens to Jo and Gabriel after their wedding? Join my reader list!

http://www.lilianmonroe.com/subscribe

Lilian

xox

Psst... Keep reading for a preview of Book 4: Broken Prince

BROKEN PRINCE

ROYALLY UNEXPECTED: BOOK 4

PREVIOUSLY TITLED KNOCKED UP BY THE BROKEN PRINCE

1

IVY

THERE'S a special place in hell for people who are jealous of their sisters. My spot has been reserved since I was just a little girl. I'm pretty sure Lucifer himself has a party planned for my arrival, complete with a thousand emerald balloons and a banner that says, 'WELCOME HOME, IVY.'

Whenever I'm near my sister Margot, I bleed green. Envy curls in the pit of my stomach and sends roots into my heart, squeezing my insides until I can hardly breathe.

It's happening right now, as Margot twirls in front of the mirror in yet another perfect, figure-hugging gown—which, by the way, she got for free. Yes, my sister is so beautiful that all she has to do is post pictures of herself online, and brands send her boxes and boxes of free things.

"Which one do you like better?" Margot asks, tilting her head. "I think the blue one might be more appropriate for a royal event, but this pink one would make a statement. Prince Luca seems like the kind of guy who would appreciate a statement." She bites the inside of her cheek. "My stylist asked me to make a decision tonight so that she can put together my shoes and accessories before the event."

Her long, false nails slide down her abdomen as she sucks in her flatter-than-flat stomach. My older sister is tall and willowy, with waist-length blonde hair and blue, come-hither eyes. All she has to do is bat her eyelashes at a man and he falls to his knees in front of her.

Why would Prince Luca be any different? I honestly don't think it matters which dress she chooses. She could show up in flannel pajamas if she wanted to. People would call it *fashion, darling* and put her on the 'Farcliff's Best Dressed' list.

Margot's eyes move to my reflection in the mirror, and her eyebrows jump up in question.

I shrug. "Yeah, either one is nice."

Margot's shoulders fall, and a pang passes through my chest. I know she needs my support right now, and I'm not giving it to her. She's meeting one of the Princes of Argyle tomorrow. The entire royal family of Argyle—the King and Queen, and two of the three Princes—have been invited to our Kingdom of Farcliff following the coronation of Prince Luca's older brother, King Theo.

The Kingdoms of Argyle and Farcliff haven't always had the best relations, but with King Theo in Argyle, and King Charlie here in Farcliff, there are high hopes of reconciliation. The formal dinner tomorrow night is an opening ceremony, of sorts, which will kick off the Argyle family's month-long visit in Farcliff.

My sister—being one of the most famous celebrities in Farcliff—is invited to the ball. Me?

Not so much.

I guess the slightly shorter, slightly chubbier, black-haired version of Margot isn't exactly in high demand.

Did I mention I'm most likely spending eternity in a fiery abyss?

I don't even know *why* I'm so jealous. That dinner sounds

like my idea of death by a thousand boring conversations. I'd rather pluck my leg hairs out one by one than spend time with the guests at tomorrow's event.

Still, I envy her.

Margot's management team has arranged to hook her up with Prince Luca, as he's apparently the hottest thing since sliced bread. They think it'll be good for her 'image' to have her dating a high-profile celebrity like the Prince. The Prince's management team agrees, wanting to bring Argyle and Farcliff closer together. It's a match made in royal Instagram heaven.

For a month, at least. All bets are off once Prince Luca leaves Farcliff again.

I swing my legs off the bed and stand up, throwing my jet-black hair into a messy bun. "Go with whatever dress you think is best, Margie. You know I'm no good at these things."

Margot throws me a look when I say her name. Her *real* name. She changed it to Margot when she started acting, because her agent told her 'Marguerite' isn't fame material. At least our mother died before *that* happened.

"I just want to make sure the Prince likes me." Her eyes return to her reflection in the mirror.

Taking a deep breath, I put my hands on my sister's shoulders. She swings her gaze back to me, and I force an encouraging smile. "He's going to love you. Everyone does. Literally everyone—even me."

Margot cracks a grin and shakes her head. With a sigh, she makes a decision. "I'm going to go with the blue one."

As the personal assistant to Farcliff's hottest star, my life revolves around my sister. It always has. Ever since she landed her first commercial when she was four years old, my sister's life has always taken priority.

Even when Mama's illness got worse and the end was near, my father would still take Margot to her auditions and modeling jobs before going to see his own wife in the hospital. That's what happens when there's an opportunity to lift a family out of poverty—everyone latches on for dear life.

Including me.

Margot is the gravy train that we all need to survive. And because my sister is such a damn saint, she doesn't hold it against us. She shares her wealth and success with my father and me without rancor or the need for anything in return.

So, every day, I swallow my jealousy and get up at the crack of dawn to make sure my sister's days go according to plan.

This morning, in particular, is hectic. I have to make sure the hair and makeup artists are here on time. I need to confirm the limo service and call her stylist to make sure she's finalized the outfit.

I need to make sure Margot eats enough so that she doesn't faint on her way to Farcliff Castle, but not so much that she'll look bloated in her pretty blue dress.

Most importantly, I need to make sure my sister is happy, confident, glowing, and ready to meet the Prince of her dreams.

Margot still has her silk eye mask on when I gently shake her awake. She lets out a cute little sigh—because even in her sleep, she's graceful and perfect—and pushes the pink silk off her eyes and onto her forehead. Her golden hair is still curled from yesterday, splayed out in soft waves on her pillow.

I couldn't look that good when I wake up if I tried.

"Hey, Ivy," she smiles. "Is it time to get up already?"

"Rise and shine, future Princess."

Margot beams at me, and pads to her ensuite bathroom. I hear a yelp, followed by a series of clattering bangs, and I let out a sigh.

My sister's single, solitary flaw is that she can't go anywhere without knocking something over. 'Clumsy' doesn't even come close to describing it. She's a bull, and the world is a china shop.

A really pretty, really feminine, blonde-haired bull, but still.

An accident waiting to happen.

She's lucky she has an entire team of people around her who hide that particular flaw from the public. The Margot LeBlanc that the masses see is graceful, kind, and pretty much perfect.

Knocking on the bathroom door, I wait for her response.

"It's fine," she calls out. "Just the shampoo bottles."

"Okay. Let me know if you need anything."

I make her bed while she showers, and check my phone when it dings. The hairstylist is on her way. Makeup will be late.

Today is all about managing Margot. Her agent, Hunter, arrives at our seven-bedroom mansion at eleven o'clock, prepping Margot with a thousand and one facts about Prince Luca.

"Remember, Margot, don't mention Queen Cara."

"His ex. Right. Got it." Margot nods. "No mention of the Queen of Argyle."

"I mean it, Margot. They were sweethearts their entire lives. When Queen Cara married Luca's older brother, it was a massive controversy in Argyle. Prince Luca was still in Singapore at the time."

"For his operation?"

Hunter nods. "That's something you can focus on—his

recovery from the spinal fracture and how miraculous it is that he can walk again. But not Queen Cara. Not even her name. When she married his brother, Prince Luca went off the rails. Talking about her is a sure way to get the Prince to dislike you."

"I *get* it," Margot repeats. Her voice has a slight edge to it —the most aggression you'll ever hear from my angelic older sister.

Hunter pulls his phone out of his pocket and stares at it as he continues: "Keep the conversation light. He likes sports— he's a big basketball fan. Just be yourself."

"Is she supposed to be herself, or is she supposed to talk about basketball?" I ask, arching an eyebrow.

Hunter ignores me.

I slink to the kitchen, tired of hearing about Prince Luca. It's all they've talked about for months. If I hear the words 'bad boy meets good girl' or 'relationship of the century' one more time, I think I might explode.

Heading for the pantry, I pull out some flour, sugar, yeast, and a few other bits and pieces. My favorite mixing bowl lives in the corner cupboard by the sink, and as soon as I feel the weight of it, my shoulders start to relax.

I love baking. I always have. Mama and I used to spend hours in the kitchen together, putting together lavish desserts from scraps of food that she scrounged from who-knows-where. She taught me everything I know about baking, and every time I make something, I think of her.

As Mama's illness progressed and her tremors became more severe, she stopped being able to bake. She'd sit in the kitchen as I did the work. Mama would coach me through the complex recipes, and then we'd eat the treats together.

It was special. It still is. Baking is the one thing that I'm really, really good at.

Right now, I need to think about something other than my beautiful sister, her impending royal relationship, and my own inadequacy.

Cinnamon buns might do the trick.

Slipping on my bright blue apron, I get to work. The sounds of the hairstylists and agents and managers fades into the background, and I inhale the scent of fresh dough. It's the scent of memories, home, and comfort. As soon as my fingers sink into the soft dough, a smile drifts over my lips.

This is where I'm happiest. If I could give up the seven-bedroom mansion and all the money and comfort that Margot provides for me, I would. I'd open a small bakery in Farcliff and I'd sell everything that my mother and I used to bake together.

The *clack-clack-clack* of stilettos on our Italian marble floors informs me my sister is coming to find me. I cover the dough to prove it, and then wipe my floury hands on my apron.

Margot comes around the corner in all her glory. In six-inch heels, she looks even more breathtaking than she usually does. Her makeup is flawless, of course, and her hair is swept to the side in elegant curls. The blue dress was a good choice—it makes her perfect figure look like she's walking around with real-life Photoshop on her body. She smiles at me, but pauses at the kitchen's entrance.

"I don't want to get flour on my dress, but I wanted to say thank you for all your help today. I couldn't have done it without you. I know it's been a tough couple of months, but once this relationship goes public, it should provide a lot more opportunities for us. We'll be real stars, Ivy."

We.

My heart squeezes.

Why am I such an ass?

Here I am, cursing my sister's name, and she's including me in all her plans. Everything she's done to be in the public eye, to make all this money—it's been for my father and me.

We stand on the opposite side of the kitchen. The distance between us is vast.

I force a smile. "I'll have cinnamon buns ready and waiting for you when you come back."

"Can't wait," she says, as if she'll actually eat one. I don't think she's eaten a simple carb in ten or twelve years.

She turns to leave, and then pauses. "Oh, would you mind grabbing my dry cleaning? Marcella didn't have time to do it today with everything going on." Without waiting for an answer, my sister blows me a kiss and disappears down the hallway with her entourage in tow.

I grimace, wincing when the door slams. "Sure, no problem!" I call out into the silence. I listen to the big, empty house, not quite sure what I'm expecting to hear.

Then, with a sigh, I take my apron off and do my sister's bidding.

2

LUCA

QUEEN CARA of Argyle looks radiant as she walks up the wide steps leading up to the Farcliff Castle doors. Her rich, purple gown cinches her at the waist, and my eyes stay glued to the spot on her lower back where my hand used to rest.

Key words: *used to.*

Past tense. As in, not anymore. Never again.

I sit in the back seat of my limousine with a sick feeling in my stomach. My brother, King Theo, smiles at the flashing cameras and lifts his arm up towards them. His wife's tiara sparkles with every photo as she stands beside him. Hot coals glow in my chest, burning me from the inside out.

My lips pinch and my gut churns. My brother, Beckett, watches me from across the limousine.

"You okay?"

I sigh. "Yeah. I'll be fine."

He gives me a tight-lipped smile. "It's good to see you again, Luca." He slides over beside me and pats my knee. "Argyle wasn't the same without you."

"It's been a long five years, that's for sure. It's good to see you too."

I smile at Beckett, and the tension between my eyes seems to ease. Besides Cara, Beckett was my best friend growing up. He's actually my half-brother—our mother had him with my father's brother, which caused about as much controversy as you can imagine—but he's as much my brother as Theo is.

"Try not to let them get to you."

"Who?"

Beckett rolls his eyes. I know who he's talking about—our brother, Theo, and his beautiful, graceful wife, Cara.

Also known as the love of my life, the shatterer of my heart, the bane of my existence, and, unfortunately, my new sister-in-law.

Beckett lets out a sigh and exits the limousine. His lopsided smile greets the flashing cameras, and I take a deep breath. I'm next.

Reaching into my pocket, I pop two painkillers into my mouth. Whenever I get stressed, my body screams with burning pain. Nerve pain. Right now, as I stare up at Theo and Cara, it's bad.

When I walk out, I don't look at the cameras. I ignore the clamoring of reporters and the death glares my eldest brother gives me. I just walk straight toward the castle without acknowledging the crowds.

What do I care about the people of Farcliff? Why should I give a fuck about the journalists and news reporters who have done nothing but tear me to shreds? They'll look for any glance, any facial expression, any word to show how heart-broken I am over Cara's wedding to my brother.

Not that it'd be hard to find something.

Theo's eyes burn holes into my back. I pause on the top step, and I can sense his approach without even turning to see him.

"Behave yourself," he hisses in my ear. "This visit in Farcliff is important."

"For you, you mean."

"For all of us. For all of Argyle. This is your first public appearance since Singapore, in case you've forgotten. It's your chance to show yourself to the world." His trimmed beard has a few white hairs growing in it. He looks old—a fact that brings me more pleasure than it should. He lowers his head toward me as cameras continue to flash. "Just don't make a scene. Your date will be here any minute."

"Wonderful." I roll my eyes. "I'm so glad you were able to arrange a suitable match for me, Your Majesty. Or are you going to take her into your bed as soon as I turn my back, too?"

Beckett distracts the photographers by stepping forward with a dazzling smile. He glances at me for just a moment, giving me a pointed stare.

His eyes say, *Don't do it. Calm down. Get through the night.*

Theo is staring at me, too—and his eyes are blazing. His anger only serves to feed mine. It pours into me like liquid heat, sending sharp daggers through my chest.

Who the fuck is he to be mad at me? I didn't swoop into his life and steal his bride away. *He* did that to *me*. And now, I'm supposed to forget it ever happened?

Fuck. That.

I'll make a scene if I want to.

Cara appears beside him, hooking her arm into Theo's. She smiles at me with soft eyes. The aggression inside me evaporates, replaced with a dull thud in my empty chest.

"Everything okay with you two?"

I incline my head. "Of course, Your Majesty."

"Luca, I wish you wouldn't call me that." Her plump, red

lower lip juts out, and I remember sucking that lip between my own not too long ago.

I arch an eyebrow. "Why not? You earned the title."

She earned it by sleeping with my brother while I was getting my spinal cord stitched back together and learning to walk again. She earned it after assuring me that she'd wait for me.

Theo clears his throat. "Here comes your date. Behave."

I turn to the bottom of the wide steps to see a blonde woman with an entourage bigger than ours. Her dress looks painted onto her perfect body, and I can't deny how beautiful she is. Her tits are plump and perky, and every step she takes as she climbs the stairs makes her look more seductive than the last. She walks in like she belongs here, flashing a dazzling smile at me, angling her face toward the cameras.

I feel nothing.

I'm empty, except for the low, simmering rage that always bubbles when Theo's near.

"Your Majesties," the woman says as she curtsies for my brother and his wife. The blonde beauty turns to me, and a slight pink tinge colors her cheeks. She bows her head. "Nice to finally meet you, Prince Luca."

I bring her hand to my lips, staring into her bright, blue eyes. Cameras flash as reporters shout for us to face them. I ignore them, but the woman smiles for the photographers.

I could fuck her for the month I'm here, I guess, if she's not too boring to listen to.

Glancing at Cara, I see her staring at the two of us. Her eyebrows draw together slightly, and she lets her eyes drift down the woman's body.

For the briefest of moments, all my anger melts away and is replaced with bright, zinging interest. I tilt my head, studying her.

Is the Queen jealous?

I quirk an eyebrow as an idea starts floating through my head. Maybe this blonde would be more useful than I anticipated. Taking my date's hand, I hook it into the crook of my arm and motion toward the castle. "Shall we?"

"Please." She smiles at me again, a little more coquettishly. In her heels, she's almost as tall as I am. She smells floral and a little too sweet. My date angles her head one more for the benefit of the cameras, and I resist the urge to roll my eyes.

Cara clears her throat, stealing another glance at us before turning away.

I grin.

Cameras flash.

Shocking as it is to say it, this might actually be fun, in a cruel, twisted kind of way.

We turn toward the big double doors that lead into the castle, and my date stumbles over the last step. Before she goes flying face-first into the ground, I catch her.

Snap-snap-snap. Cameras are trained on us.

My date smiles at me, a blush tinting her cheeks. "Thanks."

"Of course." I put my hand on her back, resisting the urge to steal a glance at Cara.

As soon as we enter the castle, someone hands me a glass of champagne. I down it in one gulp and belch in my fist. The woman—what was her name?—stares at me and then immediately rearranges her features into a smile.

"I was told you were a character." She bats her eyelashes and pushes her chest out toward me.

I guess 'not too boring to listen to' was too much to ask. I could still fuck her, I guess. Cara would hate that.

"I was told you were a good fuck," I answer. I grab another

glass of champagne on our way toward the Great Hall, ignoring whatever it is that comes out of her mouth next.

Farcliff Castle is different from the one at home. This castle just as grand, but it feels colder. There's more stone and steel in it. In the Great Hall, long tables are set up with thick, white tablecloths on them. I let the usher lead me to my assigned seat, at a table with Beckett and my date. Prince Damon and Princess Dahlia of Farcliff are seated next to us, and a few other Lords and Ladies take their seats further down the table.

The King of Farcliff, Charlie, and his Queen, Elle, take their seats at the head table. My brother, Theo, thankfully, is sitting at the opposite end of that table with Queen Cara. I won't have to stare at them all dinner, which I'm sure was done on purpose.

The more distance between us, the better.

Beckett stares at me from across the table, glancing at my date. He cocks his eyebrow as if to say, *You okay?*

I avert my eyes.

I don't know how I feel. On the one hand, I'm seeing my family for the first time in years. I'm happy to see them, but another part of me resents the fact that they never came to visit me. I want to go back to Argyle, but I'm nervous about what to expect.

Beckett stares at me and then his face twists, and he sneezes.

"Allergies?" I ask, spreading my serviette over my thighs.

Beckett grunts in acknowledgement. My brother is allergic to dust, cats, dogs, horses, pollen, peanut butter— pretty much everything except water. He sneezes again, and I hide a grin.

I used to tickle his nose with dandelions when we were

kids and run away when he'd get mad. He'd chase me, sneezing the whole time. We were kids. Our childhood was happy.

Now, that happiness seems to have slipped through my fingers.

"Can't take you anywhere," I say with a grin. Beckett sighs, frustrated. Is it wrong that I kind of like seeing people like this? Uncomfortable, in pain, and hurting?

I wasn't always like this. Before the accident, I was a happy person. I liked to laugh.

Snapping your spine and become a paraplegic has a way of changing your outlook on life, though. My family shipped me off to Singapore to get fixed up, and now that I've made a miraculous recovery, they're welcoming me back with open arms.

I'm not broken anymore, so I'm worthy of their attention.

My date shifts in her seat. She reaches into her tiny clutch purse and pulls out a pill packet, handing it to Beckett. "Here," she says with a smile. "I have allergies all the time. These antihistamines are prescription."

Beckett's eyebrows arch, and he accepts the pill with a grateful nod. "Thanks. You're an actress, right? You were in the last *James Bond* movie."

Her face breaks into a smile. "Yeah, I'm Margot LeBlanc. I loved playing a Bond girl. Something about being a villain was really fun and freeing." Her laugh is musical, and she flicks her hair over her shoulder.

Margot. Right. I silently thank my brother for asking.

"Beckett," my brother says, extending a hand. When Margot reaches over to take it, she knocks over my glass of champagne with her arm. I catch it as it sloshes over my plate, and a waiter whisks it away within seconds.

Margot looks embarrassed and apologizes. She glances at Beckett, and they stare at each other for a little bit too long. Beckett's eyes shine, and he smiles at my date like an idiot.

I'm not going to pretend like I'm into this chick, but that doesn't mean that I'm going to let Beckett swoop in on her. Apart from Cara, Margot is the hottest chick in the room. I reach my arm over the back of her chair, leaning into Margot as I glance at my brother. His smile fades, and Margot clears her throat, smiling at me.

I sip my champagne as an awkward silence settles between us.

Princess Dahlia makes a soft noise, smiling politely at us. "So, Prince Luca, please tell us about your recovery over the past few years. You must have worked very hard."

"Never thought I'd have to learn to walk twice," I say, taking another slug of champagne.

Prince Damon nods, and starts telling us about his own brush with death. His was self-inflicted, though. I remember the news reports from a few years ago. It was right before he met Princess Dahlia.

By the time we're onto the second course, I'm half-cut and dying for a piss. I excuse myself from the table, stumbling through the castle hallways, leaning against expensive paintings on the walls for support. I stumble down the hallway, poking my head into lavish rooms.

Are there no bathrooms in this fucking castle?

I pinch my lip together and finally just choose another door at random. Whatever it is, I'm taking a piss in it.

Turns out, it's a formal living room with a balcony. I head over to the balcony, unzip my pants and water one of the plants. Groaning in relief, I zip myself back up and reach into my pocket for a joint.

I can't go back in there without taking the edge off. It's too soon to take another painkiller, and the booze isn't doing anything to distract me from the pain that's starting to pulse down my spine. Weed will help.

Beckett and Margot are making eyes at each other across the dinner table, I'm zoned out most of the time, and I can *still* hear Cara's laugh from across the Great Hall. I light up my joint and take a puff, leaning against the exterior wall as I stare off the balcony.

Farcliff isn't bad, I guess. It's colder than Argyle, but that's because it's much farther north. There are more trees here than in our Caribbean climate, and the air does taste cool and fresh. It's late May, and the whole country is exploding with blooms and the excitement of late spring.

It makes me feel even more bitter than I already do.

Farcliff is like Margot—she's nice, and pretty, and sweet—but all I want to do is fuck her and leave her broken in my wake. This trip to Farcliff is supposed to be the start of a homecoming for me, but all I want to do is ruin my brother's life.

Hopefully, if all goes well, Cara will hate every minute of it. Maybe then she'll get a tiny taste of the torture she's put me through.

As I watch the smoke swirl around my head, a smile curls my lips. My PR team wants me to date Margot? That's exactly what I'll do—but I'm not promising it'll end with a happily-ever-after.

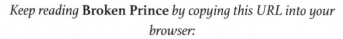

Keep reading **Broken Prince** *by copying this URL into your browser:*
https://www.amazon.com/dp/B0843P1VGF

Don't forget to sign up for access to the Lilian Monroe
Freebie Central:
https://www.lilianmonroe.com/subscribe

Lilian

ALSO BY LILIAN MONROE

For all books, visit:

www.lilianmonroe.com

Brother's Best Friend Romance

Shouldn't Want You

Can't Have You

Military Romance

His Vow

His Oath

His Word

The Complete Protector Series

Enemies to Lovers Romance

Hate at First Sight

Loathe at First Sight

Despise at First Sight

The Complete Love/Hate Series

Secret Baby/Accidental Pregnancy Romance:

Bad Boss

Bad Single Dad

Bad Boy

Bad Billionaire

The Complete Unexpected Series

Bad Prince

Heartless Prince

Cruel Prince

Broken Prince

Wicked Prince

Wrong Prince

Fake Engagement/ Fake Marriage Romance:

Engaged to Mr. Right

Engaged to Mr. Wrong

Engaged to Mr. Perfect

Mr Right: The Complete Fake Engagement Series

Mountain Man Romance:

Lie to Me

Swear to Me

Run to Me

The Complete Clarke Brothers Series

Extra-Steamy Rock Star Romance:

Garrett

Maddox

Carter

The Complete Rock Hard Series

Sexy Doctors:

Doctor O

Doctor D

Doctor L

The Complete Doctor's Orders Series

Time Travel Romance:

The Cause

A little something different:

Second Chance: A Rockstar Romance in North Korea

Made in the USA
Monee, IL
17 October 2020

45271469R00184